SWAMP

KAREN YOCHIM

ISBN: 1477424407

ISBN 13: 9781477424407

Library of Congress Control Number: 2012909097

CreateSpace, North Charleston, SC

Dedicated to the late Buddy Yochim, who first brought me to Louisiana years ago, and to the late Shelley "Pappy" Yochim, who first introduced me to the great Atchafalaya Swamp.

Thank you to all friends and family who read the manuscript and gave valuable feedback. Special thanks to Jeff Davis Taylor, Cajun extraordinaire; Twinkle Yochim, Julie Chateauvert, Tony LeClerc, Bonita Kane Jaro, Lynn Rees, Suzanne Laviolette, Curator, Longfellow Evangeline Louisiana State Historical Park in St. Martinville; Paul David, Roland Rivette, Barry Ancelet and the French Department of UL in Lafayette, and Greg Guirard.

PART ONE

Alive? He might be dead for all I know...

Childe Roland to the Dark Tower Came

- Robert Browning

1

JEAN CLAUDE'S FATHER PASSES BY

"What do you wish?"
returned Aramis, with a resigned air.
"One cannot escape his destiny."
Twenty Years After - Alexandre Dumas

The second day Jean Claude went missing, I stepped out on the front porch of our cypress farmhouse on Bayou Perdu, half an hour's ride from the tiny village of St. Beatrice, and hard by the great Atchafalaya Swamp. The morning was misty with a low pewter sky, and so thick with a heavy, eternal gray, I knew it wouldn't blow on through. It hovered, covering St. Beatrice Parish, so oppressive that the air hummed with stagnation and humidity. I needed comfort for it had been a full moon the night before, and I hadn't slept well. It hadn't helped to be worried about Jean Claude's disappearance. On that morning, I was still nervous about his safety and imagining him lying swollen and dead on some muddy bank of the Atchafalaya.

A horse approached on the dirt road in front of our yard, and I shielded my eyes with the flat of my hand, squinting to see if it were Jean Claude at last. It was instead his father, Claude Benoit, who rode onto the patchy grass at the edge of the road, as our hounds barked and raced to greet him, prancing around the chestnut stallion, so that he reared and whinnied.

"Whoa! Whoa!" Claude settled his horse and leaned back in the saddle, an expectant look in his dark brown eyes. "Any good news for me, Sidonie?"

"We haven't heard a word, sir." It was the first time that day I'd spoken, and my voice was raspy. I cleared my throat and waited.

"It's not like him to take off like this and not say anything. His mother is worrying herself sick." He shook his head and cast his eyes down, biting his bottom lip.

"Jean Claude hardly ever talks to me," I offered.

"I know you two don't have much to say to each other for now, but that will change after the marriage. You're still so young, but you'll see. Once you start having your babies and running a household, things will change." He eyed me carefully. "*C'est vrai?*"

"I don't know if that's true or not, sir. I just know Jean Claude never tells me anything."

"Has he said anything to your brother? They're such old friends."

"Maurice doesn't know anything either."

Claude blew a puff of air and slapped his reins back and forth in a distracted manner. "Well then, Sidonie. Ask your family to send word to us immediately if they hear anything. Any time of the day or night. I don't care how late it is. *Comprends?*"

"Oh yes, sir. I understand."

"I just hope and pray the boy's not snake bit out there, or lying somewhere with a broke leg." He indicated the swamp with a flourish of his hat. "Pray for him, Sidonie? For all of us?"

"You know I will, sir." I moved closer to a porch post and leaned against it, folding my arms in front of my chest. Midnight, one of the hounds sighed and flopped heavily beside me on the top step. "Maybe he's gone to visit somebody and stayed longer than he intended."

"Maybe...but it's not like him. And, if that's the case, he'll catch hell from me for worrying his mother like this." Claude set his lips in a firm line and waved his hat to me, then set it carefully on his head, pulling the brim forward to shade his eyes. "Goodbye, Sidonie. Keep yourself safe."

"The same to you, sir." I kneeled by Midnight and scratched his floppy ears as he closed his eyes, losing complete interest in our visitor. As Jean's father rode away, his stallion kicking up clouds of dust, my sister, Yvonne, limped to the doorway and stood there in shadow.

"Who were you talking to?"

"Jean Claude's father."

"Any news?"

"He wanted to know if we'd heard anything."

"Well, we haven't. So, why don't you get on with your chores?" She wiped her hands vigorously on her apron.

"I've done most of them already. I'm going to crack pecans at the cemetery."

Her forehead creased as she peered out at the overcast sky. "It's going to rain. Do it here."

"No, I'm going to the cemetery."

"*Tête dure!* Just like always! Be sure you do it right at least." She limped back inside as I picked up the sack of pecans and a basket, casting a glance at the chickens, ducks and geese still scratching and pecking at the cracked corn I'd scattered for them. I was glad to leave because I knew my work would go faster if I could get away from my miserable older sister and her never ending scolding.

As I walked the easy fifteen minutes to the cemetery where so many of our family lay buried, the breezes whipped up, and I breathed heavily of the sweet air, hoping it would clear my mind so I didn't have to suffer the black thoughts that plagued me. Not only were my grandparents and parents gone, but my *parrain* and *marrain* as well. Not even having godparents made me feel afraid at times, but visits to the cemetery from time to time helped me feel safe and protected.

As I settled myself between the graves of Maman and Papa, I patted my layers of cotton skirts down and set the sack of pecans and the basket before me. The engravings on the tombstones read: *née 1812* and 1813 respectively; the death dates the same: 1866.

A light drizzle began to soak the *garde-soleil*, the bonnet I'd tied tightly under my chin, and rainwater seeped into the thick black braid down my back. Huddling into my layered chemises, I squint-ed, blinking raindrops away.

The gravestones, flush on the ground, were still clear gray, not mossy and black as were so many of the others. Bordering the grassy clearing of the cemetery were the live oaks, graceful and serpentine as their incredibly long branches snaked out over the forest floor. Thick silver mosses draped from these branches, their gray color matching the sky and seemed to be snatched from the dark clouds hovering above. A *chat-haunt* awakened by the rain, softly hooted from somewhere back in those oaks.

Cutting my visit short to get out of the wet, I quickly spoke to my departed family, hoping their spirits were listening, and told them of my fears for Jean Claude. I believed they watched over us and tried to guide us as they had done when they were alive. It's easy to hold such beliefs in Louisiana where the very air seems alive with the voices of spirits, but that gray day I couldn't quiet my worries about Jean Claude long enough to hear anything but my own dismal thoughts.

Since I couldn't finish shelling the pecans, I'd have to do it later at the farm. In addition, I was supposed to help Yvonne put up persimmon preserves that afternoon. Yet from the cemetery it was closer to walk to my deceased grandparents' farm where my cousin, Emile, lived. I could get out of the soft rain there, get dry, and drink some hot coffee as we visited. Emile, the handsome, brilliant and thoroughly ruined attorney who had come to us from Paris two years before, fleeing scandal.

He had been trustee of a few large trust funds there, and owing to his love of horses and gambling and cards, had borrowed money from those funds that he was unable to repay. Emile had hoped blood relations in Louisiana would accept him, and our family had been pleased to have him close to us. This is how after escaping France from Marseilles and landing weeks later in New Orleans, he had eventually managed to seek us out in St. Beatrice Parish.

As I made my way toward Emile's, the gray air filtered the green of the woods that edged the bayou to my left, and smudged the leaves of the hardwoods. Even the long muddy grass by the side of the road was a dull, listless color. But it all fit my mood; I blended with it.

Yvonne's words came to me as I kicked at a clod of mud, "What a prospect! Jean Claude! To stay in St. Beatrice and marry you, lazy as you are. He's probably gone as far as he could just to get away from you!" I winced as I recalled her words, but as I approached Emile's, the smell of wood smoke spiraling from the chimney was comforting and inviting. Chi-Chi, his little white dog, wagging his tail on the front porch, then running to greet me, gave me hope and renewed energy. I walked faster.

2

EMILE

A glad smile lighted up Portho's face.
Twenty Years After - Alexandre Dumas

C hi-Chi, barking and wagging her tail vigorously, raced to
greet me as I started up the path to the front porch. She accompanied me all the way to the front door, which Emile,
as usual, had left open.

"Come in, Sidonie. I'm delighted to see you," he called. Stepping lightly over the worn threshold, I blinked my eyes to adjust to
the dim interior. Emile crouched at the fireplace, stirring something in a heavy black iron pot hanging from an iron crane over
the low banked fire. Beckoning with his free hand, he stirred with
the other. Slowly and carefully he raised an iron ladle from the
simmering sauce, waving his hand over it and sniffing the sauce.
He tasted with great care. *"C'est piquant, ça,"* he reported, making
a face. "And it burns my mouth."

Placing the ladle on a tin plate resting on the hearth, he stood
with a welcoming smile. His even white teeth contrasted sharply
with the low light of the room. "Please, come sit by the fire. I'm
starting to work on the *courtbouillon* for the *bourrée* game tonight,
but I have hot coffee and fresh biscuits to warm you."

Crossing the room to his narrow bed by the window and snatching a blanket from it, he hurried back to wrap me in it. I sat on a

ladder back chair by the fire, shoving my boots toward the warmth and drying my face with the back of my hands.

"There now, isn't that better?" he asked, watching me settle into the cocoon of the blanket before turning to fetch the coffee and biscuits.

"Oh, yes," I assured him, "much better."

"We can't have you catching a chill," he added, his back to me.

Rearranging the blanket around me, I changed position a few times, making myself comfortable. As always, I felt right at home in my grandparents' house. The chair was one Grandfather Achille had made for Grandmother Odile. The fact that the woven seat was still tight, unbowed, and didn't creak, even all these years, was testament to Grandpapa's craftsmanship.

Emile hastened to bring me hot coffee with scalded milk and a plate of warm biscuits and honey. He set these on a narrow, hand-hewn table close by my chair, and pampered me by spreading honey on a biscuit and practically hand feeding me. "These biscuits will melt in your mouth," he promised, and the charm of his smile warmed me faster than the crackling fire or even the scratchy blanket.

It was easy to understand why Emile had made friends with ease throughout the parish. Besides his naturally soothing and sociable manner, he was the only Parisian we knew. We all loved his stories, told in his deep, rich voice, about the glamour of his city, a shimmering, yet dangerous Paris.

He poured himself a cup of coffee from the white enamel drip pot, and lifted out the dark stained cotton sack of grounds. The brew was strong and black and just what was needed to drive any remaining damp from my bones. When Emile spoke, he gave me his compete attention in a way I never experienced in my own family.

"I haven't shaved yet, and I must look disreputable." He rubbed long fingers over his chin and the sides of his face. "But I was playing cards all night. And you know how I love brandy." He patted his forehead gently with the back of his hand. "*Mon Dieu!* My head is clanging!"

I reflected on the changes Emile had to make to adjust to life on the bayou. Although our lives were primitive by Parisian standards, he'd adapted with ease, switching from absinthe and arma-gnac to homemade strawberry and blackberry wine, peach brandy, and *vin de soco,* or plum brandy. He always seemed as content in his small cabin as perhaps he'd felt in his grand apartment on the Rue de Bac.

His normally handsome face was puffy and his eyes red-rimmed, more evidence of the excesses of the night before. "I'm sure I'm a sight myself, cousin. Please don't give it a thought," I said. The hot cup warmed my hands as I sipped coffee and stared into the dancing fire. As he squatted there, he turned his back to me for a moment, and I studied him. He wore mustard colored canvas trousers, a white long-sleeved shirt, and embroidered carpet slip-pers, dusty and worn, but with an intricate pattern of leaves and flowers that had once been of the highest quality needlework.

"And have you any news of Jean Claude?"

"Nothing is known. Nothing."

"Not good." He gazed at me. "And how are you with this...not knowing?" He watched me over his shoulder, raising an eyebrow.

"I feel out of sorts...and sad today. Even though I hardly ever speak with Jean Claude. He and Maurice ignore me as they go about their business hunting and fishing in the swamp. I don't think he's said more than a few words to me in my entire life."

Emile laughed. "How could anyone ignore you?" He swung his spoon with a bit of drama and drops of sauce flew to sizzle in the fire. "But look, he may come home safe and sound. Often people take off on impulse. Look at me!"

"Yes, but cousin...you were one step ahead of the gendarmes all the way...and Jean Claude had nothing to run away from." I paused. "Except Yvonne says he was probably running to get away from having to marry me one day."

"Ha!" He laughed again, throwing his head back so his ash brown hair swung around broad shoulders. "She would say some-thing like that. She's so jealous of you it shows on her furrowed brow every time she glances at you. She's....never mind." He turned toward me. "Too bad I can't feed you some of this. I can't put the catfish in until nearly serving time or it will all break up. But it's going to be...." He kissed the tips of his fingers and flicked them out in a gesture of appreciation.

"*Mais, merci.* I would love nothing better, but I can't. I have chores to do. We're putting up persimmon preserves today." I took another biscuit, nibbling carefully, mindful of the crumbs, very conscious of my manners, and aware of his attentions toward me. The humid, close air of the cabin pressed around me, and I allowed the blanket to slip off my shoulders.

"Thank you for the treat." I slid the empty plate away.

"I'm glad you like my cooking. Since I can no longer practice law, I must develop other talents."

"And in Yvonne's defense, she is also a fine cook."

"Yes, she is," he nodded. "And if she would improve her wretched personality, she may find her plain looks would no longer matter."

"It's not all her fault. After her fiancé was shot in the war, she gradually turned bitter."

He sighed. "Everyone has a different way of handling hardship. Some become bitter; some become even more compassionate than they were before because they know how hard life can be." He stood and crossed to a table against the wall to my left near a shuttered window. "And now, I'd better start mixing the ingredients for the fig cakes I need for tonight's game. Please, keep talking with me. We can visit while I'm doing this. You don't mind?" He watched my reaction from the flickering shadows.

"Of course. Go right ahead."

Emile and my brother's friends all played *bourrée* several nights during the week. Whoever was hosting the game also provided the dinner. I didn't know anyone in St. Beatrice who was not a good cook, man or woman, and the card players always expected to have plenty of food to eat during the all-night games.

As he worked, I glanced around the room at the shelves he'd put up for the few books he'd been able to pack in his two trunks when he fled Paris. My only schooling had been when Maman had the time to work with my reading and copying from the French Missal or the Almanac. Fortunately, Emile had taken it upon himself to work on my French and some history, almost as soon as he'd arrived in St. Beatrice, although Parisian French is quite different from our bayou French. "You must be educated to the world, There are many worlds beyond this one here on the bayou. You may never leave from here, but you need to know about the rest of the world just the same."

He had entertained with tales of the Bourbons, their queens, powerful mistresses, and crafty cardinals. I learned of poisonings and deceit and of Mesdames Pompadour and du Barry, and then of the horrible events of the French Revolution. Emile's narrative of French history was so real, I would shiver at his stories. And when it came to Napoleon, he would draw diagrams of his campaigns, so that I learned the geography of Europe, even though my knowledge of American geography was poor. I learned of Napoleon's coming to America, and of the Bonapartists who traveled to Demopolis on the bluffs of the Tombigbee River in Alabama, hoping to grow olives and grapes, so they could make a fresh start here.

But even though Yankee soldiers had trudged and burned their way through our bayous, I was ignorant of most of the facts of our own war. They had come so close to us, I'd smelled the smoke from a burning sugar mill in St. Martinville. I didn't know much about the Yankee War even though my brother's black eye patch and facial disfigurement were a daily reminder of it.

Emile left his work at the table then to stir the sauce again, steam creating a halo around him. I wondered how I'd ever summon the will to leave my cozy relaxed place there and return to my work at the farm. A few sparks flew from the fireplace, landing on the wide grey cypress planks of the floor. He half turned to make sure they hadn't landed on me as I ground them out with my foot.

"But, look at that! We can't have you staying in those muddy boots." He laid the long handled spoon by the firedogs, slowly bending to examine the condition of my boots. He carefully placed his long hands on my left boot, pulling it gently toward him and stretching my leg in a comfortable, but altogether unexpected way. Glancing up at me from his kneeling position by the fire, he appeared fully recovered from the puffy and red-rimmed state of my arrival. His hazel eyes were bright even in the dim light.

Shrinking back and embarrassed by his touching and closeness, I pulled my foot away. "Oh, no, no, Emile! I'll clean them when I get home. They're just going to get all muddy again when I take the shortcut through the woods along the bayou."

"But it's not...." He broke off, and still staring at me in that bright way, grasped my boot again, and then, with a dreamy expression, allowed one hand to rise toward the top of my clumsy, worn ankle boot, where it lingered, forefinger slowly tracing the rim of the stiff leather. His hand slid quickly up the thick knitted stockings of my calf. "See? Your stockings are wet. Please let me dry them for you before you go home." His hand felt hot through the coarse knit, and I pulled back, even more embarrassed and conscious of the roughness of the stockings.

"Emile, please!"

Startled by my anxious tone, he snatched away his hand. "I'm so sorry, little cousin. I didn't mean to..." He reddened. "I'm so very sorry. I forget myself."

Remaining kneeled before me, he continued to watch me with that somber expression, so unlike the laughing and smiling Emile I knew. "Please forgive me. I must not be in my right mind today."

A faint smell of alcohol drifted in the air as we remained in limbo for a few moments there in the flickering firelight. As my clothes warmed, the smell of wet wool and caked mud rose as well. I fervently hoped I didn't smell like the stables besides, as I'd been mucking out Solange's stall earlier that morning.

The atmosphere in the cabin changed as we stared at one another, and the entire episode took on a dreamlike quality. Frozen, as we can be in dreams sometimes, I was unable to speak or move. After a few moments, I recovered, blinking rapidly as though coming awake from a deep sleep. Emile jerked his head around to look at the fire sputtering and popping, then quickly busied himself with the iron poker rearranging some of the glowing coals at the base of the fire.

"So..." I nervously began, trying to break up the long silence. "They'll just keep searching for Jean Claude until they find him."

"Oh, they'll find him," reassured Emile, his back still to me as he poked at the fire. "He's probably made camp somewhere and forgotten to tell his family where he was going."

Still confused about the strange experience between us just a few moments before, I rattled on, unsure of what else to do. "I pray he's not dead!" I clasped my hands together. My palms were clammy, so I wiped them on my skirt.

"He's not dead. He's tough. Don't be worried. Go home and help your sister put up preserves." He continued to avoid looking at me.

Emile had never suggested I go home before. Feeling instantly hurt, I immediately rose from the chair. Chi-Chi began barking then and raced out to the road as a man approached the path to the cabin. Emile turned from the fire, still avoiding my eyes, and looked outside. Leon Hebert was making his way to the porch.

"Emile!" He cupped hands around his mouth, then continued energetically toward the steps. "What time tonight?" Chi-Chi romped in circles around his legs.

"The usual. Seven o'clock will be good."

Still hurt, I stepped quietly out onto the front porch, preparing to leave by the side of it, toward my shortcut through the woods. Leon planted a boot on the second step, tilting the black slouch hat back off his forehead.

"*Bonjour,* Sidonie....Emile. *Comment ça va?*" He focused dark eyes on Emile.

"What you cooking for us tonight, you?"

"Courtbouillon and baguettes and fig cakes." Emile placed both hands lightly on his hips and straightened his shoulders, his expression once again relaxed and pleasant.

"Then we're in for a treat, aren't we?" Leon smiled, revealing a broken tooth, souvenir of a fistfight with Hippolyte the year before, over a *bourrée* game.

Emile nodded cordially, casually leaning back against the doorway. He had become once more the man I was familiar with, sociable and relaxed in the company of others, confident and regal in posture and manners.

"Maybe tonight I'll win back some of the money I lost to you over the past year, no?" Leon again pushed back the brim of his hat with his thumb, then leaned forward, resting palms on his knees. He squinted up at Emile, deepening hundreds of fine lines around eyes and mouth, etched there by years of hard work in the fields and in the swamp. His hands were gnarled and crosshatched with dark creases from trapping and farming. His short and stocky body contrasted sharply with Emile's lankiness and far more delicate bone structure.

"So then…until tonight." He clapped a square hand on his thigh to punctuate and straightened with a polite nod to me as I prepared to slip away for home. Turning to leave, he paused to ask, "Are Hippolyte and Maurice coming tonight?"

"Yes, and so are Alex and Gerard."

"That crazy Gerard." Leon shook his head. "He should give up playing cards, him. He always loses."

"He learned cards from his father, Ètienne. He always loses too," laughed Emile.

"Malchanceux en cartes, chanceux en amour." Leon pursed his lips.

"He's lucky at love all right." The two men were referring to the great beauty of Gerard's wife. I sighed, wishing my hair was as long and shiny as hers, and that my skin was as finely pored and smooth.

"I'm bringing muskrat and beaver skins to bet tonight. Amelie and I have prepared some three hundred skins for my next trip to New Orleans. I'll have to sneak some of them out of the house. She'll never let me take them to gamble at cards." Leon flashed a quick, sly smile.

"Goodbye, Leon. Goodbye, Emile." I half-heartedly waved at the men, and still feeling hurt, hurried toward the woods at the back of the property, anxious to disappear among the trees and quickly put distance between myself and Emile. Pressing forward into the cool shadows of my beloved forest bordering the bayou, I longed for the privacy and solace of my sleeping loft, but knew I would have to work alongside Yvonne all afternoon, putting up the preserves.

Slowly, I made my way home, in no hurry to spend the rest of the afternoon with my sister and her acid tongue. Vines and thorns snagged my skirts, but I paid them no mind. Songbirds serenaded, but I barely heard them. The visit to Emile's had not accomplished what I'd hoped for: a break from my gloomy thoughts about Jean Claude. Instead, I felt even worse. My best friend had just told me to go home! Moving closer to the shoreline, I admired the gumbo-colored water and the greenish tint where thick gum, oak, and willow trees cast reflections as their graceful long branches trailed in the lazy current.

Being near the bayou always calmed me and I felt better as I carefully picked my way around the roots of the trees along the bayou bank. Watching for snakes, I breathed deeply of the moist sweet air. Flashes of sunlight glinted on the brown and green water and two killdeer, disturbed by my presence, flew off with high-pitched cries. They landed on the opposite shore near a log with eight *tortues ventre jaune* sunning. It had been a while since Maurice had trapped any of the yellow belly turtles so Yvonne could stew them in a sauce piquant. I wasn't going to remind him of this as it pleased me to see them warming themselves in great numbers on half submerged logs and snagged branches all along the bayou.

Pausing for a few moments, I watched a *gros-bec* on the opposite bank studying the water for his next meal. Remaining as still as the heron, I admired his patience and wished I had more of it. Then a mockingbird scolded a cardinal, chasing it out of its territory, making me laugh, so that by the time I reached home, I felt less distressed by Emile's strange behavior. The peace of the woods and the shimmering of the bayou overcame my worries, so that I felt quiet inside. These tranquil moments never failed to give me hope that my life in this bayou world would improve.

3

HIPPOLYTE BRINGS NEWS OF JEAN CLAUDE

This evening I wish to be free.
Twenty Years After - Alexandre Dumas

I had been home only half an hour when Leroy Viator, the constable, rode up to the barnyard and called from the saddle as his horse, a big gray, danced a few feet, stepped sideways, then snorted, blew air and kicked up dirt as the hounds leaped about him, howling as if the devil himself had come calling.

The geese and ducks and chickens raced around in circles screeching, honking, and frantically clucking. Two geese ran toward the horse, long necks stretched out fiercely, honking wild warnings, as the constable waved his hat at them.

"Go on! Get out of here! Get!"

Tigre and Midnight, the older hounds, charged from beneath the house, yelping, ears flopping, and crisscrossing one another, made territorial half circles, protecting the farmhouse.

"Quiet! Quit your barking!" I hollered at them, but they carried on anyway, until Maurice, who was on the roof nailing down loose cypress shingles, yelled one time.

"Quit!" His deep bass voice hushed them, and he called to the constable, straightening his back and wiping his gleaming forehead with a red handkerchief.

Leroy's bulky shadow loomed large on the dirt as the sun angled west. I studied his shadow, as for some reason, I felt shy about meeting his gaze. "Sidonie?" I had to look up when he called my name or look rude, and it was just then that Yvonne stepped out onto the creaking porch in back of me.

"You seen any strangers around here?" he asked, squinting at me. Silently I shook my head as he held my gaze, barely noticing Yvonne.

"What is it?" she asked, voice higher than usual. "Bad news about Jean Claude?"

My sister was in the habit of anticipating bad news and calamities.

"No, no, Yvonne. No news yet. He's probably off trapping somewhere and just forgot to tell anybody."

Leroy, Hippolyte's uncle, sat heavily in the saddle, appearing weary as though he carried all the burdens of the village on his stout frame. He knitted heavy black eyebrows which gave him a menacing expression, yet I knew him to be always polite and serious minded, but never intimidating.

"There were reports of this stranger, a logging scout, passing through the village and buying supplies, but nothing more than that," he reported, swinging his hat at one of the hounds still sniffing around the horse.

"Get on now!" Leaning way over in the saddle, surprisingly agile for such a stout man, he swatted the hound hard enough on the nose to make the dog yelp and back off.

Then straightening in the creaking saddle, he gazed at me again, eyes suddenly sad.

"Why would a logging scout be wandering around here?" I asked.

"To see about taking those giant cypresses out of the swamp." He rubbed his fingers against his thumb making the sign for money.

"You mean actually cut those giant trees down?" A cold chill raced down my spine.

"Somebody's planning to do it or that scout wouldn't be nosing around down here." Leroy firmed his lips in displeasure as red splotches appeared on his cheeks. "Damn a Yankee! They're always causing trouble. Always! Don't you know that yet, Sidonie?"

Tigre commenced leaping about the horse again, and Leroy swatted his hat at him so hard that Tigre let out a howl. Straightening once more in the creaking saddle, he gazed at me with a peculiar melancholy look as though he'd lost something valuable. "I've got to get on with it then. If you hear anything about a stranger, let me know."

"If it's a Yankee they're looking for, who cares what happens to him?" yelled Maurice from the roof.

Leroy laughed, then spat to his left, away from where I was standing. "Now that's a damn fact! But I have to look like I'm doing my job." He secured his hat firmly on his thick black hair, adjusting it carefully so the brim was just so over his eyes. "Of course people around here will understand if I don't look around too hard for him, now won't they?" He peered at the sun just beginning to cast long shadows along the east side of the house. "You all take care now." He wheeled his horse back toward the road, waving his arm with a flourish. As his horse trotted off, our hounds loped along behind, following them down the road, kicking up mud clods before they slowed as of one mind and, bored with the chase, sauntered back to our dirt yard to flop heavily into their customary resting positions, long ears spread out on the ground like leaves.

Yvonne limped over to sweep a cobweb from one of the porch uprights until the smell of scorched milk drifted out the windows and open door. "The bread pudding!" she yelped limping fast into the house.

I quickly returned to weeding the garden so she couldn't figure out a way to blame me for the scorched milk. Squatting between rows of onions, I tried to figure out why any logging scouts would be interested in our swamp. It seemed impossible to cut down the giant cypresses; they were too huge. Nevertheless I had a bad feeling about this news. It was one thing to cut down a cypress and float it out to the sawmill to build a house or barn in the parish. It was quite another to think about strangers coming down from the north to log our precious trees and hauling them off for profit hundreds of miles away. My stomach tightened at the very thought of logging our swamp. I weeded the rows of onions and then the greens, but my heart wasn't in the work, and I continued to feel unsettled about the constable's visit.

Another reason I felt uneasy about Leroy's visit was because of the way he'd stared at me. It occurred to me that he often did that when I'd see him in the village or at community gatherings. I paused in my weeding to pull some sorrel by the edge of the garden to chew some of the sour leaves while pondering.

"Sidonie! Quit daydreaming and come help me!" Yvonne barked from the kitchen window, her tone quite different with me than with Leroy Viator. I winced as her sharp tone brought me back from my reverie and sighed, walking slowly back toward the house, still munching sorrel.

An image of Emile passed before my eyes as I brushed dirt and weeds from my skirts before entering the house. The day so far had been most confusing, and I couldn't make much sense out of any of it. Shrugging, I gave up wondering about it, resolving instead to put my attention on the work at hand.

A dog howled from the farm down the road, and I figured Leroy must have arrived there. Our hounds raised their heads, and I expected them to join in the howling, but instead, they quickly lost interest and dropped their heads back to doze. Saying a quick prayer for Jean Claude's safety, I entered the house to begin the afternoon's work.

I hardly spoke to Yvonne for the next two hours, as we worked side by side, putting up preserves. She kept complaining about how I did each and every detail of the preparation. Everything I did was wrong; nothing was done right.

"Be careful, you're dripping that! Don't put that there. Watch out! You'll spill it all on the floor. That's too hot. Look what you're doing. You can't do it that way. See what you've done now. You're making a mess. I should do it all myself and never ask you for help, you clumsy careless girl!"

I kept working despite her cruel tongue and attempted to let it all slide off my ears, pretending she was talking in gibberish, and I couldn't understand a word of it.

It helped to make excuses for her: she's lame; she's bitter; she can't help her twisted personality. I withdrew inside myself and thought of other matters, such as Jean Claude's possible whereabouts, and also what I might have done to offend my dear cousin, Emile. I'd lost my parents only two years before and hadn't fully recovered from that as yet. I'd possibly lost my fiancé, and on top of all that, certainly couldn't bear to lose my closest friend.

As I reflected on how much Emile had done for me - opening my eyes to the world beyond the bayou, teaching me so much of history and language and French writers - I realized that his friendship had made it possible to bear the cruel loss of my parents. Yvonne's criticisms wore on and on, but I barely heard her as I came to this realization.

Visualizing his face as he excitedly leaned over a book, pointing out a phrase to me, I felt gratitude for the time he took with me and for the way he'd taught me to love the wonders of a great story. Because of Emile's help, the world of literature had become a refuge from the harsh realities of my life the past few years.

Once when Yvonne came too close to my ear with her abuse, I purposefully turned and caught her with my elbow, knocking her back a few steps. I would have done more than that if she wasn't lame, but then of course, after knocking her off balance, I felt guilty for my behavior and she then had even more fuel for her anger.

"Now look what you've done, you clumsy fool!" and the nagging continued as she collected her balance and turned to the work table where the clean jars awaited the remaining persimmons. As soon as we were finished, I left the kitchen, relieved at escaping her, and went out the front door to get on with the rest of my chores. I took a deep breath and exhaled slowly as I stood on the porch and thought about all the work I had yet to do. I was glad to have chores that must be done as it made the day go faster and helped keep worries at the back of my mind.

The yard was an extension of our small house, and the wide expanse of it greatly increased our living space. While I was sweeping the porch and front path, I watched our fat glossy black rooster, T'Neg, who was perched on the seat of the wagon between the outhouse and stable. His glittering black eyes kept watch over a dozen *jacguard* or black and white speckled hens and two young roosters, so young they were just learning how to crow. As they scratched and pecked for bugs and worms, he stayed alert for chicken hawks circling above or other predators that might endanger them. T'Neg stretched his neck and beat his wings so hard, it sounded like sheets flapping on the line in a strong wind. Then he crowed such a loud *err-err-err-errrr!* that he teetered on the frame of the wagon and had to catch his balance.

The clucking of the busy hens and the dogs scratching fleas and making muffled sounds under the porch were all soothing to me as I swept with our coarse handmade broom. When I'd swept enough, I prepared chicken feed by dropping handfuls of dried corn into the *pilé*, a hollowed out cypress log which stood upright on its base. Then I cracked the corn by vigorously shoving a pole called a *pilon*, up and down into the grain at the bottom of the *pilé*.

Gathering my apron to make a pouch and making a cluck-ing sound to call them, I toted cracked corn into the yard and scattered it about for the fowl to peck. They immediately rushed forward, geese, ducks and hens, to the feast, and T'Neg flew off the wagon to join them. I felt peace as I strolled the yard fling-ing handfuls of corn, as the smell of wood smoke from the stove, the pine needles from the woods along the bayou, and the moist turned earth of the vegetable garden all drifted toward me on a southern breeze. The cries of crows at the border of the garden in the cane patch calling to other crows in the cornfield, and the flight of two mockingbirds to one of the gnarly pear trees, lifted my spirits even higher.

For me, all the sights, sounds, and smells of nature were the real world. Life within the house didn't feel as true to me as the great outdoors. The drone of cicadas and the flash of yellow and purple butterflies busy at the flowers were like tonic to me. There could never be a potion I could take that would equal the healing powers of nature. The hounds, their somber eyes world weary, watched the activity in the yard from their lazy positions on the porch and beneath it.

Solange whinnied as I finished flinging the corn and swiped my hands together to brush off the remaining corn. "I'm on my way," I called to her as I went to bring her in from the pasture west of the stables. After toting buckets of water to fill her trough, I got to work laying out fresh hay for her bed, mindful of the six-foot gold and brown rat snake that slithered out of my way, disappearing through a gap between the boards.

While I was busy in the stables, Hippolyte arrived on horseback and tied his gray, Gris-Gris, to the hitching post in front of the porch. He strolled to the side of the house where he greeted and patted the barking hounds. Then he spoke a few words with Yvonne who still worked at the stove by the open window.

He swung his hat, with its band of alligator teeth, into the air and caught it as I called from the stables, picking straw from my skirts. An outgoing, energetic, wiry man, he shouted to me, as was his custom. Whenever Hippolyte was around, he demanded everyone's attention with his loud voice and restless, fidgety behavior.

At times Hippolyte's energy was too much for me to tolerate for long. He was the sort of person who did all the talking and whose feet and hands were always tapping or shuffling. He would squirm in his chair or leap up and pace the room. That sort of unnerving behavior permits no one near him to feel peaceful. He interrupts and barely listens if anyone else gets a chance to say something.

But, my brother never seemed to mind all this whiplash energy. He and Hippolyte, close friends for as long as I could remember, were opposites. Maurice hardly ever spoke. When he did, his remarks were short and bitten off. Whereas Hippolyte was restless, Maurice was still, his expression forbidding. His usual deeply furrowed brow and tight jaw revealed pent up anger, unlike the anxious rapid movements of his friend. How Maurice could stand to go off into the swamp for hours and hours, and put up with Hippolyte's continuous talking and restlessness was a mystery, but somehow these two balanced one another. The two friends, unchanging in their ways, provided each other camaraderie, and they seldom missed a day of being together. How I wished I had someone like that...a close friend to spend time with each day.

Hippolyte brought my attention back to the present. "A man in St. Martinville says he thinks he saw Jean Claude over there the day before yesterday." Tossing his hat again, he opened his mouth wide as he snatched it back with his right hand. Twirling the hat, he suddenly broke into a raucous laugh and smacked it on his head. He looked quickly at me to make sure I'd seen his performance. Then, very carefully, he ran thumb and forefinger along the broad rim, adjusting it to a precise angle over his forehead.

"So!" He took a deep breath, fully expanding his chest, then puffed out his cheeks as he exhaled. "Don't worry. He'll be back soon. I'm sure of it." He then stood on tiptoe at the window, sniffing the aroma of duck gumbo. "And," he sniffed again dramatically, "Tell Maurice I'll be by after dark to get him for bourrée at Emile's."

"And after you're done losing all your money, go get me some frogs. I want to make smothered frog legs tomorrow, me," demanded Yvonne. She leaned out the window, motioning toward him with a long wooden spoon.

"Give me some of that gumbo, and I'll bring you all the frogs you want." He raised up on tiptoe and leaning on the *tablette,* stretched his neck so he could inhale deeply. "And don't go swinging that long-handled spoon at people unless you're planning on supping with the devil," he teased.

"Don't you speak of the devil around me! Go on! Get going! You're in my way. It's not ready yet. You must learn patience." She turned back to the stove. "Something you will never know." But even though she was in the dim interior of the house, I saw a rare smile on her face.

Then, as is customary with Hippolyte, he laughed, leaped up, and whirled about like a dancer. Waving his outstretched arms, he trotted back toward the hitching post to untie Gris-Gris. Collecting the reins loosely in his hand, he swung up onto the saddle with a great flourish, then wheeled Gris-Gris, and circled the yard as chickens, ducks, and geese flapped their wings and scattered with a great clamor. With an echoing yell, he kicked Gris-Gris into a fast trot. Off down the road they clopped, as Hippolyte whooped and hollered. Clods of dirt flew from Gris-Gris's hooves as they headed west toward Hippolyte's mother's house, where he still lived at age thirty-three.

The hounds, excited by all the noise, scrambled from beneath the cool of the house, and broke into a run, racing after Hippolyte and Gris-Gris. They joyously yelped and cavorted down the road until they smelled a fox squirrel. In an instant, they veered off into the cane field across the road, tearing after the red-tailed squirrel until they were hidden from view in the thick of the tall, graceful sugar cane.

Suddenly weary from the long day, I headed back for the house where I planned an escape to my narrow cot in the loft. I hoped to read a few pages of the Dumas that Emile had given me to improve my French. As I lay on the crackling, moss-filled mattress, holding the unopened book on my stomach, I stared at the rafters, eyelids heavy. Yvonne's voice carried up to the loft from the kitchen. She grumbled and mumbled about how lazy I was, and how she had to do everything herself.

An old memory of Yvonne came to me. Years before, someone had tried to drown some puppies in the bayou. I had found them in a drenched sack lying half in the water and half on the mossy bank. One puppy was still alive, its little eyes not even open yet. Crying, I'd run with it to Yvonne. "Poor little thing," she'd said softly, hurrying to heat hot milk. Together we'd nursed it by soaking a rag in the milk for it to suck. We put the puppy to bed by the stove so we could take turns looking after it. My father, cursing whoever had thrown that sack of puppies into the bayou, buried the drowned litter and allowed us to keep the lone survivor. That puppy had grown into a healthy hound, and became one of our favorite dogs: Midnight.

Within minutes of this reverie, I was fast asleep and dreaming of an anguished Jean Claude staring at me, trying to communicate with dark, sad eyes.

4

A VISIT TO THE SWAMP

Hoofbeats pounded on the moonlit road.
Twenty Years After - Alexandre Dumas

That night as we sat at the table eating, our family, as usual, ate in silence without the conversation I had heard at other people's houses. Only sounds of chewing, scraping cutlery against the tin plates, or setting down bowls of rice or gumbo, interfered with this measured silence.

Maurice was a noisy eater. His jaw made grinding noises as he chewed because the right side of his face had been severely damaged by a black powder explosion in the war. The entire side of his face was covered with puckered red scar tissue and part of his ear was missing. He wore a black leather patch where his eye had been, and his right eyebrow and part of his beard had never grown back. He had been injured during the first year he joined the 18th Regiment in Lafayette when the rifle of the soldier standing next to him had exploded. He had never been of a cheerful disposition, even before the accident, and by the time they sent him home from the hospital at Fausse Point, he had turned mean and hot-tempered. None of this had affected his keen eye, however, for he could still spot a squirrel from seven *arpents* away.

Besides being a noisy eater, he also ate fast and was in a great hurry to leave the table as though sitting with us made him uncomfortable and restless. He took greedy bites with his right hand, while keeping the other in a loose fist firmly planted on his hip. He positioned himself always half turned toward the door in his haste to be away from us and out the door into the night – either to his room in back of the stables, or to his nightly adventures in the swamp or at cards.

I had always made excuses for Maurice's rude behavior and told myself it was because of his injuries and that he'd eventually improve as he adjusted to his losses. But I was beginning to grow weary of always trying to be polite to someone who regularly bit back with hurtful words. Over the past few years, as I gradually met other survivors of the war in our community who had sustained terrible injuries, yet who managed to treat others with respect and friendliness, I found it even more difficult to live around Maurice.

That evening, I ventured a comment about what Hippolyte had said that afternoon, as Maurice cut an onion with the knife from his pocket, and ate a chunk of it wrapped in a thick slice of dark bread. "Hippolyte says Jean Claude was seen in St. Martinville." I looked at him closely while carefully holding my fork midway between the bowl and my mouth, pausing for an answer.

His damaged jaw made that harsh grinding noise as he chewed the onion and bread. I examined his face as I waited, the dark moustache, the downturned corners of his mouth expressing a bitter view of the world. His skin was dark as a beetle's from being outdoors most of his life, and his brow was deeply furrowed as he frowned at me, his good eye glittering in the candlelight.

He suddenly laughed while leaning his chair back so it rested on two legs. "You are so stupid always. That story is rubbish. Old man Bouchard is half blind anyway, and he says now he doesn't even remember much what Jean Claude looks like." Maurice laughed again, shaking his head. "You're such a *couillon!*"

"She'll believe anything," Yvonne jumped in, not looking up from her gumbo as she spooned another bit of rice into the bowl. "She probably likes Hippolyte," she added with a smirk, still not looking up.

Feeling a stab of anger at this injustice, I once again let it pass. Hippolyte's news had given me hope that Jean Claude was still alive, but Maurice's words dashed those hopes, and I was once again fearful that he was dead somewhere in the swamp. "Well then, I'm sorry to hear that. I was beginning to hope Jean Claude was alive and well somewhere."

"Don't worry about that one. He's too tough to kill," offered Yvonne.

"He's tough all right," agreed Maurice, rocking his chair back onto all four legs with a loud thump. "And you mind your business, and don't go believing everything you hear," he said gruffly, pointing a finger at me.

In Acadiana there is an abiding affection for all family members, relations, and friends. All look out for one another, and the ties of family are much in evidence anywhere you travel around the bayous. It was for this reason that I often kept trying to hold a normal conversation with these two, and that night persisted as usual, despite their rude talk. "You're going to Emile's tonight to play cards, no?" I asked Maurice, keeping my voice low.

"What do you care?" he responded without looking at me. His voice was so sharp that Yvonne finally peered up from the gumbo bowl looking like a witch leaning over a cauldron.

"Hippolyte said to tell you he'd be by for you after dark," I continued.

Maurice sniffed. "I already knew that. What of it?" He shoved his chair back and stood, cleaning his knife on his trousers. He returned it to a leather sheath hitched to his belt.

"Are you going to the swamp later on?"

"Maybe. So?" He still hadn't met my gaze.

"I want to go along."

"Ha! And why would we take you?" He finally met my eyes, brow knitted, black eye patch glinting in the candlelight.

"Please, Maurice," I urged. "I want to help look for Jean Claude. At least one time."

"It'll be too late. We won't get done with cards until well after midnight." He turned to leave.

"Please. I really want to go along." I half stood, holding onto the planks of the table with hands tightly gripping the wood.

"It's too late for a young girl," Yvonne growled.

"Please, Maurice. I never ask you to do anything for me."

"As well you shouldn't, little girl." He rubbed a hand over his mouth and wiped it on his trousers. "What good could you do out in the swamp?"

I ignored Yvonne. "Please. Papa took me sometimes."

"Maybe. Who knows? If you're not asleep we may come back for you, but probably not." He strode for the door, never thanking Yvonne for supper, and slammed it behind him, so hard the broom by the doorway fell. His heavy steps crossed the porch, and then he whistled to the dogs as he returned to the stables. I knew from his words that he would probably come back for me unless he got too drunk at cards and forgot. This gave me the energy I needed to clear the table and clean up the dishes.

"I'm going to bed early," Yvonne said. "My foot is hurting tonight. I've been on my feet all day." She hobbled off to her narrow room by the kitchen, and I gratefully watched her retreat. She closed the door to her cramped space, and I heard her rummaging in the trunk at the foot of her bed.

My chores completed, I scurried to my loft and retrieved the leather bound copy of the book Emile had entrusted to me in order to improve my French: *Twenty Years After.* Then back down the ladder, I poured coffee from the dented pot on the stove and settled myself at the table with the book and coffee so I could amuse myself reading until Maurice and Hippolyte returned from cards to collect me.

Opening to a blue jay feather I used as a bookmark, I felt with pleasure the worn scratched leather cover and the pages as thin as a Missal. Within minutes, I was lost once again in the great adventures of d'Artagnan, Porthos, Athos, and Aramis, on Cardinal Mazarin's intrigues for the court of Anne of Austria, the Queen Regent.

I had read for perhaps an hour and a half, when I suddenly remembered to pat wood ash on my face and hands to protect my skin from the giant swamp mosquitoes. I got up and tended to this, then poured more coffee, which grew stronger and blacker the longer it kept warm on the stove.

Trying not to feel jealous of those who were sharing Emile's warmth and hospitality that night, I nevertheless wished to be among the group playing cards. I knew how to play bourrée because my father, Gros Louis, had taught me. I pictured the men eating Emile's stew, drinking his wine, and laughing together as the card game wore on. The poker and bourrée pots in those days were slim compared to the lavish games in New Orleans, but as each economy values its exchange, so did ours, and our exchange reflected the trapping, bartering, and hard to come by coins these men could collect for their furs and crops in Baton Rouge or New Orleans.

As I gazed around the shadows of our house near midnight, the moon rose, and creamy moonlight spilled through the kitchen window onto the rough planks of our table where I sat, *Twenty Years After* lying open before me. Somehow the moonlight bewitched me in its silver glow, and I began to feel almost sorry for Yvonne and Maurice. He had sounded so harsh and unfeeling at the supper table and didn't want my company in the great swamp, for surely my presence would hamper the usual rough talk he and Hippolyte normally used, their talk coarsened even more by the wine or brandy that Emile had served at the card game. They would not be able to talk of their women and curse about anything that was bothering them.

When the moon had risen high in the sky, hoofbeats pounded on the road, and I closed the book, quickly carrying it up to my loft to hide it from prying eyes. I did not want my sister or brother to know I had a book belonging to Emile. They would be sure to make cruel remarks about this, and no doubt ridicule my learning more French. Hurrying down the ladder so I could run out to meet them, I yanked a wool shawl off a peg by the door and softly closed the door behind me.

Maurice hissed from where he sat on Theotiste as I stepped off the porch. The yard was silvery gray in the moonlight. "We're going to old man Delcambre's cabin. It's faster if we take his pirogue." He jerked his head toward Hippolyte who held his reins taut, and blinked drunkenly at me. "Well, go on. Get Solange! What are you holding us up for?"

Running to the stables, I entered Solange's stall where she must have wondered why I was bothering her so late at night. I reassured her and stroked her mane, bridling her with the help of the moonlight, then led her out and using a wooden box by the stables, pulled up my skirts, and swung up bareback, nudging her into a walk. The two men, already out on the silver road, were disappearing fast around the bend by our field, and I urged Solange into a gallop so we could catch up. In the course of our journey to the Delcambre cabin, not only black woods, but also flat and silver rice fields stretched for acres to the north of the road.

The peace of midnight was a time I seldom got to see, unlike the two men, who stayed out all night most of the week, seldom needing but a few hours sleep. We rode the two miles to the cabin without speaking, hoof beats drowning out the night sounds of the crickets and owls. When we neared the cabin, I could smell the swamp, the bayou muck, and the leaf mold bordering the banks, moist and fresh, and like no other smell.

Whenever I am at the threshold of the great Atchafalaya, I feel happy and also in awe of its sprawling size, and huge capacity for growth and renewal. It's a great simmering stew of budding plant life, fish life, and millions of insects and birds. This great drowned cypress forest harbors endless numbers of tiny eggs, cocoons and little creatures which add up to thousands of small deaths each night by predators in this thick swamp soup.

Gros Louis and Grandfather Achille had frequently brought me as a child to teach me the extravagant wonders of the swamp, so I felt on familiar ground as I entered its dreamy shadows. As we tied the horses to a post in front of the Delcambre cabin, the insects' screaming, screeching night song billowed around me with enfolding arms, pulling me toward the swamp. I associated the Atchafalaya with Papa and Grandpapa, and I felt the warmth of their love as we made our way toward the bank.

Old man Delcambre stepped carefully down the path from his little cabin to speak with us, lantern held high, casting a welcome glow over the dark bushes and undergrowth of the banks of Bayou Perdu. He was in his late seventies and somewhat stooped, but had a firm, steady voice and confident step.

"Going frogging, you?"

"Yes, and we'll bring you back a sack of them as always, old man." Hippolyte's voice sounded like the ride from the farm had sobered him.

"I'll wait up then." He nodded to me pleasantly. "Take this, Sidonie." He handed me the lantern and began to make his way back up the path in the moonlight. His cabin on stilts looked inviting with mellow flickering candlelight at the windows.

"Well, get in then!" Maurice ordered as they scraped the pirogue into the water, grunting with the effort. I stepped into the moving boat, quickly kneeling and settling comfortably, as Hippolyte hung the lantern on a pole at the stern.

Maurice's hair was tied back with a scarf, pirate style, and Hippolyte wore his usual slouch hat with the alligator teeth gleaming in the moonlight. He pushed us off with a long pole, and we began to float easily north toward the Atchafalaya River and then beyond to the thick of the swamp. Birds, disturbed by our passing, clacked and rustled in their night perches, then resettled after we passed. The insects' drone amplified to ultimate force as Hippolyte poled us deeper and deeper into the thick of it. Occasional screeches and shrill cries of fear and death came from the tangled vines and shadowy undergrowth near the banks. The willows trailed long graceful branches into the water, further shrouding the predators on their nightly hunt. The cypress trees grew thicker and taller as we progressed. Their trunks were so gigantic, it would take four men stretching their arms to form a circle around them.

The canopy of their branches intermeshing over our heads shut out the moonlight, and we were in darkness as we rounded a bend, reaching a bay of the swamp. Hippolyte began to have trouble navigating us around a multitude of cypress knees. They were great humps in the black water, and difficult to see in the density of the shadows. Despite the blackness, the screeching and the growls surrounding us, despite the red eyes of the alligators on the choked banks, and the whine of the mosquitoes, I felt safe and protected in the great swamp. Everything we had, we owed to the swamp. Our bountiful way of life, our rich dirt were all owing to the noble Atchafalaya. Our farms were irrigated from it; and the very air we breathed was filtered by those hundreds of thousands of watery acres.

So, even though it was long after midnight, and we were in a narrow boat of ten feet, surrounded by wilderness, my only feelings were of comfort and pleasure. This was an extension of our home, even though the farm was miles away. I was aware that every house and barn were built from these giant trees, and all the hand-made furniture within. No matter how many tales Emile told us of France and Paris, and no matter what adventures I read of the brave Musketeers, this was my home and I never wanted to leave. Even when we died, our coffins would be built of cypress.

The fact that we were on the eve of the great destruction of these ancient trees by Yankee logging crews, was unknown to us that night as we made our way along. We were still innocent of the painful devastation of our wilderness that lay ahead. As we round-ed another bend, there was a break in the overhanging canopy, and moonlight glinted on the black slow moving water. Gradually, we were able to make out a pirogue at rest near the opposite bank just yards ahead.

"Arsène!" my brother hailed, and as we drew nearer, I recog-nized Arsène who had lived in the swamp as long as I could re-member. The only times I ever saw him were on trips to the village to take cane to the pressers or to buy supplies at the tiny store. I knew he lived in a camp just beyond the next bay. Arsène stretched out a strong arm to steady our craft against his own, but the two boats bumped and bobbed until he used both arms and Hippolyte was able to jam his pole into the mud of the river bottom.

A *pichou* screeched as a breeze moved some of the overhanging canopy, and moonlight outlined Arsène's features so that he also looked like a wildcat. His straggly beard, heavy black eyebrows and long black hair took on a forbidding look in the night, but I knew Arsène's eyes to be kind and serene, for I had seen him close up in the daylight and knew him to be a mild, easy going man.

"No sign of Jean Claude?" asked Maurice.

"Nothing." Arsène tossed his head to flick the long hair over his shoulder. "I never stop looking for him though when I'm in the boat."

We sat quietly as insects screamed around us. Fish jumped, and the frogs we'd come after croaked in rhythm to the insects' cry. To an outsider, the night noises of the swamp might seem deafening, but for me, it was all music that soothed my spirit.

"What are you after tonight, you?" Maurice asked.

"What do you think?" Arsène laughed, and held up a string of *gaspergou.* Then he peered at the moon, and back at me. "Is that Sidonie out so late?"

"She made us bring her along."

"And why do you want to be here instead of your warm soft bed?" He strained to keep the boats steady with his long arms.

"I wanted to help hunt for Jean Claude."

"You will find nothing tonight. I've been out for three hours. There is no sign of anyone out here."

"I believe you. You know everything that moves out here. But I promised Alcide Delcambre and Yvonne some frogs," said Hippolyte.

"We'll check Jean Claude's catfish holes too," he added, drawing himself up straight to begin poling again.

"Go ahead, but I already did that." Arsène pushed us off, blowing out a deep breath.

We drifted along a hundred yards as Hippolyte worked silently, never allowing the pole to touch the boat. I batted whining mosquitoes away from my face, but the wood ash was working, and they weren't biting me.

Maurice laughed low. "That Arsène is half alligator, and he lives in an alligator cave under the water."

"*C'est vrai!*" laughed Hippolyte, "and his mother was an alligator and his father was a *pichou.*"

As we rounded another bend, willow branches caught at my scarf and face, and I breathed in more insects, causing me to sneeze. Another half hour more of Hippolyte's steady poling, and we had reached our destination. The men pulled the boat onto a bank, took the lantern, and sloshed off into the murky undergrowth. Moments later, Arsène's pirogue glided out of the darkness, coming to rest a few feet from the bank.

"You all right here by yourself in the dark?" he asked, peering at me through the gloom.

"Oh, yes, thank you. They're close by, and the moon is full."

"I'm going back to camp, but I'll stay and keep you company if you want."

"No. You don't have to do that. They're close by."

"Here then. Keep this with you." He handed over a small tin of a foul smelling salve. "Rub this on you. It's better than wood ash. My mother makes it. She's a *traiteuse.*" He raised a hand in farewell, pushed off, and disappeared within minutes into the gloom. I hadn't known that his mother was a faith healer. Our family had used one for years, Miss Ozime. We believed in the power of her prayers and herbal cures. It was only when Miss Ozime's treatments hadn't saved our parents from the fever that we called in a doctor. His medicine couldn't save them either. The fever had proved too deadly for treater or doctor.

I smeared the salve on the backs of my hands and on my face, wrinkling my nose at the strong smell. I was, however, no stranger to strong smelling concoctions. The *huile de cocodrie* my parents had forced on us to prevent colds and fevers when we were children, had such an awful smell that we'd run away whenever we saw Maman reach down that alligator oil bottle from the kitchen shelf.

She always persisted, hunting us down in our hiding places, and we always ended up grimacing and taking the spoonful. It must have worked because we rarely got colds or sore throats. Maman continued keeping up the supply of oil by rendering alligator fat until she took sick with the fever. No one in our family made up alligator oil after my parents died, although many others in St. Beatrice continued to use it as medicine.

"Thank you, Arsène!" I called into the inky shadows downstream, but the only sound from that direction was the water falling from his pole as he glided away into the night.

5

A VISIT TO THE SISTERS OF THE HOLY REFUGE

The two friends drew near.
Twenty Years After - Alexandre Dumas

Before I went to bed that night, tired as I was, I took the time to draw water at the pump and fill my basin so I could sponge off some of the ashes and salve from my face and hands. A few places around my collar and my forehead itched, but I was so worn out, I didn't care. Once falling into bed, I drifted off to sleep wondering about the whereabouts of Jean Claude, but feeling hopeful now that I knew Arsène was searching for him in the swamp every day and night. If anyone could find Jean Claude, it was Arsène, the swamp rat.

The roosters awakened me the next morning, but I pulled the quilt over my head. I couldn't fall back to sleep however, and placing the pillow over my head to shut out the light and the gentle cooing of mourning doves didn't help either. Finally giving up and swinging my legs over the side of the bed, I dressed quickly, brushed and braided my hair and peered out the loft window to see a clear and dry day. T'Neg was making so much noise, I was tempted to put him into the cook pot. Rubbing my eyes and yawning, I stumbled to the edge of the loft and descended the ladder, thinking only of coffee and cold water on my face. Yvonne already had *couche-couche* sizzling in the pan, as I groped for the coffeepot and poured out a cup.

"Well?"

"Well what?"

Steam from the *couche-couche* billowed around her face. She stepped back from the stove. "How did it go last night?"

"All right." I sat heavily onto a chair and hunched over the coffee, sipping the strong brew and closing my eyes to shut her out.

"Nice big frogs though. I don't suppose you caught any of them." I shook my head. "Didn't think so," she muttered, wiping the shelves of a wooden cabinet. Yvonne was obsessed about cleanliness. She spent her life cleaning things. If she were in heaven, she'd be cleaning everything up there too. As for myself, I couldn't even see the invisible dirt she attacked every day, and didn't worry about it. As she wiped vigorously with a cloth, she stirred up a bit of dust, and the motes were floating in the beam of early morning light that angled through the kitchen window.

"I'll be cooking those frogs today. See that you clean a chicken for me and pull some onions. I want to make a pot of rice dressing besides." She washed the cloth and wrung it over the edge of the *tablette*, the shelf that extended from the kitchen window. This is where we kept the dishpan, so we could toss wash water out into the yard. "Go on now. I'm going to knead bread here." She crossed to the table where I slumped, still trying to wake up after only a few hours sleep, and began wiping the table.

"I need another cup of coffee first."

"Take it outdoors. You're in my way." She wiped the table so hard with her red and chapped hands, she almost knocked my cup over. The smell of lye soap was strong on her.

"Why are you hands so red and chapped?"

"Because all I do is cook and clean for you and Maurice, that's why." She bit off every word.

Pouring more coffee, I escaped to the front porch, settling myself on the warped top step in order to drink it in peace. The hounds came around and began licking my hands and wrists, laughing, their tongues hanging out, hoping I'd hurry and feed them. There was stale cornbread in the kitchen and some meat scraps saved for them, but that could wait. First, I had to cure my headache with the chicory coffee. I burrowed my face in the soft neck and ears of Lulu, a yellow cur, who was almost eleven years old.

Finally, scratching a few mosquito bites on my neck from the night before, I stretched and stood to get on with my chores. I fed the hounds, the chickens, ducks, and geese, gathered up the eggs in the henhouse, and led the horses out to graze while I mucked the stalls, throwing pitchforks of manure into the manure wagon for the garden. I filled all the troughs. We had three of these for the horses and the dogs. I hauled water from the well by toting buckets back and forth until the cypress troughs were full.

When I'd postponed the job of killing a hen as long as I could, I finally selected one and wrung her neck, closing my eyes as I whirled the doomed bird, meanwhile imagining the little hen to be Yvonne. Hating this task, I rushed through it; submerging the body quickly into scalding water and plucking out the feathers as fast as I could. As hard as I tried to contain the feathers, I knew some of them would fly out of the basket I dropped them into, and that would result in another round of scolding from Yvonne about what a mess I was making in the yard.

As soon as my chores were done, I intended to get away and go visit my friend and advisor, Claire, at the convent a mile down the road, where she lived with her fellow sisters in a convent they'd built five years before. She and the others had arrived from France to build their community. Sister Claire had befriended me one day when I was in the *sucrerie* in the village, where Maurice and I were awaiting the pressing of our cane, two years before. She had stopped by our wagon and asked me about the loss of my parents and invited me to visit them at the convent that very day to eat with them.

I was enchanted by the convent, the flowers they grew in the bountiful garden, the charming little chapel, and their cheerful welcoming ways. The visit was such a success, I returned weekly to visit them ever since that afternoon. Claire gave me a volume of Psalms that first visit and instructed me to read one daily, and this became as strong a habit as my nightly prayers. It was through Sister Claire's instructions so soon after the deaths that I was able to bear the shock of losing my parents.

As I rode Solange to the convent, she seemed pleased to be making a day trip. The hounds escorted us part of the way, then growing lazy in the heat, they hung back and soon returned to their naps on and under the porch. Solange kept a steady pace down the road. The mud had dried, so dust rose as we trotted along, and I leaned into her mane, sniffing that deep horse smell in the coarse hair.

We passed cane fields brilliant green in the sunlight with glossy black crows here and there vivid against the intensity of the graceful cane. The wind from the south felt warm as it touched my skin, and it was so good to get away from the farm. As we neared the Convent of the Holy Refuge, I sat up straight and observed the sisters hoeing and weeding among the bright reds, blues, and gold of the front flower beds. Some of the nuns were bent over, while some kneeled as they worked. One nun's face was surrounded by pink blossoms, and she smiled at us as we approached, her round, rosy face blending with the flowers. One of my favorite sisters, Genevieve, was so absorbed in her weeding, she didn't notice us, her face almost hidden by a *garde de soleil.*

"Hello, Sisters Genevieve, Monique, and Louise," I called, "and Sister Lorraine." I waved to them all before dismounting. Tying Solange to a spreading fig tree, I hurried along the brick walk toward the main building as the nuns waved to me. It was close to the time when we would all enter the chapel for prayers before the noon meal. I regretted leaving the farm so quickly I'd forgotten to bring them some preserves.

Sister Claire opened the front door, her mouth widening into a bright and welcoming smile. A delicate perfume wafted from roses and lavender in a vase behind her in the hallway, so that it seemed to be coming from her. Claire's face was plain, some might even say homely, yet her sweet disposition softened her looks. A network of lines creased the skin around her sky blue eyes and mouth, and her jaw line was blurring with age. Her smile, however, was generous and bright which took years off her face, so that she seemed much younger than her seventy years.

"Sidonie! I've wondered when you were coming to visit." She opened the door wide and beckoned me inside. "Come in. Come in." She took my hand, escorting me down the narrow hallway to a tiny room at the front of the building, sparsely furnished with four ladder back chairs and a low table and bookcase. "Sit down and tell me what you've been doing."

I settled into a chair, with a glance at the crucifix on the wall and the portrait of the Blessed Mother beside it. I bowed my head when I saw the Blessed Mother's likeness, and hoped she would forgive me my cruel and unkind thoughts toward my sister, such as imagining I was wringing her neck instead of the poor little hen's.

"Nothing new really. Except I did go to the swamp last night with Maurice and Hippolyte to help look for Jean Claude."

"You're too young to be traveling about in the swamp at night," she chided, settling herself and folding chubby hands on her lap.

"I insisted. I'm worried about him. He's missing now three days and no one has any idea where he is. But at least, we met up with Arsène, who is truly a swamper, and he looks for him day and night when he's out fishing and trapping. That made me feel a little better."

"And what else have you been doing? Catch me up. Tell Claire."

"The usual. Putting up with my sister who has the tongue of a viper. Same for my brother. I'd be better off living in the swamp, me too." My eyes felt suddenly wet. "Never a kind word from either of them."

"I'm so sorry you have to put up with the two of them. They're going to miss you when you marry and leave them with all the work at the farm."

"Miss me? I doubt that very much. They will dance for joy." The air in the room was still and hot. I tugged at the collar of my blouse, pulling it away from my throat. "And the work is good. It gives me something to do outside of the house all day." I squirmed in my chair. "I'm sorry to be complaining so much. It's just that lately, it all seems worse because my dear cousin, Emile....I think he's annoyed with me about something, and I have no idea what."

"Really?" She waited patiently as my face grew hot.

"Maybe he doesn't want to be my friend anymore. That's what I fear, and that hurts."

"You're having a bad time lately. But Emile may not be annoyed with you. It may be something else altogether that has nothing to do with you. You may find you were wrong. I hope so. He's such a gentleman. And *you*, you're quite the brave one. Out in the swamp at night!"

"You came all the way from France to build all this," I made a sweeping gesture to indicate the convent and the chapel and grounds. "How many people would have the courage, and at your age, to sail for weeks to a strange land…and do all this?"

She tilted her head. "Hmmm. I never thought of myself like that." She laughed, blue eyes crinkling. "So maybe we're both adventurous?"

A shuffling sound in the hallway made me turn, and there was Sister Brigitte standing at the door, watching me and licking pale, dry lips. She stepped three times to the left, then three to the right, and repeated the ritual. Her delicate nose quivered, and she pursed dry cracked lips, frowning as she concentrated on performing those precise movements. Then she raised a finger to her lips as if to say, "Wait. I have to do this first."

Claire said softly, "Sister Brigitte counts steps each day whenever she goes anywhere. She has to count steps before entering rooms, and at other times. We are praying for her. It's some mysterious inner need – a disturbance she developed recently." Turning toward Brigitte she said, "Join us when you can. We won't disturb you." Brigitte began a new ritual then, stretching her arms high to tap the doorway with the tips of her fingers. Her lips moved silently as she kept counting. Claire and I resumed our conversation, ignoring Brigitte as she continued on with this strange behavior.

"So, as I was saying, my dear," Claire went on. "We will all pray for your serenity, and I will add your problems to my own private prayers. But, in the meantime remember the old saying: *God laughs at our plans.*" She narrowed her eyes at me for emphasis.

"I don't understand."

"In other words, we mustn't worry so about the details of our lives. Our natural state is one of happiness. Our nature is to love. When people like your sister make you feel badly, that is because you are forgetting to love her. Her state of mind is not a happy one, or she wouldn't be so unpleasant. Take refuge in your woods and with your animals as I know you do. But remember to love her as you go through your day. Your love can melt her anger."

"I can't do that."

"But, of course you can, dear friend. It's your natural state. And when our love tames an enemy, our Lord is especially pleased. If you are wearing the armor of love, no hateful words can penetrate."

"Armor of love?"

"Love protects you!"

"Then you don't know my sister....or my brother."

"Oh, yes I do. At least your brother is gone all the time, so you don't have to put up with his anger too often. That's a blessing you can be grateful for."

The bell started ringing for *Sext*, the midday prayers. Claire rose from her chair. "We're going to have to help move Sister Brigitte along, otherwise it will take her all day to get to the chapel. Let's go help her."

"I feel better already just talking with you for a few minutes."

"You know we're always glad to see you here, Sidonie. You're welcome at any time. And remember, never doubt the power of love for even an instant." We turned toward the doorway to help Brigitte progress toward the chapel.

As we slowly passed the perfumed flowerbeds on a tidy brick walk toward the vegetable gardens, delicious smells from the outdoor kitchen in back of the convent drifted toward us. We passed rows of cabbages and Brussels sprouts, cauliflower and dark curly beet greens. I felt hungry, yet knew I'd have to wait another half hour at least.

The chapel was small, not much bigger than our bayou home. Brigitte's hand twisted in mine as she tried to break loose, but I held on tightly. Claire had a grip on her right arm, despite Brigitte trying to squirm away from us. Sister Louise was yanking on the bell cord, clanging the bell high up on a pole in front of the chapel. Each time the bell clanged, Brigitte jumped, and Claire and I would steady her.

"It's all right. Come along. You're safe with us. Breathe deeply of the roses." Claire kept reassuring her in this manner, but at the door to the chapel, Brigitte began to pull back and count aloud. "Come inside now," Claire told her. "No more counting. We're going to walk right inside and sit down."

The gray painted steps were worn bare from years of use, going in and out for predawn, morning, midday, evening and night
prayers: Matins, Louds, Sext, Vespers and Compline. I felt relief as
we finally got Brigitte seated in the cool dim interior of the chapel.
"Dear Lord and Savior," she whispered, briefly squeezing my hand
as she fell to her knees on the kneeler.

A vase of yellow roses decorated the altar. The single stained
window above the altar had been brought from New Orleans. The
window showed the Savior praying in Gethsemane, and purple
and green shafts of color angled down from the stained glass onto
the altar. As we repeated the prayers, each side of the aisle taking
their turn, I watched over Brigitte, fearful she'd break away from
us. She touched each finger of her hand with her thumb and silently mouthed numbers instead of the prayers. I tried to comfort
her by taking her hand, but she yanked it back, every now and
then turning her head from side to side in a measured ritual only
she understood.

As we emerged into the bright light, I blinked to adjust my
eyes, and saw that Solange had somehow gotten her rope untied,
and was serenely munching grass on the other side of the road. "I
must go, Sister Claire. Look." I pointed.

"She'll be all right. Come eat with us."

"No, thank you. I'd better get back. Thank you so much for
talking with me. I feel so much better now."

Brigitte stepped in place beside us, her lips still moving. "You're
sure?" Claire motioned toward the sisters slowly moving toward
the outdoor kitchen. "We'd love to have you stay."

"I'll be back soon. I promise."

"Remember…practice that feeling." Nodding, I impulsively
kissed her cheek, then did the same to Brigitte, who didn't re-
spond, except to rapidly flick her eyes back and forth.

As I rode away from the convent on my little mare, I gazed
around at all the wildflowers in the ditches, the billowing clouds
tinged with gold against the sharp blue of the sky, and practiced
Claire's direction to love everything I saw. Not burdened with
thoughts of Yvonne and Jean Claude, I admired the sorrels, the
dandelions, the swamp mallow and the bright pink and blue pas-
sionflowers on twining vines. The light was no brighter than when

I'd first set out that morning to visit Claire, but now it seemed to illuminate the roadside weeds and wildflowers with a radiance that stunned me as we trotted toward home.

As Solange veered into the yard, I gave out a yell, "I'm home!" Chickens, ducks and geese scattered, clucking and honking wildly, and the sleepy hounds yawned and shook themselves alert, tongues lolling as they trotted out to greet us.

"Stop that yelling this instant! Are you insane?" Yvonne banged out of the house, shaking a long spoon.

"It's a beautiful day! I can't help it!" I called out, refusing to be shaken from my new cloud of happiness.

"There's no reason to act like a fool!" She shook the spoon like a weapon. "You are an embarrassment to the family when you act like this!"

I laughed at her and led Solange back to the stables. Sinking heavily into the straw, I thanked God for my friend Claire who helped me endure and overcome. Breathing deeply of the sweet hay, I gazed with loving eyes on Solange as she munched straw. I absently stuck a piece of straw in my mouth and admired the light rays angling in through chinks between the boards, and the lone hen who was not outside pecking for grubs and worms, but making soft serene clucks from her precarious position directly above us in the rafters.

6

EMILE TELLS ME OF THE GOLD COINS

"And with what do you make these twelve thousand francs?"
said d'Artagnan, "with your poems?"
Twenty Years After - Alexandre Dumas

I slept fitfully that night and dreamed of the great swamp. Drifting in a pirogue, my hand trailing in the dark water, (something I would never do when awake for fear of moccasins and alligators,) the current carried me swiftly in the narrow boat. Bumping into a bank at a curve in the bayou, I opened my eyes from this twilight sleep and watched as a giant cypress turned into a man I knew to be Arsène, but couldn't really make out his features in the darkness. Feeling fear and not being able to move, I wanted to guide the pirogue away from the bank and hasten on down the bayou, but could not. It was not Arsène I feared, but something else, something hovering just beyond us, out of reach, and out of sight, but menacing nevertheless.

I awakened to the roosters' crowing and felt wet with perspiration. In addition to that discomfort, I had a bitter headache left over from that tense and unpleasant dream. Throughout the chores that morning, I kept seeing wisps of that dream in my mind's eye. My throat would tighten each time I recalled these disturbing dream fragments.

Yvonne called out the kitchen window mid-morning to tell me to go to the woods and hunt mushrooms when I was finished with the chores, as she wanted to serve them with the baked chicken we were having for dinner. This was good news for it meant I had a perfect opportunity, once in the woods, to write a poem to Emile. I hoped in a poem I could let him know how upsetting our last visit was to me. All I had left to do was hang up the wash on the clothesline. It was hard to buy material after the war, but we hadn't gotten desperate enough to haul Maman's old spinning wheel and loom out of the stable where they were stored. It would take four days to spin enough cotton to make a skirt, so it was important for Yvonne and me keep up with the washing, for we each had only a few changes of clothing. What we had were either on us, in the wash basket, or folded in the trunks at the foot of our beds.

Once I'd escaped the house, I took off at a fast pace toward the woods at the edge of the property. Our farm was about fifty acres of fields and woods around the house and stables, so finding mushrooms would not be difficult since we'd had a good deal of rain that month. As soon as I stepped inside the protective shadows of the woods and smelled the damp of leaf mold, ferns, and mosses, I felt safe. Inside the woods, my privacy assured, I could breathe again without feeling tightness in my chest.

My body felt loose and free, and I set out eagerly to hunt mushrooms. Slowly moving through the trees, I bent over, carefully studying the forest floor. When I came upon a mossy spot under a spreading live oak, I sank gratefully to the ground, leaning my back against the tree. Closing my eyes for a moment, I listened to the cicadas' sleepy drone, the varied melodies of the songbirds, and the soft rustling of the leaves as a light breeze lifted them. I ran my fingers through the cushion of dark green moss, loving the velvety feel of it. As my head lolled back against the bark, my thoughts drifted, and the lines of a poem to Emile began to form. A mockingbird on a branch above sang fervently, as if he were singing encouragement just for me.

I composed a few lines in my head, resolving to write them down when I returned to the house, as soon as I could manage to slip upstairs.

Je Me Souviens
Je me souviens, me souviens.
Ou que tu sois,
Ou que tu puisses etre a l'instant.
Me souviens.

And there the inspiration stopped. Hoping more would come to me as the day wore on, I left my resting place to resume foraging. I was anxious to find enough mushrooms to satisfy Yvonne so I could hurry home and write down what I had composed before I forgot the lines. It didn't take much longer to gather a dozen of the fawn-colored mushrooms. Tying them in my apron by folding it into a makeshift sack, I walked home reciting the lines of the poem over and over so I wouldn't forget.

Fortunately, Yvonne was in her room when I entered the house, so I crossed to the worktable and untied my apron over it. The mushrooms tumbled lightly onto the surface. Then as quickly as possible, I climbed the ladder to my loft and scrambled for the writing papers kept hidden under the mattress.

Under the loft window, I had made a crude desk with rough boards resting on wooden crates. Carefully uncapping the ink, I dipped my pen and began to work. The nib made a scratching sound as I wrote on the rough paper. When finished, I stared out the window as the rest of the poem came to me in a rush of creativity. I wrote it down as fast as I could.

Je Me Souviens
Je me souviens, me souviens.
Ou que tu sois,
Ou que tu puisses etre a l'instant,
Je me souviens.
Nous ne pouvons pas vraiment etre separes.
La pensee peut toujours rejoinder le coeur,
Peu importe la distance qu'elle a a parcourir.
Je me souviens, me souviens.
Nous serons toujours unis
Par une invisible ficelle argentée.

I Remember
I remember, I remember.
Wherever you are,
Wherever you are now,
I remember.
We cannot really be apart.
Thoughts can always touch the heart.
No matter how far they have to fly.
I remember, I remember.
We will always be connected
By an invisible silver thread.

I didn't sign it. If Emile was not at home, I would slip it under his door. If somehow, one of his friends should chance upon it, they would not be able to tell who wrote it. Only Maurice would recognize my handwriting, and it was unlikely he would ever go there except for card games. Tiptoeing from the house, still not hearing Yvonne, I ran across the clearing toward the woods once more. Taking my usual shortcut, I walked fast past the oaks, sweet gum and swamp maple trees, alert for vines, snakes and deadfalls.

As soon as I reached the clearing around his house, it was easy to see he was home. Argent, his horse, was in his stall, and smoke spiraled from the chimney. Slowing to catch my breath, I tried to improve my appearance and wiped my face with the sleeve of my chemise. I shook my skirts, hoping he wouldn't notice the dusty hem, and smoothed my hair with my hands as I made my way toward the house.

Chi-Chi was sleeping in his spot by the door, and didn't wake up to my quiet approach, so I tiptoed up the steps, hoping they wouldn't creak. But, I needn't have bothered, for he woke up and jumped around, wagging a tail and barking a welcome.

Emile came to the door. "Sidonie, how lovely to see you." He took my hand. "Come in. Come in." Shadows underscored his eyes. "I'm just having tea. Would you like a cup?" He urged me inside, and we crossed to the fireplace. His fingers trembled as he reached for the heavy iron pot on the hearth.

"What's the matter, cousin?"

Lifting the heavy pot, he poured steaming water into a china teapot on an oval table between two chairs. "I'm afraid I have a small emergency today. Quite upsetting."

Feeling awkward, I remained standing by the chair.

"Sit, Sidonie. Please. I'll bring this to you. And I have biscuits. They're cold, but still good." Sitting, I leaned forward, concerned.

"I'm afraid I'm missing quite a bit of money." He brought me a cup of tea.

"What money?"

"I had hidden gold coins safely in the lining of my trunk when I fled Paris. And even though I make myself live on what few coins I can win at cards, I occasionally have to go into the trunk to grope for a few coins. Then I take them to New Orleans when I need a stake, or when I want to buy presents or supplies.

"I haven't had to go into the trunk more than a few times since I've been here, as we have most anything we could want growing around us here in St. Beatrice." He paused. "Don't let me keep you from your tea." He waved a hand toward the table. "Don't let it get cold.

"Then today I just happened to be looking for something else in the trunk and thought to check on the coins. I tore the lining apart to find them. But, no…there are no coins there. I took everything out of the trunk just to make sure they hadn't slipped out somewhere." He lowered his eyes and shook his head in a slow despondent way, so unlike the usual Emile.

"They are absolutely gone! Gone!" He gazed sorrowfully at the fire, which popped and spit.

"How much is missing?"

"Four thousand francs." He bit his bottom lip. "Most upsetting, I must say."

Four thousand francs was a huge sum to me, as I hardly ever saw money at all.

I gasped. "But, do you have any idea who might have done this?"

"None. No suspicions."

"Who could have known you even had that much gold?"

"All I can think is that someone was lurking about one night and saw me go into the trunk. Or maybe someone just came in

one day or night when I was gone and searched. Looking for anything of value."

"When did you last see the coins?"

"It's been a while." He hooked thumbs into his belt.

"Is anything else missing?"

"No. Actually, I have a few other things that are valuable….if
they'd looked further they might have found them. I'm grateful
whoever it was didn't keep looking." He gave me a brave smile.
"I'm so sorry to spoil your visit with this dreary business."

"Is there any way I can help? Shall we search the trunk again?
Sometimes…"

He waved a hand impatiently. "No, no. There's no way I missed
anything. Believe me, I really went over every inch of that trunk."
As he pulled his chair closer to me, I could see his mouth was lined
with worry.

"But who would have spied on you like that?"

"I have no idea. My friends come here once a week to play
cards, and we take turns going to each others' houses. But I sus-
pect none of them."

"Have you won a lot at *bourrée* lately?"

"Not really. Not by my standards anyway. And we don't usually
play for money anyway. Hardly anyone has any. We use whatever
we have. Food, furs, nuts, berries, fish…quite different than in
New Orleans."

"Has anyone lost heavily?"

He pressed a hand to his eyes. "Not that I can remember. But
my thoughts aren't that clear today. It's been quite a shock."

While his eyes were covered, I quickly took the poem from its
hiding place tucked into my waistband, and slipped it onto the table between us. Then taking a deep breath, I watched him closely
as he moved the hand from his eyes and sat straighter.

"Well, there's nothing to be done about it, but cut my losses
and resolve to live even more carefully. It's all my fault. I'm the
one who ruined matters in Paris, and I'm paying the price for it.
It's better than years in a dark dungeon, as I'm well aware. And
I'm especially blessed to be here safe and free, accepted by your
family." He smiled warmly at me, and the creases of his face vanished.

Absently, I touched the small concave spot at the base of my throat. He leaned forward, his left hand starting to reach out, but he drew it back just as quickly, looking away, and staring once again into the fire.

Emile was still acting peculiarly, I thought. But this time I didn't feel hurt because of the theft of his coins. Who wouldn't behave strangely if they'd had their treasure stolen? Eying the folded poem on the table, half hidden by my tea cup, I admired Emile's profile as he gazed sadly into the flames. "I'm sorry you've had this bad luck. If you want to join us at the house later, ride on over and have dinner with us. Yvonne is roasting chicken, and I've picked wild mushrooms to go with it."

He turned toward me. "Thank you, but I'm afraid I'm not good company today. I'm planning a trip to New Orleans to recoup my losses."

"At cards?"

He raised an eyebrow. "Oh, I can be very good at cards, when I'm properly motivated…as I am now after this theft."

"Not good enough though, or you'd still be in Paris."

He gave me a rueful smile. "You are wise for one so young."

I wanted to be gone before he found the poem, so I stood and turned toward the door. I knew he'd find it as soon as he cleared away the cups. Emile walked me to the door. "I'm charmed, as usual, by your visit."

I nodded a thank you. "And you'll tell the constable right away?"

"Oh, no." He put a finger to his lips. "Better to let the thief think he's safe. He might get careless and make a mistake, if he thinks I haven't discovered the theft yet."

He blew me a kiss, and I hurried down the steps, Chi-Chi yelping and running with me. As I crossed toward the woods, I turned once to wave, and was pleased to see Emile was still standing on the porch watching me depart.

Happy that the visit had made clear that our friendship was still strong, my eyes were more alert, and I quickly spotted more of the fleshy chanterelles and bolettes, sheltered and safe in their snug pockets of leaf mold. I felt light and airy as I added more mushrooms to my folded apron. Continuing on my way, my happiness was interrupted by more worries about Jean Claude's whereabouts, but I put those thoughts aside, as I preferred to enjoy this new found relief and happiness.

In this state of mind, it seemed possible, even certain, that Jean Claude would be found; my sister would become sweet-natured; Maurice would become less angry and more civilized; and Emile would recover the stolen gold coins. Beginning to feel hungry, I hurried on along the bayou bank toward home.

7

A MIDNIGHT VISITOR

It was, as we have said, a misty dark night.
Twenty Years After - Alexandre Dumas

I couldn't get to sleep that night. At periodic intervals, I awakened from cryptic dreams that floated in and out of my mind
like drifting mist. Half asleep often during the night, pieces of
these dreams filtered into my waking moments, and then I'd feel
incomplete, wanting to slip back into the dream world to collect
missing pieces of those mysterious dreams.

The air was clear, the crickets especially loud, and many owls
hooted as they glided back and forth among the grand oaks of the
forest. I didn't know their language, yet somehow believed if only
I could unlock the secrets of my dreams, I would also understand
what the night birds were saying in their dreamlike, ghostly night
flights.

Then a pack of coyotes yipping and yowling as they passed
miles away on their nightly hunt, made sleep even more impossible. Kicking off the quilt, I lay there in my chemise, feeling hot
with the stillness of the night air. I remember abandoning the bed
in frustration and shuffling to the tiny window under the eaves
to see if the shutters were closed. As I grasped the sill with both
hands, I could see the shutters were wide open to the night, and a
light breeze stirred just then, refreshing me.

Grateful for the relief, I noted movement below me near the house. I could make out a shadow like that of an animal or person hiding near the wall, perhaps even peering up at me silhouetted in the loft window. Afraid, I pulled back into the shadows of the room, still able to look out, but with only the black forest in view.

After a few minutes, the shadow slipped through the darkness toward the tree line, blending immediately into the black of the trees, silently swallowed by the woods. As I'd been in and out of dreams all night, it occurred to me that I could still be dreaming all this. I glanced toward the bed to orient myself. The empty bed, covers hastily thrown back, convinced me I was awake. Taking a deep breath, I exhaled slowly, then strained my eyes once more to see if any more mysteries would emerge from the woods.

Wide awake from the experience, I doubted I'd sleep any more that night, but the fear was gone. It was as though beneath the startling effect the moving shadow had on me, a part of me knew it was all right and there was no need to fear. In fact, as I stood by the window, I felt a special sort of calm, the calm that circulates when body and mind are fully in tune. A fox streaked across the yard, tail straight out behind him, but I knew the chickens were safe in the rafters of the stables and the hen house. Then an owl with huge wingspan glided out from the trees to scoop up something small on the ground. The creature briefly shrieked, then was silenced.

Toward dawn, I returned to my bed and as happens when I drift off that early in the morning, I fell into such a heavy sleep that Yvonne's piercing wakeup call from the foot of the ladder felt like cut glass in my brain. I awakened befogged with sleep and dragged out of bed, rubbing my eyes.

Stepping out into the morning to check the weather and see what chores must be done first, I spied a small object left by the front door. It was a small whittled bird, carefully smoothed and polished so none of the carving marks were visible. It was so small, just a few inches long, that I almost missed seeing it. Kneeling to pick it up, I thought I understood. This was the reason for the midnight visit. The night visitor had come into our yard to leave this gift for me. Or for Yvonne? Or Maurice? Yet, as I cradled the little bird with folded wings in my palm, I felt instinctively this present was for me. And it was a gift that took considerable time and talent so as to achieve the perfection of the little bird with its outlines of feathers and sharp beak and eyes. It was so real, it even seemed to tremble in my hand. I thought of different possibilities. Maybe it was somehow a signal from Jean Claude that he was all right, and for some reason not coming out of hiding. This was heartening. However, it would be surprising because Jean Claude had never given me a present, and I'd never known him to be a woodcarver.

With experience, I have learned not to expect people to depart too far from their customary ways of behavior, but at that time of my life, anything seemed possible. One thing I was sure of...I wouldn't tell Yvonne or Maurice of the bird as they would only make some hurtful comment about the gift. Since I wasn't sure who brought it, I decided to keep it a secret. Slipping the beautiful bird into my pocket, I reentered the house and hurried up the ladder with it.

"Where are you going? I need you to dig potatoes as soon as you eat something."

"I'll be right there," I cried out, and shoved the carving safely under the mattress.

And while I was on my knees beside the bed, I said a prayer to the Blessed Mother thanking her for this new sign that possibly Jean Claude was still alive.

"And also, Blessed Mother, please keep him safe wherever he is, or whatever it is that he's doing. And please help my dear cousin, Emile, to find his gold coins and help him stay safe on his trip to New Orleans."

"Sidonie. Get down here!"

"And Blessed Mother. It's almost impossible for me to love my sister. Please help me to feel some sort of love for her as Sister Claire has instructed me. I find it impossible to do this."

Later that day, when my work was finished, I decided to walk over to Emile's and see if he'd somehow found the missing coins. I also wanted to offer to take care of Chi-Chi while he was in New Orleans. As I entered his yard, Argent was pulling grass with de-

termination halfway between the house and the stable. Hurrying
to the porch, greeted by Chi-Chi, I called to Emile, hoping I didn't
look too messy from my farm chores and fast walk through the
vine tangled woods.

He came to the door dressed again in canvas trousers, white
shirt and slippers. Smiling broadly, he hailed me. "Sidonie. Come
in. Come in. We'll have something to eat. Can you stay?" He
beckoned me inside as Chi-Chi returned to the knucklebone he'd
been gnawing. "I just made a cream sauce for the fish a friend
brought me last night. Come and sit by the fire."

The smells of chicory coffee and pecan butter sauce tempted
me. "I'd love to try some, please." I gratefully settled myself in the
chair.

"I found your poem," he said gravely. "It was very good...and
I'm so proud of your French." He served some fish with sauce,
placing the plate on the oval table with a flourish.

The sauce was delicately seasoned and the fish delicious.
"Umm. This is a perfect sauce."

"*Merci.*" He regarded me gravely. "As for you, why, I didn't know
you wrote poetry."

"A few times." I felt embarrassed, and kept my eyes on the
plate.

"I'll give you a volume of the great Francois Villon to study.
Would you like that?"

"Thank you, I would very much. And are you still planning on
going to New Orleans? Because I'll walk over every day and feed
Chi-Chi if you like."

"That would be a wonderful help if you could take care of him
for me. I'm leaving tonight. And I'll bring you back something
beautiful from New Orleans for your trouble."

"You don't have to bring me anything. I'm glad to do it..." I
protested, and then hurried on, "and I have some news. Someone
left a hand carved bird on our doorway last night. I'm hoping it
was some sort of message from Jean Claude that he's all right."

"Hmm. Could be. Has he ever done this before? Left things
in the middle of the night for you?"

"No. He's never given me anything. But I can't think who else
it could be. I've kept it a secret though. Only you and I know."

"I won't say a word."

"I hope it's Jean Claude. If he's dead..." I crossed myself. "I'll end up like my sister as a spinster for the rest of my life."

"You a spinster?" He threw back his head and laughed so hard tears formed in his eyes.

"Why is that funny?"

"Because, dear *cousine*." He wiped his eyes. "You are easily one of the most beautiful women I've ever seen." He laughed again.

"Me? But, all those women in Paris...and your friends there. What you're used to..." My throat felt dry, and I stammered. "How could you think that?"

"And you would put all of them to shame if you were in the same room with them. All that powder and rouge covering God knows what...compared to your clear, tan complexion. And your hair. It's like shining silk!"

"Thank you, but..." I lowered my eyes, speechless. No one had ever called me beautiful before. Far from it. We didn't speak for a few long moments. Finally, I looked up and found him staring at me, but this time he wasn't laughing. Then slowly, he put his cup on the hearth and moved toward me, half crouched, then kneeling, as he had that day he'd first touched my boots. The smell of tobacco and strong soap and Bay rum rose from him.

Tentatively, he touched my cheek with the tips of his long fingers, then drew his hand back as though he'd burned it. Once again he touched my cheek, then slowly stroked it. "Such fine skin, like velvet," he whispered. Heat came off his palm and I literally could not move, feeling tingling wherever he touched me. My heart began hammering, and I felt the pulse in my neck and temples.

Suddenly however, he backed away from me, turning once again toward his chair close to the fire. "No," he half muttered to himself. "What sort of man would I be to compromise my little ingénue? My lovely country *cousine?*" He wiped his mouth with the back of his hand.

"Compromise? But...I don't understand. We are the best of friends. We..." I felt thoroughly confused. And to make matters worse, a moth flew in the doorway and fluttered around my face. I waved it impatiently away.

"You are very beautiful to me, Sidonie, and I am a used up scandal. I drink too much. I gamble too much; and I have ruined the first half of my life. I will not ruin yours, and I will not ruin the second half of my life. I have another chance here in St. Beatrice. I will not betray you or your family. Your family that has given me that chance." He kept his eyes averted.

"But...we are such good friends. I have learned so much from you. You've been so good to me. How is that compromising me? I'm not even sure what the word means."

He met my gaze, fear and confusion in his eyes, then abruptly closed them as if to conceal his emotions. "There is nothing to worry about," I kept on, not understanding his distress. I clasped and unclasped my hands as he sighed and opened his eyes, all fear and confusion gone. He stood, his expression most serious, slowly moving forward. When he reached my chair, he leaned over and pulled me to my feet, enfolding me in his long arms.

We stood together like that, lost in some sort of strange dream-like state, then he grabbed me by my shoulders and, pulling me to him with a roughness I'd never seen in him before, kissed me fully on the lips. I was startled as I'd never been kissed before, other than the affectionate cheek and forehead kisses of childhood. It was fortunate that he was holding me up, for emotion swept over me in such a wave that I felt weak, but he held me securely, his arms wrapped around me. After long moments, his lips left mine, and he kissed my face tenderly.

"Sidonie. *Chère.*" He held his head back then, eyes veiled with desire. Blinking at him, I felt dazed and unable to speak. It was then that he lowered his arms to his sides and shaking his head, murmured sadly. "*C'est trop tard.*"

"Too late for what?" I managed to ask, despite my emotional turmoil.

He shook himself as though just becoming aware of where he was, then moved away from me toward the fire, staring into the flames and leaning with one hand against the mantel. A spark from the sputtering fire flew toward his trousers. He brushed it off, then turned back, took two steps toward me, and wrapped me again in his arms.

"I love you, Sidonie. I think I must have always loved you…
since the first day we met." He rocked me back and forth, pressing my head against his chest as he stroked my hair. "But I never
allowed myself to entertain thoughts of you and me. Here I am,
almost forty…twice your age. You're so young…but, may God forgive me…today I couldn't help myself."

He kissed the crown of my head and continued stroking my
hair. The collar and top buttons of his shirt lay open and my face
was pressed to his chest. I had never been that close to a man
before. Enchanted, and in a kind of trance, I felt warmth and excitement rise within me. Placing a finger under my chin, he slowly
brought my face up to meet his and kissed me again, but this time
his kiss was gentle and soft and lasted much longer than the first
one. As he kissed me, his hands moved across my shoulders and
down to the small of my back. At one point, he broke his mouth
away from mine in order to bring my hand to his lips. He kissed
the tip of each finger in turn.

"Come sit with me," he whispered, and still holding onto me,
he sat in my chair and pulled me onto his lap. Then placing my
head on his shoulder, he ran his fingers through my long hair. We
remained like that, silent, for a long while as the fire crackled and
the sparks sputtered, while he held me tightly, his breathing deep
and steady. I felt so safe in his arms, as though I belonged there,
and had always been with him in this intimate way. I remained
very still, not wanting to break the spell of our closeness. I felt his
chest rising and falling, and I matched my breathing to his, so that
in our closeness we were breathing in unison. I could not ever remember feeling happier in my entire life. I felt cradled in delight
of a nature I had never known.

He finally spoke. "I never dared speak of love to you. You were
to marry Jean Claude. How could I interfere? I've never dared
touch you in all this time. I knew if I did…this would happen.
And I knew once I began holding you, I'd never be able to stop."
He traced my profile with a finger. "How could any man stop loving you once he'd begun?"

Still stunned by all that was happening, I remained silent, afraid
of breaking the spell by saying the wrong thing. I closed my eyes

because the reality of it all was too much for me, and then afraid it was all a dream, I opened them wide again. It was real. Emile was holding me, telling me he loved me, and saying things I'd never even dared imagine he would say.

"When I came here to Louisiana, I never thought I'd love again. I loved someone deeply in Paris. Her name was Catherine. She was my mistress and the mother of our little daughter. They're both gone now. And I remain, a deeply wounded, sinful man who has somehow been blessed with you. I don't understand how I earned this, but I embrace you, and my heart is open to you. And it has been silent and closed for years...since their death."

"What happened to them?"

"They died of cholera," he said softly, lips tightening. "The scourge of Paris."

He paused, then took my hand, kissing the palm. "And I, missing them to the point of death and wanting to die, drank and gambled like a mad man. I believe we each have a shadow side, a secret self, that is not goodness and light. And I am a living example of someone who has expressed that shadow self far too many times, and so now look at me." He released my hand. "I have even shot and killed a man over cards in Marseilles. It was self defense. He didn't want me to take my winnings and pulled a pistol from his vest. May God forgive me, I shot him in the throat."

He shook his head as though to dispel bad memories. "So here I am. Dissolute, still gambling – far from my native land, my beloved Paris – all because of my shadow self on a rampage. But thank God, I made it across the world to Louisiana, or I would never have met you. For this, I am immensely grateful." He raised his eyes to heaven. "And now that you know how I feel," he hesitated, "...What about Jean Claude?"

"Jean Claude?" The thought of Jean was far from my mind.

"Do you want to marry him? Assuming that he returns home safely?" Emile watched me carefully.

"Oh no," I said, without a moment's hesitation. "We hardly even speak. I don't know him except to see him ride off with Maurice."

"This is very important. Are you certain of this?" His tone changed as he questioned me.

"Oh, yes. I'm very certain. I don't want to marry him...but I always thought I had to because of the old arrangement between our parents."

He spoke low into my ear. "Then, will you consider marrying me?"

Suddenly I felt dizzy and placed my hands over my face like a child.

"I've upset you?"

I let my hands fall from my face and protested. "Oh, no, no. I'm just so happy, I don't know what to say."

He laughed and pulling me against his chest, held me tightly. "Does that mean you'll think about it? About marrying me?"

"But I don't have to think about it. I already know what I want."

"And what is that, *chère?*"

"I want to marry you. I never even dreamed you'd ask me."

"Thank God you feel that way. We are blessed indeed. Thank you for saying you'll have me. I'll make very sure you never regret it." He kissed me again, and I felt the heat of passion spreading quickly over me. He twined my hair around his hand and gently pulled my head back away from his. "I've got to stop kissing you," he said hoarsely, "Or I'll be doing something I'll regret."

"What do you mean? Have I done something wrong?"

"No, no." He kissed my cheek. "It's very hard for me to wait for our wedding night to make love to you. So I have to stop this now. Instead, I'll serve us some coffee and give you a present to honor our engagement."

He lifted me from his lap and stood me on my feet. "There, I did it," he smiled.

"I stopped kissing you. I must be stronger than I thought." He sat me back in the chair, as I smoothed my skirts. Then he poured us each a cup of coffee from the pot kept hot beside the fire, and adding a splash of brandy to his, lifted his cup to mine.

"A toast, *chère.* To our lives together."

I touched my cup to his and smiled shyly, feeling so happy I didn't think I could bear it. He drank from his cup, then set it down, and turned toward a cypress plank that served as a shelf to the right of the fireplace. He pulled two books from the shelf, both leather bound with gilt lettering on the spines. "In one of these lies a secret," he said. "If only I'd used this hiding place for the coins as well. Let that be a lesson to you. Always hide valuables in different places around the house. At least the thief didn't get these."

"I don't have any valuables."

"Oh, but you do now." He opened one of the books and inside, in a hollowed out space about three inches wide, lay a blue velvet drawstring bag. "See?" He placed the books on the little table between the chairs, and withdrawing the velvet bag, untied the drawstring. He carefully coaxed the velvet open and with two fingers drew out a gold chain and sapphire pendant, dangling it before my eyes. The pendant slowly swung, sparkling as it caught the light from the window.

He delicately raised it to my eye level. "You like it?"

"Do I like it?" I was dumbfounded. "It's like nothing I've ever seen."

"I hope you will wear it always. And close to your heart to remind you of my love for you." He regarded me with grave eyes. "Turn around and I'll fasten it."

Gathering my hair on top of my head, I turned so he could lower the necklace onto my neck and close the clasp. He kissed the back of my neck, then turned me by the shoulders. "Let me see it on you."

"You are incredibly beautiful anyway…but wearing this? You are perfection!"

"I want to see."

"There's a mirror." He gestured toward an oval shaving mirror hanging over the ewer and basin on a washstand near his bed. Hurrying to it, I stared at the reflection of the beautiful antique pendant. "That necklace was worn by a lady in waiting at the court of Louis XV," he said softly. "I won it at cards years ago."

"I love it. I can't believe you're giving it to me." Timidly, I dared to touch it with just one finger.

"Go ahead. You won't hurt it," he laughed.

Slowly I touched it again, turning the pendant back and forth as I admired it in the mirror. "I must keep it hidden under my chemise or Yvonne will see it."

"Whatever you like. That is, until I return from New Orleans. Then I will have a talk with your family." He circled his arms around me as I continued to stare at the necklace in disbelief.

What he said jarred me alert. "Meet with my family?"

"Yes, of course. They need to know my intentions. I'll sit down with Maurice and Yvonne and tell them I want to marry you. We'll give them a date."

"But…" Gazing dumbly at him, my brain worked slowly after all that had happened between us. I had trouble finding the right words.

"But?"

"But they're only my brother and sister. What do they have to say about it?"

"It's only respectful. That's all."

"And you're leaving tonight?" I felt a chill on the back of my neck at the thought of his going away.

"As soon as you go home, I'll begin packing."

"I don't want you to go. I have a bad feeling about it."

"Don't worry. It kills me to leave you. But after our wedding, we'll never have to be apart again." He turned me toward him. "Take care of yourself while I'm gone. I'll be home as soon as I can. And after that, I will take the best care of you always, I promise."

I pressed my face against his chest. "Please be careful. Remember what you told me about that man in Marseilles who drew the pistol on you."

"I don't miss much at the card tables. Don't worry. I am never more alert than when I'm gambling. And I won't be long. Two weeks, maybe less with any luck. It depends on how fast I can make my money back. I'm not going to marry you without the money to take proper care of you. Now go home, *chère*. If you stay any longer…." He broke off and turned away from me.

I made my way toward the door, feeling dismay at every step I took away from him. Emile loved me and wanted me to be his forever! Stunned by this revelation, I somehow managed to walk out the door, across the porch, and onto the clearing. Once on the grass, I forced myself to put one foot ahead of the other and made my way toward the shadowy trees.

Chi-Chi accompanied me as far as the edge of the woods, where he sat down and watched my departure. Head tilted with one ear pointing up, he made a soft whining sound as though to change my mind so I'd stay. "I'll be back to take care of you, Chi-Chi. Don't worry. And believe me, I don't want to leave." I turned to look back and Emile was still standing on the porch watching, as I knew he would be.

8

YVONNE AND I FIGHT

'Ah!' said Porthos. 'What a dreadful day, my dear d'Artagnan!'
Twenty Years After - Alexandre Dumas

I don't remember walking home that day. I'm sure this is because I was spellbound and remained that way throughout the
journey to the house. I do remember crossing the porch slowly as if in a dream. Becoming aware of my surroundings, I picked
up my pace before I passed through the door, blinking hard in an
attempt to bring myself back to reality. As I hurried into the house,
hoping to avoid any confrontation with Yvonne, I saw her washing
a bowl at the kitchen window, the dishpan resting on the *tablette*.
She tossed the water from the dishpan out the window and turned
abruptly.

"Where have you been all afternoon? I've been calling and
calling for you!"

"I fell asleep in the woods. I was hunting mushrooms and fell
asleep beneath a tree."

"And where are the mushrooms?" She limped closer to me,
squinting in the dim light of the room.

"I...woke up so quickly, I scattered them all, and ran home."

"Hmm." She put her hands firmly on her hips. "Well, you'd
better be about the rest of your chores. Daylight's fast fading."

She stepped closer to me. "And by the way, I don't believe
you," she scowled. "You're a terrible liar. What did you really do?

Go see your precious nun? You love the nuns so much, why don't you join the convent? I mean now that you won't be getting married, now that Jean Claude's vanished…why not? Then maybe we can have some peace around here." At that point she turned away, but something changed, and she abruptly turned back toward me, her face gone pale. Even in the dim late afternoon light, I could see the difference in her. "You've been with Emile!" She glared at me, wide-eyed, aghast.

"What?"

"You've been with Emile! Making love with him!" she called out, lips drawn into a grimace. "You…Emile!" She picked up a tin cup from the table and flung it at me so that it caught me on the shoulder and clattered to the floor. Then she kicked at me, missing and almost falling.

"What are you talking about?" I was at a loss as to how she'd concluded this. I looked at my clothes. Was I disheveled? What clues were there? Nothing seemed amiss.

"You look in vain for something wrong. You…" Here she stopped herself. "I smell his Bay rum on you!" she screamed, and she pinched her lips together so that they turned white. Her forehead furrowed, her nose dilated, and the total effect was so frightening, it appeared as though a demon had taken shape before me.

"His what? What is wrong with you?"

"I smell his cologne on you. Don't deny it. He's been making love to you!" She stepped forward and tried to kick me again, this time tripping on her skirts and falling forward. I lunged to grab her. She looked so pathetic as she fell, hobbled and lame onto her knees on the bare floorboards.

"Yvonne, don't!" Not able to catch her in time, she fell all wrong and screamed as her ankle buckled beneath her.

"Oh, my God! I always knew you were wicked! How could you? Look what you've done now!" She tried to stand, but fell again, and as I stretched to help her, she beat at me with white-knuckled fists.

"Yvonne, please! What's wrong with you?" I thought she'd been drinking, or gone mad, or both.

"You are so evil! Now I can't even walk…"

"Stop!" I held her wrists, surprised to find I could control her easily, and that my strength was more than I realized. Hard daily work around the farm with the crops and horses had paid off in many ways. Instantly, I understood. Our eyes caught, and I had the impression I could read her mind. "You're jealous…of Emile and me." I choked on the words.

She continued to glare at me, the pain in her ankle distorting that angry stare to hatred, giving her such a frightening expression that she appeared to be a witch in that shadowy gloom, before the lamps were lighted. Pursing her lips, she jutted out her chin and then looked away, the fight in her eyes slacked and her wrists went limp. Dark blotches appeared on her cheeks.

"You wanted Emile for yourself," I said softly. The frown deepened, and the smell of fear rose from her body. She looked down at the hurt ankle, pretending not to hear. I shook her wrists. "How long?"

She looked up at me then, and this time the anger changed to triumph, as her face lighted up. "For months he has been visiting me late at night when you are asleep, you stupid, ignorant, wicked, useless girl!" She laughed at me. "And you were too *coullion* to see it. He loves to be with me." She spit out the words, and they cut me like slivers of glass. "He can't get enough of me. I have to push him away just to get him to go home before you or Maurice find him in the house." She laughed bitterly in my face, and I smelled blackberry wine on her breath. So she had been drinking!

The attack continued, even though I was still reeling with the shock of it. "He's an insatiable lover. He can't get enough of me. Me! Poor lame Yvonne. The one nobody wants. The one everybody feels sorry for. Ha!" She bared her teeth, frightening me anew with the whiplash of her hatred.

Falling backwards, I hit my elbow on the floor. Then, scrambling to my feet and numb with the shock of her poisonous words, I abandoned her there and fled to the ladder to scurry up to my loft for safety, to hide, and to somehow recover from the fury of her attack. But, it was there in my haven that I realized I couldn't leave her lying with whatever was torn or broken and, surrendering to my conscience, reluctantly descended the rough rungs of the ladder once more, and silently returned to her side. Hunkering down, I reached out with both hands for her shoulders.

"Pull me to my room!" she ordered. Sliding my hands under her arms and stepping backwards, I pulled her along to her tiny room on the opposite side of the kitchen. We said nothing further as I breathed harder with the effort and clenched my teeth as I steadily pulled her through the narrow makeshift door of the room and toward her cot, trying not to think of what she said had gone on in there. After I'd managed to slide her onto the bed, I wrung out a cold cloth and brought it to her, pressing it gently around the swollen ankle. Then without a word, I left her alone, walking through the twilight gloom of the house and onto the porch.

Sitting quietly out there, the hounds coming around for affection, I absently patted their heads, not fully aware of what I was doing. I was so numb, I could have been petting alligators and not known any better, for I was so preoccupied with Yvonne's revelations and accusations. After sitting on the porch for I don't know how long, having lost all track of time, I collected myself enough to go back inside and start some sort of meal.

By the time it was fully dark, I had prepared a simple potato and cabbage soup using a chunk of stew meat for the broth. My face felt hot, not from working at the stove, but from embarrassment and shame for believing Emile and falling so much in love with him. I could not forgive myself for being so naïve and stupid. Barely able to speak and with no desire to do so, I dully trudged into her room with a steaming bowl of the soup, setting it silently on the nightstand by her bed.

Yvonne, her arm slung over her eyes, dramatically twisted in the bed, and sat up abruptly, glaring at me with the glittering eyes of a feral creature. "Soup! You probably poisoned it. I'm sure you're that jealous of Emile and me!" She waved a few fingers over the rising steam and drew some of it toward her face. "It smells all right. What did you put into it?"

I wheeled and exited the room without speaking. If she suspected me of poisoning her soup, let her. *So go hungry*, I thought to myself as I returned to the kitchen and began to put things away for the night. I had no appetite and did not want to eat. In the morning, I would give the hounds the remainder of the pot.

If Maurice came in some time after midnight looking for something to eat, at least there would be some soup. As I prepared to withdraw to the refuge of my loft, I glanced around the house, wondering if I could even bear to stay there any longer. It was the only home I'd ever known. Still, I envied Maurice the makeshift room he'd fashioned in the rear of the stables. I'd be better off out there than in here breathing the same air as Yvonne.

That night I wanted to run away so badly, I even fantasized throwing together a makeshift hut in the woods, but told myself I was hurt, tired, and in need of sleep before making any decisions. I had such a bad headache I could hardly see as I pulled myself steadily up the ladder. Once in the loft, I rubbed my forehead trying to get rid of a headache, and felt the tender places on my face where Emile's whiskers had rubbed when he kissed me. I was near tears, but too numb to cry, and my heart felt like the small carving of the bird, fragile, yet made of wood.

As I kneeled to say my prayers at bedside, the owls hooted and glided outside. I fervently wished I too could glide through the filmy shadows of the night, wild and free. But instead I felt constrained, confined, and bound. My chest felt tight, and it hurt just to breathe. Feeling beneath the mattress where I'd hidden it, I pulled out the bird carving and held it close to me for comfort. At least I had one friend: whoever had taken the trouble to carve this little bird for me. I spoke a silent thank you to whoever that person was, and felt the delicate carving of the feathers with my finger, admiring the workmanship.

Then, still holding the bird as I prayed, I told the Blessed Mother of my love for Emile and all else that had happened that day. His proposal, the gift of the necklace, his promises to return soon, the horrible fight with Yvonne – all of it. When I'd finished praying, I waited on my knees for a few moments in silence, then rose, deciding to remove the sapphire necklace and hide it in my trunk until I saw Emile again. I would give it back to him when he returned from New Orleans, but not wear it in the meantime. Twisting my long hair over my shoulder, I undid the clasp and carefully wrapping it in a piece of flannel, I hid it in the bottom of my trunk beneath an old blanket that my grandmother had woven on her loom, many years before I was born.

Tired as I was, I didn't think I could sleep with my head aching so badly, so I sat at the window staring out and watching the owls glide back and forth, wondering how far along Emile had managed to travel on his journey, and of the whereabouts of Jean Claude. A line of bats swooping out from a vent high up near the roofline of the stables crossed my view and disappeared into the dark forest on their nightly hunt for insects. As I watched the night creatures going about their business, I forgot about my headache and my problems, and began to feel more and more drowsy. I had had enough for one day, and within minutes of sliding under the quilt, I fell asleep.

9

A CRISIS

"It is the demon in person," said Aramis,
hastening at the call of his friend.
Twenty Years After - Alexandre Dumas

T he next morning I felt no better than the night before, despite my hopes that sleep would help my despair. Emile's face hovered before my eyes as I went about my chores, and still angry at myself for being so naïve, I'd shake my head to rid myself of these images. After tending to the animals, I took Yvonne breakfast and coffee, but she waved me away and struggled to her feet, wincing and crying out from the pain of the swollen ankle. "It's not broken. It's sprained. I can walk with my old cane," she insisted as she hobbled from the bed.

Still not speaking to her, afraid of what I might say, I took the coffee and food away and went about the rest of my chores, ignoring her. I was able to work out some of my anger that day around the farm. Within an hour, I was wet with perspiration, from working so hard in the stables and garden. My thoughts were all on Emile, so much so that I thought at times I could even smell his cologne and the lingering fragrance of his freshly washed hair. I was so full of emotion I wanted to cry for the relief that tears would bring, but no tears came.

What if we'd made love! I'd been alone with him in his house, and we had felt such passion. What if that had happened, and

I'd gotten pregnant? To be pregnant and unmarried would have been so unbearably shameful that I felt dizzy just thinking about the possibility of it. I knew of one woman in the village who had drowned herself because she was pregnant and unmarried. These terrifying thoughts kept racing through my mind making me more and more upset, so I just worked harder to quiet my thoughts.

Toward mid afternoon, I smelled smoke. Trying to figure out where it was coming from, I hurried out to the road. Yvonne had hobbled out to the porch to see as well, and was peering at the sky in the east, hand shading her eyes. Great clouds of black and gray smoke rose from somewhere far down the road from the farm. We silently watched for several moments, then I started for the stables. "I'm riding over there to see what's going on," I called.

"No! You stay right here with me."

"I'm going."

"I told you to stay with me!" Ever the controlling one, she could never stand not getting her way. Ordinarily I might have stayed, telling myself that she was lame and frightened of the fire, but that day I continued toward the stables to fetch Solange. The smoke grew more intense as I led Solange from the cool of the stables into the light. She whinnied with displeasure at the biting smell of smoke and raised her head in the direction of the fire.

"You're a selfish, willful girl!" Yvonne called out as I hiked up my skirts and climbed on Solange. I almost felt sorry for her as we trotted down the road. I glanced back at her where she still stood at the edge of the porch, clutching her cane. But, quickly putting her out of my mind, I rode on, turning my attention toward the fire.

As we passed Emile's house, Chi-Chi merrily raced after us barking excitedly. Seeing the shutters closed with the wooden latches holding them secure, and no smoke rising from the chimney, made me feel abandoned and desolate, and very lonely. Chi-Chi followed along behind us, and Solange whinnied again as the smoke grew thicker. She slowed and tried to turn back to our house, but I urged her on, kicking with my heels, something I hated to do to her, but the situation was urgent. Reluctantly, she trudged forward once more. The smoke bit at my nostrils, and I held my sleeve to my nose as we pressed on. By then, I was beginning to get a location on where it was coming from, and feared it might be the convent.

The thought scared me. The convent had only been built five years before. How could it be burning? It was afternoon, and lamps or candles wouldn't be lighted yet. Maybe it was a grease fire in the outdoor kitchen where the sisters worked with large pans. In that case, the fire would not be so devastating as the cookhouse was detached and well to the rear of the main building. Rounding a bend in the road, and circling a patch of sheltering trees, we came upon a view of the fire itself. It wasn't the outdoor kitchen; it was the chapel. The fire was in full raging force, and the red-orange flames were consuming the precious frame building like the very fires of hell.

The nuns were standing in the road watching helplessly for the flames were far too powerful and out of control to fight with buckets of water drawn from the well. Claire was to the side of the huddled sisters, and holding Brigitte firmly with her stout arms wrapped around her quaking shoulders. Brigitte began struggling with her, and then two sisters quit staring at the flames and rushed over to assist Claire.

As we drew closer to the group, the flames danced through the windows of the chapel and through holes in the roof. One whole wall buckled and with a great whoosh of sparks and black smoke billowing from the roof, a third of the shingles fell into the chapel as a great gasp came out of the charring shell, like the moan of a dying man.

Solange, eager to turn around and bolt back home, strongly resisted, but I was able to slide off her and taking the reins, urge her toward the sisters. Chi-Chi, confused and frightened, looked wildly around, yipped once, then took off racing for home. Trying to comfort Solange, I smoothed my hand over her mane as we walked toward Claire, my nose smarting from the acrid smoke.

"Claire!" I called abruptly and turning for just a moment, she acknowledged me with a blink of her sad eyes, then quickly turned her head back to watch the destruction of the chapel. Brigitte attempted to slip from beneath her arms, and as she struggled to free herself, she stepped on my boot. I reached out to steady her and to help Claire hold her.

"Demons!" she screamed at an ear-piercing pitch.

"We have to lock her up, Sidonie! Help us get her under control." Two of the sisters were already breathless, and one had to let go to sit by the side of the road as she held one hand over her heart, trying to recover.

Sister Lorraine, red-faced, continued to hang on to Brigitte, although right then she bucked and began screaming again. "Let me go! I have to burn it all down. They are ordering me to burn it all!" Her voice rasped and crackled like the boards of the chapel, and I could feel the power swelling from within her, so strong that she almost threw me off. As the others came to our aid, we finally were able to restrain her using all of our combined strength.

Worried about Solange, I looked around for her just in time for she was trotting away. I broke away from the group and ran after her, catching up with her and snatching at her mane. As I caught my breath, I stroked her, then tied her reins to a persimmon tree as far away from the commotion and smoke as I could. She eyed me sideways as I talked to her and calmed her, promising we'd go home as soon as possible. She snorted in discomfort. Fortunately, the air was still and the flames were rising vertically, with no breezes blowing sparks toward the convent, a safe hundred feet away. As we struggled with Brigitte however, the south wall caved in, and within minutes the whole structure collapsed in upon itself. The flames, while not dying down yet, were not expanding, as they continued to feast on what wood remained.

Sister Louise pointed to us. "Let's all walk her to her bed. She needs a potion to make her sleep. We can't keep fighting her."

"I don't think the flames will spread. Let's go now," directed Claire as she led us toward the convent. "We'll lock her in her room and then we can return and see what has to be done."

We moved forward as one. I kept pressing against Brigitte's back, almost pushing her over one time as she stumbled on a flagstone. "Let me go! Let me go!"

"She's so sick, poor thing," said Claire, shaking her head as we moved her along the walkway.

"It's the devil talking to her," offered Anne.

"I've seen this before in France. When they become deranged like this, they don't know what they're doing," said Claire. I marveled at her tone. Her voice was soothing despite the emergency. Brigitte let out a mad shriek then, and a moment later, as though the scream had released something inside of her, her head slumped over onto her chest, and she went limp all over. She was like dead weight, which made holding her up even more difficult.

"Let's lay her down," said Claire. It is a testament to her personality that she was instantly obeyed by all of us. We laid her gently down on the grass, and Claire smoothed the wet hair from her perspiring, pale face. Tendrils of hair lay as though glued to her forehead and streaks of soot stained her cheeks and mouth. "Poor dear Brigitte." Claire crooned to her as Brigitte stared straight ahead, eyes gone vacant as though she'd slipped into a trance.

"Each one of us can take an arm or a leg, and we'll be able to get her safely to her bed," Claire told us. And this is how we were able to carry her on through the front door and into the much cooler air of the building. As we moved over the threshold, Brigitte came to life again and screamed. "No! No! I can't go in there! They'll kill me! Please! Oh no, please no!" Our little entourage persisted, despite her agonies and as we finally made it to her room, two sisters met us by the bed, holding long strips of flannel to restrain her.

Brigitte's room was unadorned, except for a metal cross on one whitewashed wall and a small painting of the Virgin over her bed. I shuffled across the bare wood floor, almost tripping as I scuffed up the edge of an oval braided rug at bedside. At last we managed to lay her down on the thin mattress, neatly made up with muslin sheets and quilt. "Take her wrists and tie them firmly to the bedposts," said Claire.

The nuns looked reluctant to do this, but with one more bloody scream from Brigitte, they hurried to obey Claire. Brigitte fought them but they were able to secure her wrists, and then, as we held down her legs, her ankles were restrained, and she was finally unable to kick or beat her fists. "Sister, run and fix a sedative. Please hurry," said Claire to Lorraine, who hurried from the room, long skirts flapping.

Sister Anne, petite and frail, soaked a cloth in the basin on the washstand, wrung it out, and applied it to Brigitte's forehead.

Gradually Brigitte's outbursts became more like crying, and her pulse visible at the blue veins of her pale temples, slowed. Lorraine returned with a cup of the sedative and we supported her head and urged her to drink. She clamped her lips together at first, but Claire ordered her to drink, and she finally did, spilling only a little.

We waited beside the bed until the drink seemed to take effect, and then Claire asked us to release one of her wrists. Annette kept reapplying cool water to her forehead until her eyes closed. Claire nodded. "There. Now you can release her other wrist. She'll sleep for a while and someone will stay with her at all times." She turned toward me. "Sidonie. I'm so glad you came on this terrible day to help us. Thank you so much." She crossed to the door. "Come on. Let's go back outside and make sure the fire is contained. And then you better get back to your farm or they'll be worried about you."

"Oh, no. I won't leave yet. I must make sure all of you are out of danger."

"A true friend!" Except for Lorraine and Annette, we followed Claire out of the room and down the cool hallway toward the front door. As soon as we stepped outside, the acrid smoke bit at our nostrils so that I really did want to get away from it and go home. But I couldn't leave my friends just yet. Smoke, black and ominous, spiraled above the desolation of those charred, crumbling uprights that still stood in the smoldering mess. The stench of the aftermath of the fire was nauseating. A few neighbors had arrived and were dumping buckets of water from the well onto the embers and sludge of the foundation of the chapel.

Three men hauled water, their faces smudged with soot. "There's nothing left. Nothing!" whimpered Monique. "Cover your face. Don't breathe this horrid air. It's like hell itself. There's nothing we can do until those embers die out." The sisters stood at the edge of the garden, looking helpless and stunned by the crisis, the black of their habits blending with the blackened ruins of the chapel.

One of the neighbors, Pierre Bonin, dumped his bucket on one of the last patches of glowing embers, and wiped the sleeve of his sooty undershirt across his streaked and grimy face. "God in heaven," he asked, shaking his head. "What happened here?"

"We don't know," Monique said quickly. "We think maybe a candle overturned."

She looked quietly around at the other nuns and narrowed her eyes.

They all nodded. "Candles. Yes, it must have been the candles."

Pierre returned to the well as though not expecting an answer. "Lucky nobody got hurt," was all he said.

Monique made a sign of the cross, and I supposed it was in order to ask forgiveness for lying to protect Brigitte. Nothing would be served by the constable locking her up in the dismal jail in the village for burning down the chapel, although I was quite certain Leroy would never do such a thing.

"That wasn't really a lie," Monique whispered to me. "She really did start the fire with a candle." I nodded, and then decided it was safe to head home. so I said my goodbyes, and went to untie Solange.

The heavy thick hot smell of smoke followed us on the trip home, making me yearn for a bath. I reined in Solange at Emile's so I could check on Chi-Chi. He was safely curled at his favorite spot on the porch, and ran to greet us. Emile had left his food in a bin on the porch and I filled his food and water dishes, then wearily climbed back on Solange.

As we returned to the farm, Solange headed straight for the high grass by the trees at the rear of the stables. She started munching before I'd even slid off her back. Her long, graceful neck stretched in a gentle curve as she savored each clump that she yanked loose, and seemed oblivious to the adventure we'd just had. I smiled at her contentment, rubbing her elegant neck, then headed for the house.

Wiping my face with the back of my sleeve and seeing the gritty black soot on my clothes, I decided to waste no time filling the tub that hung from a nail on the back wall of the house by the back stoop. But first, I needed to face the unpleasant task of going inside the house and facing Yvonne in whatever evil mood she'd worked herself into during my absence.

She was nowhere in sight as I entered the house. I called her name, but there was no response. Walking to her narrow room,

I tapped on the rough planks of the door. There was still no response, so I jiggled the black iron latch, but she had barred the
door. This recent withdrawing was not like my sister. Far from
it, she was always annoyingly in the middle of the house, so it was
hard to stay clear of her.

"Go away! I have a hideous headache. It's all your fault for
upsetting me and running off like that."

I jiggled the latch again. "Open up. I want to tell you about
what happened. The convent. It was the chapel."

"Go away. Leave me alone."

"I'll fix you something to eat."

"I don't want anything."

"You need to eat. Maman always made people eat when they
were sick."

"I'm sick of *you*! Food won't help."

"I'll make mint tea."

"Stay out of the kitchen. You can't cook anyway."

"I'll get Maman's *livre de recettes,*" I called through the door, and
spun around to fetch the handwritten cookbook that Maman had
made up. She sewed the pages together with coarse black thread
and kept it on the top shelf of the cypress cabinet Papa had built to
hold kitchen utensils and crockery. The book was seldom used, as
Yvonne knew all its dog-eared pages by heart. The book held dried
lavender flowers, which released a faint smell as I leafed through
the pages, welcome after all the drifting smoke I'd inhaled.

Memories of Maman were stirred as I leafed through the
booklet. She had written *Gumbo de Okra et Poulet* in her spidery
handwriting. The ink had faded to a dark brown tint, the color
of strong tea. That seemed like a good choice. In my mind's eye,
I could see Maman seated at the kitchen table carefully writing in
her homemade book. I was glad Maman didn't have to witness the
terrible things Yvonne had said to me the day before. But then, I
believed she looked down on us from heaven, so that meant she
may have seen that pitiful scene. I consoled myself by hoping she
hadn't been looking in on us at that particular time.

I gathered up the ingredients, and after chopping and slicing,
and browning the roux to the rich color of bayou mud, I started
putting together the gumbo. As I stirred, I reflected on the recent

changes in my life. No longer was I willing to work around the house as servant to Yvonne. The servant who emptied the *pots de chambre* each morning into the *cabinet*, our cypress outhouse. The servant who fed, killed and cleaned chickens and ducks, plant-ed and tended the garden, foraged the berries and mushrooms, cleaned the fish and game Maurice carried home, mucked the stalls and groomed the horses. The list of my daily duties rolled on and on through my mind as the gumbo thickened.

"There are many changes coming around here!" I vowed aloud as steam from the *chaudière noir* rose before my eyes. Like the strong and dependable iron pot I was using, I was taken for grant-ed in my family, but I was going to change roles. I would become the fine creator of cuisine as well. I too would make the pralines, bread pudding, and fig *gateau* that I loved. I too could make the *boudin* and the *tasso* and the *etouffées*.

Despite my misery over Emile's failings, I felt strength rising within, and the growing hope of finding my own way, even after learning of his backdoor treachery with Yvonne.

"There are going to be big changes around here!" I repeated, continuing to stir the pot, feeling better by the minute, and hav-ing no idea of just how substantial and far reaching those changes were going to be.

10

A GRISLY DISCOVERY

"Don't be alarmed," said d'Artagnan.
Twenty Years After - Alexandre Dumas

The next morning, I was relieved to open my eyes and discover the smoke smell had cleared and once again the air was clear and clean with the extra freshness of morning dew. The squirrels chased each other in the trees, chattering and playing as they loved to do early in the morning. Sticks cracked and fell as they played, along with the soothing sounds of mourning doves gently cooing.

Yvonne and I didn't bother speaking as I took my coffee outside and whistled up the hounds so I could give them all a scratch behind the ears and a few encouraging pats on the head. They clustered around me, each seeking attention, when I happened to look up and see Arsène approaching on horseback. His expression was strange and forlorn, and in back of him, slung across the saddle, was a lumpy, heavy looking *sac de pitre*, the coarsely woven sack we used for potatoes or most anything else we needed to carry. He tethered his horse to the hitching post and solemnly met my gaze.

"Good morning, Sidonie." He nodded politely, tipping his hat. As he came up to the porch, I saw how bedraggled he was. His clothes were rumpled and in disarray, his trousers strained with crusted mud and black smudges. He looked like he'd been out all night fishing or frogging, and because of the peculiar look in his eyes, I wondered if he was drunk.

"Is Maurice home?' he asked, his voice dry and raspy as though he hadn't spoken for a while.

"Yes, but you'd have to wake him up. He's been out all night."

"Please do that." He stood in a wide stance as though to support himself better, and his strange behavior, the dark shadows of his face and the tightness of his jaw told me not to ask why he wanted me to fetch Maurice. I turned immediately and ran for the stables to wake up my brother. I could tell something was very wrong, so I fled into the cool shadows of the stables and hurried along the central passageway toward the tack room, where Maurice had made a bed for himself.

Flinging open the plank door, I called, "Maurice! Get up! Arsène is here. Something bad has happened!"

He mumbled and stirred beneath the worn woven cover where he lay sprawled on his rough mattress on the floor. Tack hanging from pegs on the rough walls made deep shadows in the dim interior. Sunlight could barely streak through the dense cobwebs at the window. Papa's grinding wheel and Maman's spinning wheel were both stored in the shadows of the back wall. Maurice still used the grinding wheel from time to time, but the spinning wheel and its treadle were cocooned in dusty cobwebs.

"Maurice! Wake up!"

He rolled over and blinked at me, puzzled, as though he didn't recognize me. Then, groaning, he sat up and rubbed his face with the palms of his hands. He took a deep breath and noisily yawned. "What? What is it?" He scratched his chest through the faded brown shirt he'd worn the night before.

"Arsène is here to see you! Come out front. He's got something to show you, and you've got straw stuck in your beard!" He frowned and picked at his beard. Solange whinnied for me then, so I left him to stir himself, and went to her stall toward the front of the stables. I lovingly stroked her velvet nose and led her out of the stall so she could graze in the pasture. Maurice finally trudged down the passageway, his outline blurred in the dim light and floating dust motes from the scattered straw on the dirt floor.

"What does he want?" His voice was deep and fogged with sleep.

"Whatever it is, it's not good," I told him as he passed. I began to groom Solange as she munched grass, her flesh quivering with pleasure as I brushed her. Within five minutes, Maurice returned to the stable, an air of urgency about him as he hurried back down the passageway. By then he was wide awake and breathing hard.

"I have to ride to town. *Maintenant!*"

"Why? What is it?"

"Never mind what!" he yelled from the tack room, and then he reemerged with Theotiste's bridle swinging from his hand and disappeared into the stall next to Solange's.

"I have a right to know!"

"Shut your mouth and get out of my way!" He led Theotiste out of the stall and out into the sunlight.

Outraged at being talked to like that, I left Solange's side and followed him toward the front of the house. The poultry, disturbed by all that was going on, fluttered and cackled and ran to and fro. The curious hounds milled around Arsène who was remounting his mare, the mysterious sack still slung over the horse's rump. Maurice swung up onto Theotiste's bare back.

"Arsène! Wait!" I called, catching up to them. "Where are you going?"

He turned, surprise in his eyes. "We're just going to the village. We won't be long."

"What's in the sack?"

"Nothing much." He spoke abruptly and his jaw ground as he spoke. A chill ran up my spine. Something was very wrong, and if trouble had a smell, then I smelled its scent that day.

"Please, Arsène! You can tell me."

He eyed me intently, then nudged his horse to leave. Maurice was already almost to the road. "It's...nothing you need to know."

I reached out boldly toward the sack. Arsène brushed my hand away. "Don't!"

Maurice stopped at the road and turned to yell again. "Damn you, Sidonie! I told you to stay out of this! Now get back to your chores and leave us alone!"

I grabbed at the sack again, and Arsène again brushed away my hand. But I caught a feel of what was hidden inside, and it reminded me of a side of meat. My hands flew to the sack again, grabbing at it in what was fast turning into a battle.

"Stop! Or I'll come over there and slap you!" Maurice yelled from the road.

With the full force of my anger, I snatched at the rough material again, and this time the fabric ripped, making a foot long tear. What looked like human skin was revealed through the torn sack.

"What is that?" I demanded, startled at the sight of flesh and the impact of the smell of death, both sweet and repulsive at the same time.

"What the hell is the matter with you?" yelled Maurice as he dismounted, dropped the reins, and ran over to us. "Look what you've done now, you stubborn girl! My God, get in the house before I knock you down!" He raised a fist to me, but Arsène flashed one arm out and blocked it.

"We have to get another sack now," he said grimly, arm still raised to protect me from Maurice. He looked steadily at me. "Go! Get another sack."

Yvonne emerged from the house, leaning heavily on her cane at the doorway. "What's going on out here?"

"Nothing! Nothing's going on! Get back in the house!" raged Maurice, panting with anger, a vein throbbing at his temple.

Yvonne, never taking orders from Maurice or anybody else, stomped off the porch, and began limping toward us. "Don't order me around, brother! I want to know what's going on." As she came closer, Arsène tried to cover the split in the fabric with his hand.

"We need another sack is all. Go, Sidonie."

"It's Jean Claude, isn't it?" I whispered.

"We don't know who it is," scowled Maurice, first at me and then at Yvonne who had halted near the hitching post. "Now both of you get out of here before I hurt you."

"Let me see," I insisted.

"You better let me see," warned Yvonne, "or you're the one who's going to get hurt!"

"It's a piece of bloody meat. It could be anyone," said Maurice. "Whoever it was has been half eaten by something...probably an alligator. We're taking it to Leroy Viator…that is, if you two would leave us alone to do our work."

"Where did you find it?" asked Yvonne of Arsène. She clutched her cane so tightly, her knuckles were white.

"In the swamp. Back around Bayou Chêne." Arsène bit his lip. "I think some trapper got torn up by a gator. Could be two gators fought over him after he was dead. There's no telling. He's too ripped up to know."

Yvonne's hand flew to her mouth, and she squeezed her eyes shut.

"An alligator….got Jean Claude?"

"We don't know that!" Maurice yelled so hard, spit flew from his mouth. "Now get out of our way before this corpse starts stinking even more than it already is!"

Arsène spoke softly. "Whoever it was might have slipped on the bank. Broken a leg. Maybe he was drunk and fell down. Who can say? Both arms and a foot are missing, and the face is in such bad shape…"

I ran back to the tack room to get another sack from the dusty pile on the floor and while there got the idea to ride Solange into town with the men. How could they stop me? I grabbed her bridle from the nail on the wall and hurried out of the building to her.

"Hurry up! What are you doing?" Maurice yelled.

I rode Solange to the front yard, and tossed the sack to Arsène.

"Where do you think you're going?" sneered Maurice.

"Oh, I'm going along with you," I barked back. "That could be Jean Claude."

"You're not going anywhere!" Yvonne ordered, wiping her eyes with her apron.

"You're going to stop me?" I laughed down at her from my seat on Solange. "I don't think you can move that fast!" Yvonne's jaw dropped, and it was then that I learned the lesson that bullies back down faster than anyone, because they're not used to anyone speaking up to them.

Arsène and Maurice tugged the sack partially over the ripped material, and then Maurice, giving up on me, sauntered angrily to the road to remount Theotiste. "There, Rubis. There, boy," said Arsène, steadying and calming his horse who was beginning to skitter and stomp. He quickly mounted Rubis and slapped the reins to start the ride to town. Yvonne stomped back onto the porch as fast as she was able with her injury, and then slammed the door so hard, sparrows flew off the roof.

Maurice glared at me as we all three started out down the road. "You don't have the sense you were born with." He shook his head in disgust. "What kind of girl would want to ride along with a dead man?" He and Arsène took the lead and Solange and I fell behind. I smiled in triumph. I had stood up for myself to them for the first time, and I had won! With a deep sigh of relief, I realized I was becoming free of Yvonne and Maurice's dominance. Never again would I surrender this newly found sense of independence. It felt too good to be free.

With an eye on the gruesome cargo up ahead, draped over Rubis' flank, I thought about the many alligators I'd seen on trips to the swamp with my father, their red eyes glowing in the dark. I'd watched both my grandfather, Achille, and Papa kill them and skin them. On one occasion, Papa had shot an eight-foot long alligator out by the stable. They had taught me a good deal about alligators, so I was familiar with their habits, and how they have a dry mouth and must allow their meat to decompose for that reason. And that's why they like to drag it into their caves beneath the water line so it can rot. The thought of the missing parts from that corpse hidden away in some cave made my stomach turn over, so I turned my thoughts to Solange, speaking to her as if she were a person.

"We're free. Did you know that? No matter what happens, we're free now, my sweet girl." As I stroked the coarse brown hair of her mane, she twitched her soft ears in answer. The road was dry and dusty, and occasional drifts of the awful leftover smell of smoke from the burned chapel, floated on a light breeze. Two vultures circled above us, their flight lazy and slow, as they followed the scent of death we carried. Horse flies buzzed around us, and I waved them away with exasperation. Another vulture soon arrived, and joined the others all the way into the village.

The constable lived at the outskirts of town in a cypress house, larger than our own. At the far left corner of the house, he had built a huge cypress cistern, and to the rear of the property stood a large barn. That day Leroy Viator was working in his garden, hunkered down and digging weeds among neat rows of okra. When he spotted us, his bulky barrel chest puffed up, and he hailed us with a wave of his hand.

"We've got something to show you," called Maurice, dismounting and tying Theotiste to the hitching post. Arsène, silent, slung a leg crossways over the saddle and hunched over, waiting. Crows cawed in the cornfield beyond the house, their cry piercing and demanding. Leroy strolled toward us, drawing a handkerchief from his pocket to wipe his damp face. His shirt, wet from working in the sun, clung to his body.

"What you got, you?" he asked as he approached, the smell of alcohol and sweat rising from him. He directed his comments toward Maurice, but shot a glance at Arsène and me. He stopped and placed his hands lightly on his hips, nodding curtly to each of us in turn. "Well?"

Maurice twisted his mouth as though reluctant to speak. He looked to Arsène to answer. I scanned the sky to see if the vultures were still there. Two more had joined the death watch, and they lazily circled above us. "I found this half-eaten body at an old abandoned camp out in the swamp. He's been chewed up, maybe by alligators, and he's half covered with mud. His face is such a mess, it's hard to say who he is," Arsène said slowly.

Leroy sighed as though this news meant unwelcome work when he'd rather get back to his garden rows. He kept mopping at his brow as he stared at the lumpy sack. "Well, heave it down on the ground then. Let's have a look." Arsène slid off Rubis, and he and Maurice hauled the body to the ground, then Arsène kneeled beside it to untie the rope that secured the sack shut. He worked the coarse material down to display the grisly contents, and as he did so, Leroy's forehead furrowed and his mouth screwed up in disgust.

"Whew!" He flapped his hat across his face and shook his head in disbelief. "We're going to have to take this over to Doc's. Close that thing up again, and Doc can lay him out on his examining table. That's as bad as I've seen. No telling what chewed him up."

As the men heaved the body back onto Rubis, the constable backed off. "That's a bad business. I don't know why you brought Sidonie along. She doesn't need to be seeing such as that."

"Tell her that. We didn't want her along," grumbled Maurice.

"Sidonie. Go home! This isn't for you to see. Might give you nightmares," Leroy said.

"I have to know if it's Jean Claude," I said firmly, sticking out my chin. Leroy stared at me for a moment, then gave a curt nod. "Have it your way then." Soon our party of three was moving along again, down the dirt road toward the village. I felt annoyed with all of the men and yet was proud that I'd refused to obey even the constable.

Doc's modest house was situated at the very edge of the village surrounded by sheltering oak trees. In the village of St. Beatrice lying just beyond, were a crude store, a blacksmith shop, a *moulin a scie*, or sawmill, a *moulin a riz*, a rice mill, and a *sucrerie*, or sugar mill. As we reached Doc's low whitewashed fence and gate, Maurice shuddered. "I can't stand that smell anymore. Let's drop it off here at Doc's and get going. I need to jump in the bayou and wash the stink of death off me."

He dismounted quickly and headed up the brick walkway, leaving us behind, and knocked on the front door. The vultures were still with us like bad habits, and flies were reorganizing around the sack. I felt itchy and in need of a bath as well, but didn't complain. Arsène glanced over at me and with a slight smile of encouragement, slid off Rubis and waited at the gate.

Doc opened the door wide, spoke briefly with Maurice, then waved us all inside. Maurice returned to help carry the body. I tied up the horses to the hitching post outside the gate, and we made our way to the front porch. Doc patted my head as though I were still a child. He had been very kind to us when our parents died, and helped as much as he could during their brief illnesses. "It's always good to see you, Sidonie," he said.

My memory of Doc is always the same. If I think of him for any reason, I see him taking a cup of *café noire* in the kitchen at the wooden table with Maman when grandfather died. In this memory, he doesn't speak, just sips the steaming coffee, then squeezes his eyes shut with fatigue, placing thumb and finger on the bridge of his nose. Despite seeing him for days at bedside when my parents were mortally fevered, and despite countless other times in the village, this is the memory that replays in my mind whenever I think of him. I wonder how people remember me. I wonder what I'm saying or doing in the picture of me that plays in their mind from time to time.

Doc had migrated from Germany to New Orleans, then to St. Beatrice, years before. He lived alone with his hunting dogs and whiskey as his best friends. He was grizzled with a tobacco-stained beard and long dull gray hair. He usually wore a black suit flecked with cigar ashes, but that day wore only a plain blue shirt and tan wrinkled trousers.

Generally, bayou people took care of their ailments on their own, or with the help of a *traiteur* or treater. We used sassafras, *mamou, la mauve,* hot pepper, elderberry, turpentine, whiskey, sulfur, spiderwebs, peach tree leaves, boneset, and *tête de cabri* for various ailments. But when the problem was too much for our remedies, then Doc was asked for help. He also had to be called to pronounce someone dead before we could bury them.

Sharp disinfectant bit my nose as we pressed ahead into Doc's office past the messy rolltop desk by the door with its stacks of papers and files. The metal examining table in the center of the room gleamed as sunlight cut through the tall sill windows. I surveyed the examining room in wonder. A heavy wooden side table held bottles of powders, vials of liquids, a mortar and pestle and a scale, where Doc mixed compounds and elixirs for his patients. A glass-front bookcase, reaching almost to the ceiling, held shelves of leather volumes. A skeleton was suspended on wires from the ceiling, which Doc used to help explain various ailments to his patients. Next to the skeleton stood a wide wooden cabinet displaying jars of yellowish tape worms and kidney stones and even an albino baby alligator that I'd stared at wide-eyed as a child, while Doc had worked on Yvonne's foot injury.

As the men heaved the body onto the examining table, the smells of swamp muck and death overcame the disinfectant. Doc passed around a tin of peppermints. "Here. Suck on these. Helps with the smell. I make them myself." He smacked his lips and frowned, studying the lumpy sack and fishing in the pockets of his baggy trousers.

Leroy joined us then, stomping into the office and squinting at the body as he wordlessly took a mint from Doc's tin. Maurice slapped his hands together, then rubbed them on his pants, wrinkling his nose in distaste, and groaning in complaint. I knew he wanted to take his leave right away as he edged toward the door. Doc took over then, unfolding the knife he'd taken from his pocket and delicately cutting the sacking that held the corpse until he completely uncovered the entire bruised and torn, fish belly white body of the victim.

"Good God Almighty!" barked Leroy. Arsène made the sign of the cross, and I did likewise, biting my tongue in distress as I stared in shock at the ragged wounds and dark blood-stained clothes. I forced myself to look at the face, half-hidden by black soaked hair, but the damage was so severe, the nose and mouth one muddy, bloody gaping hole, that it was impossible to tell if this was Jean Claude. The shredded clothing and one remaining boot were so ruined that I couldn't recognize them as belonging to him.

"No arms, no foot."

"His face is so mangled, his own mother wouldn't know him."

"Give me time. Something always shows up," Doc assured us, beginning to hum a tune, yet appearing totally engrossed and in deep concentration as he peered intently at the body. He leaned over so that his face was inches from the stinking flesh. He tilted his head and angled his body awkwardly, as he peered at the ragged wounds. Finally, he straightened, his back creaking and cheeks hollow from sucking on the mints. "I'll be studying on this for the rest of the day, people. I'll send word to you, Leroy, if I find anything that may help identify him." Placing his hands firmly on his hips, he dismissed us all with a look.

As we all filed out onto the porch, he called after us, then showed up at the door as we were making our way along the walk toward the gate. "This can't be Jean Claude," he announced, wiping his hands on a towel.

"That's some good news at least," said Leroy, still sucking on a mint.

"I don't know who this man is, but it's not Jean." He smiled at us. "Relieved, eh?"

"How can you tell?" asked Leroy.

"Jean got dragged by his horse when he was sixteen years old. I had to put fifty stitches in his back. This man is in terrible shape, but his back is still intact. It's definitely not Jean Claude."

"Maybe it's that missing logging scout then," I offered, looking at Leroy.

"Just like an ignorant Yankee to wander around in the swamp and get himself killed," said Leroy, spitting what was left of the mint onto the grass.

We thanked Doc, and he closed the front door, as we all breathed gratefully of the fresh air. I was so relieved the body wasn't Jean Claude, I said a silent prayer to the Blessed Mother and made the sign of the cross.

"Thank you for bringing the body to me, Arsène...Maurice," Leroy turned to me reluctantly, "You too, Sidonie, although I still don't approve of young girls having anything to do with such as this."

Arsène was mounting his horse as Leroy walked toward him. "That was a long haul out of the swamp. You did good. Some would have left him there and made me get in my boat and gone to see for myself."

Arsène nodded. "If I left him there, there would be nothing of the body left to show you but a few scraps of skin and bone."

We all mounted our horses to head out. I couldn't wait to ride home and get that smell out of my nostrils with some fresh air. Solange needed no encouragement, and she took off with the same spiritedness she'd shown getting away from the chapel fire the day before.

"I need to drink a whole bottle of wine after touching that stinking corpse," called Maurice to Arsène as they cantered ahead of me. "You come drink with me. You earned it."

"Thanks, but it's time to get back. I've got to ride all the way to my mother's place where I left the boat."

11

MY FLIGHT INTO THE SWAMP

Rage showed itself in d'Artagnan's face.
He frowned;... he was red to his temples.
Twenty Years After - Alexandre Dumas

The rest of the time during Emile's absence slogged along without incident. Yvonne and I had little to say to one another. Her usual nagging was mostly replaced by a sullen silence, although she still managed to bark at me from time to time. I continued to do my usual chores and, of course, daily rode over to tend to Chi-Chi. Those times that I found myself recollecting Emile's arms around me, I angrily turned my thoughts to something else. And as trying to change my thoughts was useless, I would stop whatever I was doing and throw myself into some sort of work.

The only odd thing that happened during that time was one night toward dawn. At *point vierge,* or the time right before the dawn, I woke up hearing Maurice coming home and leading Theotiste to the stable. In a few moments he was wandering by the side of the house, and I got out of bed and peered out the window to see what he was doing. He was standing on something by the cypress cistern, and stretching up toward the eight-foot high rim. Curious, I waited quietly at the window and watched.

Rubbing my eyes to see better in the gloom, I pressed my face forward as best I could, as he strained to stretch his arms to reach something. Then, he drew something out of the cistern. Once he'd retrieved whatever it was from the collected rainwater, he pulled it over the edge of the cistern and, clutching it tightly to his body with both hands, skulked away toward the stables. Drinking again, I decided. He must have lowered a bottle of wine into the cool water to keep it cold, and gone back to his tack room to finish it off and drink himself to sleep.

Thoughts of drinking brought a mental picture of Emile in the middle of an all night poker game in New Orleans. I pictured him sitting in some velvet cushioned chair, a gilt lantern hanging above him, a pile of gleaming coins in the middle of the table, and elegant gentlemen of many different nationalities, smoking cigars, drinking brandy, sitting around the table, and guarding their cards by holding them closely to their embroidered vests. I could almost smell the cigar smoke as I imagined him studying his hand through half-lidded eyes while clinking more coins into the pot.

My heart grew heavy as I once more felt the despair from Yvonne's revelations. As this sorrow once again washed over me, I angrily talked to myself. "There you go thinking of him again. Stop it right now!" Never again would I be that stupid, I vowed. If Jean Claude ever returned, I would marry him as planned and start making our home and having babies. Forget about love and passion, I told myself. It's all illusion and fantasy.

I cooked more than ever during those days because it hurt Yvonne to be on her feet more than an hour or two at a time. Then she would have to go to her room and lie down to rest her ankle. When I could get away I would ride to the convent and help the nuns with their work cleaning up the charred mess from the fire. I never revealed the whole story to Claire, but I did tell her about the theft of the gold coins and how he'd gone to New Orleans to make up his losses at cards.

"He lost his gold coins and we lost our chapel. But there is nothing to fear in all this. It appears bad now, but it will all work out somehow. Remember what I tell you, dear friend, if we keep learning to love and keep our faith strong, all that works against us will melt away."

"But how are we supposed to know what's best to do? Sometimes it's hard to know."

Claire patted her heart with a plump hand. "We know by our heart. Does it feel right in our heart that we're doing the right thing?"

In those days, even my heart was confused, so that advice didn't help. One thing I knew for certain was that I somehow wanted to get away from the farm and my sister and brother. But, with Jean Claude still missing, the only way I could do this was to join the sisters at the convent. I gave some thought to this, however, I knew Claire would see it for what it was...a means of escape. And I knew she would never permit me to enter the order for that reason.

Almost two weeks after the fire, I was mucking out the stables, when I heard hoof beats and then the hounds barking and scrambling to greet the visitor.

"Hellooo!" the visitor cried out. That voice stabbed through me, jolting me upright in shock. Emile had returned! Without a moment's hesitation, I threw down the pitchfork and raced along the narrow passageway toward the back of the stables and the woods.

Breathlessly, I charged into the thick of it, running as fast as I could, ignoring the vines and brambles that tore at my face and clothes, not caring as I sped away, deep into the forest, stumbling over deadfalls, tripping on roots, always regaining my balance and hurrying on, as far from the house as I could possibly get.

As I fled further and further, I heard him making his own way, snapping twigs, and coming after me into the cool and the dimness and the shadows. "Sidonie, my love. I'm home!" He sounded so happy, so cheerful and excited. And here I was, pressing through vines, thorns scratching my face and tearing at my hair. Why was he so happy? He should be ashamed and hiding from me after what I'd learned from Yvonne, but he had no way of knowing what she'd told me.

"Sidonie. Answer me." His voice, so full and deep, soothed me despite my anger. "Are you all right?" I tore loose of the wretched vines and plunged ahead into the thicket, hurrying toward Bayou Perdu. When I came out onto the bank, I would follow the bank as deeply into the swamp as I could. Anything to get away from all of them. Sprinting ahead, I could hear Emile crashing and forcing his way through the undergrowth. "I hear you. Please stop. I have so much to tell you."

It was then that I tripped on a fallen tree, landing so hard on the ground that I saw stars, and all the wind was knocked out of me. For a moment, I couldn't catch my breath. Finally, I was able to choke in some air and could push myself up onto my elbows, spitting dirt. I continued to crash through the blackness, until a barbed vine scratched my eyelid so badly at that moment that I had to stop. Carefully easing the razor like barbs from my brow and eyelid, I heard Emile approach closer and closer.

"I've missed you so much. I have gifts from New Orleans. I have gold. Come see." He laughed, like this was a game. I struggled to my knees, brushing off twigs and pine needles and leaves from my scratched face, hair and skirts. And then he was there, grabbing me from behind, and pressing me to him. "Sidonie. Sidonie!" He sheltered my body with his long arms, clinging to me and rocking me back and forth so that we cast one long shadow along the thicket. He smelled of a mixture of tobacco and rum and French cologne, as he rocked me silently in the darkness.

And I could do nothing. I felt numb and paralyzed, but this was not the paralysis of despondency, but rather the enchantment of his presence. The warmth of his body and touch held me like chains. My brain screamed: *Break away from him! Run! Fight!* But I could not. My mind just could not make my rebellious body move away from him. So I remained in his embrace and soaked up the warmth of him as if it were balm to the dying. I was powerless to resist his hold and what is more, I felt my blood warming and tingling with his touch, so that I began to come alive again after the fear and dismay of that dreadful day with Yvonne.

After long moments, he whispered in my ear. "Why were you running from me?"

I could not speak and let him know what happened, what I'd learned about him and Yvonne, because that would break the spell I was under at that moment. The spell of being held in his arms that was healing and cleansing me of all the grief I'd felt for so many days.

"Sidonie. Why?" He stopped rocking me and taking my face in his hands, he gently turned my head, so he could see my wet eyes and trace the course of the tears down my cheeks.

I finally spoke, but my voice broke. Clearing my throat, I tried again. "Yvonne told me."

"Told you? What was that?"

"About you and her."

"Yes?" He held my face with both hands and peered at me through the darkness. I could see the whites of his eyes, but his face was shrouded in shadow.

"About your affair with her."

"My what?" His hands jerked, his back went rigid, and he was no longer bending over me, but scrambling back to his feet. I could see the shock in his face even through the gloom.

"She told me all about how you and....how she's been with you... you and her...together...for months." I stammered.

"But...you didn't believe her? You couldn't have believed her!"

"Of course I believe her. She's my sister! Why would she lie?"

"You mean you heard these insane accusations and took them to heart...without asking me first? This is Emile! Yours, all yours, and I love you so much. How could you believe such preposterous lies?"

"You should have told me."

"Told you what?"

"About you and her. That you've been with her."

"Been with her? Been with her?" He shook his head, blinking, his mouth gaping. "But, no! This is not true. I have never even touched the woman! It's never even crossed my mind to touch her. Why would I? I swear this before God!"

Wiping his white sleeve across his mouth, he kneeled before me. "Please! Don't listen to these lies. I have no idea why she would lie to you like this. She must be demented to make up such things." Remaining silent, my mind whirled with his words, and I felt the excitement from his touch evaporating, as my body grew heavy once again with sadness.

Part of me struggled to believe him, grasping at the hope he was offering, and part of me was repeating over and over, *Of course he is going to lie about it. He can't admit it to you. Don't listen to him.* But, the rising volume of the crickets' steady rhythms lulled me along with the warmth of Emile's hold on me. Slowly, I weakened, turning to him in the darkness. "Do you swear you never touched my sister?"

"I swear," he said solemnly.

"But, why would she make up something so scandalous and wicked?"

"Jealous maybe. She's older and no one's coming around to court her. She invents this melodrama to amuse herself. Or perhaps she truly believes it. People who are unhappy hate to see other people be happy. They will destroy another's happiness if they can."

My thoughts whirled. "I need time to think," I finally said.

"Of course, *chère*. Take your time. Think it over. But, in the end, you will realize the truth…in your heart." He kneeled again, held me in his arms and rocked me to and fro, there on the forest floor with the creatures of the forest our witnesses. As he held me, I tried to make the choice between listening to my heart and listening to my mind.

"All right, then," I whispered. "I accept your story."

"Thank God!" He gently turned my face so he could look into my eyes. "How devastated I would be if I lost you." Slowly, we rose and he took my hand. "Come. Let's go back now."

Pulling back, I resisted. "I don't want to go back there."

"You must. We need to confront her with this hurtful, dangerous lie."

"I can't stand the thought of returning there."

"That is still your home…for now…not for long though."

He kissed me then, and I felt such a powerful desire for him, it was as though nothing had come between us. His long arms held me so closely that I felt warmth flowing into me. The feelings of the last occasion we had been together rushed over me, and I knew I loved him as I could never love another. He had overwhelmed me emotionally and changed me for life. I would never be the same.

He shook his head. "I can't bear this separateness. I want this mess straightened out today, and I also want plans for our marriage decided today. I can stand being away from you no longer." He gently turned me toward the house. "We can't stay here. I won't be able to control myself, and…" he broke off, swallowing hard. Slinging an arm around my shoulders, we made our way back through the forest, hearing the whoosh of an owl gliding overhead and the sudden scream of a small animal.

As we started for the house, the rich smell of leaf mold from the thick carpet of rotting leaves wafted from each step we took. Although I was reluctant to face Yvonne's evil temper again, I was glad to be able to face her with the truth at last. Scratches from the barbed vines still stung, and then I was scratched again in the same place by a low hanging branch, but we at last emerged from the thicket and stepped onto the clearing that surrounded the house without further incident.

As we entered the front door, she was nowhere in evidence, and I assumed she'd gone into her room to lie down. "Yvonne," Emile called, his deep voice ominous.

"I'm lying down," came her raspy response. The house lay in shadow, except for one lone kerosene lamp, its chimney black with soot, which flickered from the kitchen table. The eerie shadows from this yellow light danced upon the floorboards and the walls by her closed door.

"May we speak with you?" he called out.

"I'm too tired. Go away."

"But, this is rather urgent," he insisted.

"I want to be left alone. Go away!"

"Then tell Sidonie the truth from your bed!" he demanded, his tone that of a general on the battlefield. My muscles instantly tightened, and I felt a sharp pain in the shoulders as my neck stiffened.

Finally, there was a stirring in her room, and rustling as the quilt was thrown back. A long shadow appeared on the floor as she threw back the door, the candle in her room casting a wavering glow around her. As she limped from her room with the help of the cane, her fury was evident in the way she careened from the doorway and lunged forward into the main room. "You! You dare to deny what you did to me? Over and over and over? Lusting and desecrating me?" Her face was in shadow, yet even in the low light of the room, her grimace was visible as she approached us, striking her cane on the floor with each step.

She fell against Emile pounding on his chest with her fists and screaming at him like a madwoman. She rained blows on his shoulders, her fists hitting him again and again. He grabbed her forearms and held her at arm's length as she frantically struggled to continue hitting him.

"Satan! Deceiver! You said you loved me. You lie! Lie! Devil!" She spit and sputtered as he held her away from him, and she fought against his hold on her.

When she began to tire, and her struggle weakened, Emile attempted to speak calmly to her. "Please, Yvonne. For God's sake, tell her the truth!"

"The truth? You want to know the truth? You have two women now. And who knows how many in New Orleans or scattered throughout the bayous? And this one is pregnant. There's your truth! Now, what will you do, deceiver? Father of Lies!"

I felt like I'd been kicked in the stomach. So he *had* lied to me. No wonder Yvonne was hysterical. Pregnant! Not married! The scandal of this would be intense in our village. The air in the room suddenly felt stuffy, heavy, humid, and unbearable. I turned and raced from the house, fleeing back to the safety and privacy of the forest. I was like a wounded animal seeking a cave to lick my wounds. I pushed through the forest once more toward the bayou. Somehow I had to find Maurice's boat in the darkness and use it to go deep into the swamp. At that point, I didn't care about the dangers of the Atchafalaya. They were of no consequence to me. Getting away from Emile and Yvonne was all I cared about.

As I tore through the gloom of the woods, the moon rose, and though waning and not quite full, I could still make out general shapes of the trees and bushes. Even though shadows obscured most of the scene, this time the forest yielded to me, as though knowing I belonged there. It seemed to bend itself for me to aid my escape, and allowed me this time to make my way through the thickets, dense vines, and protruding roots without incident.

Veering north toward the bayou, I knew somewhere on the bank, I would find Maurice's pirogue, and with that I'd be able to venture up the bayou toward the bay off the Atchafalaya River where Arsène lived. I vaguely knew my way toward his camp. I hoped, if all else failed, I could count on him to protect me while I had time to sort out my life and make a plan for my future. My future which at the moment seemed lost and hopeless, was maybe not all lost if only I had time to think.

I recognized that I was in shock and very tired, and because of this, everything seemed overwhelming. My faith had taught me that we are never alone, that we have invisible help from the spirit world, and I tried to repeat this to myself to summon courage. As I twisted my way through the forest, I smelled the bayou close by. The bayou has a rich smell of vegetation and slow moving water and mold, mosses and ferns. I slowed, and carefully picked my way toward the bank, where I kneeled and caught my breath, listening to the night sounds, encouraging myself, and allaying fears of getting lost that arose with the raucous insect volume that swelled and swirled around me.

My precious owls hooted softly back and forth as unseen animals cried and shrieked. Swatting a few horseflies and mosquitoes, I pondered my situation. Maurice's pirogue had to be near because this was a direct route from the house. I waited for my eyes to adjust to the dark as Emile's calls from the vicinity of the house told me he was beginning to come after me again. In desperation, I pushed toward the edge of the bank, slipping once and getting my boots full of mud. Regaining my balance, I peered into the gloom.

Carefully stepping and picking my way along the bank so I wouldn't slip again, I finally spied the pirogue tucked beneath a willow whose branches hid it partially from view. Wasting no time as Emile's cries grew more and more desperate and ever closer. I shoved the heavy boat, gradually angling it toward the water, and then with the strength born of anxiety, I gave it a final hefty shove, and it slowly slid into the black waters.

Pleased with myself for achieving that much, I felt a surge of energy that came from pride in my flight so far. Quickly I jumped into the boat and, taking the pole in hand, nosed it toward the north. My plan was to navigate into the heart of the mysterious swamp, where Maurice, Yvonne, and Emile could not find me, and where I could collect my thoughts, summon my energies, and heal the wounds of my heart.

PART TWO

...Who is my mother? And who are my brethren? Matthew 12:48 KJV

12

ARSÈNE

I have hired a little felucca,
narrow like a pirogue, swift as a swallow.
Twenty Years After - Alexandre Dumas

O nce upon the black waters of the bayou and free, my pounding heart slowly returned to a calmer pace. Rumbling thunder in the distance only increased the thrill I felt at this new freedom, and the deep menacing tones underscored the drama of the evening. Breathing hard with the exertion of poling, the wet air pressed against me, and I was filled with excitement as I pushed on. I had broken away from all that had bound me, oppressed and disappointed me. Gros Louis had taken me along some of the bayous and the great river that flowed through the swamp, and I blessed him for teaching me all that he had. I imagined he was there with me in the boat, encouraging me as he always did, to not be afraid, and to keep on with whatever I was trying to do without ever giving up.

"Gros Louis," I whispered. "Papa. Help me find my way tonight." I felt a lunge in my heart and a lump in my throat, which caused me to press my lips together so I wouldn't cry. *Now is not the time for crying.* I imagined him saying. *Save the tears for when you get where you're going, you.* I could feel his powerful arms around me, and just by imagining he was with me, I felt such a sense of peace and calm, that I easily continued on my flight.

Owing to living beside the great swamp all my life, it had become for me a symbol of refuge. No church or cathedral, not even the pictures of Notre Dame or Sacre Coeur that Emile had shown me could equal the sense of awe that I experienced that night as I, for the first time alone, entered the mystical space of the great Atchafalaya, the unending swamp of the towering cypresses, that region of shadowy mystery and strange night music.

I could still hear the echoes in my mind of Emile's cries, as I kept working my way north, as the screams of night birds, the loud chorus of frogs, and an occasional growl from a bull alligator kept me company. Pressing forward, I guessed it would take almost an hour to find Arsène's camp. I hoped the smell of his cooking fire would lead me on. The bay on which he lived was not so big that I couldn't locate him by stubborn determination. Yvonne and Maurice had always told me how stubborn I was, and that night I was definitely living up to it.

Part of me felt cold and afraid however, for all my bravado. My neck felt like ice. What if? What if I couldn't find Arsène? What would I do all night in the swamp? How could I protect myself from predators with only the pole I held in my hands? I had no knife, no gun. I pushed these thoughts out of my head knowing I couldn't give in to fear, or I'd not be able to pay attention to what I had to do.

Sister Claire had always taught me about having faith, and about knowing that I was protected as a child of God. *Be grateful for the gift of faith. You are in a state of grace. Be ever thankful for this precious gift*, she often reminded me. It comforted me to remember her words as I worked my way up the bayou, the huge, ancient cypresses towering above me. I looked upon them as my friends, my guides, and protectors. They were mythic in size and solemn in their great stillness, and they also comforted me.

My back and shoulders strained from poling, and I thought briefly of guiding the pirogue to the bank and resting for a while, but then the splash of something large near by spurred me on, and I rejected any ideas of resting until I found Arsène's camp. I had never seen him much at all, but Papa had always spoken well of him and talked about him with admiration for his self-reliant nature. *That is a good man, him. He knows how to make a good life in the swamp by himself. I like that old swamp rat, Arsène! Some people they hate to live alone. Some people, like him, they do just fine off by their self, and him so young to be doing dat!* I remembered Papa talking about him one day when we saw him in the village trading some pelts for sugar and coffee at the general store.

Then the rains began. The mist and downpour combined to obscure my vision as the silver rain blended with the black of the night. Crooked lightning cast eerie daylight all around, then just as suddenly, all was somber once more. The rain streamed down my face, and I had to wipe my eyes by twisting my face onto my shoulder as I steadily poled. Shortly, the sleeve was so drenched, it hardly helped to wipe my eyes. As the streaming water on my face almost blinded me, I thought again of pulling over and waiting out the weather in the shelter of a giant cypress. But the red eyes of the alligators here and there along the banks kept me moving along as fast as I could.

Their red eyes reminded me of all the *loup-garou* stories I'd ever heard as a child. The fact was, if I was honest with myself, I'd have to admit part of me still believed in werewolves, and this caused me to feel a *frisson* of fear that night. Papa had laughed at my fears concerning *loup-garous*, and managed to convince me, at least a part of me, that they were just made up stories. And when I was still a child, and Maurice would try to scare me with a threat such as, "The *loup-garou* is going to get you!" Papa would scold him harshly and tell him to go away and leave me alone.

Stopping every few moments to bail water with an old can left in the boat tired me at first, but my sorrow and anger and frustration filled me with energy and the fire I needed to continue, so that outer discomforts didn't prevent me from pushing on through the murk of the liquid night. I wondered if my own eyes didn't also glow with the red of anger, for every time I thought of Emile and Yvonne, my eyes and all of my face felt hot despite the rain.

After half an hour of downpour, the moon began to shine through once again. Drenched and chilled and miserable as a wet cat, I could see then to make my way toward the bay where Arsène lived. From the vague sense of where he made camp, I thought I might have only another half hour to go as long as the rain didn't start again. The frog chorus swelled in volume in the aftermath of the rain, so loud that it drowned out my thoughts. When I started shivering my teeth began to chatter, yet I could still whisper pleas to the Blessed Mother to help me find my way to Arsène's cabin.

Presently, the silver mist lifted like a dream, and water dripping from thousands of leaves lulled me gently, so that my hopes gained strength once more. The swamp was not murmuring that night; it was screaming. High pitched yowls and screeches from birds and animals and insects were almost deafening and came from all around me. Mosquitoes collected in a noisy haze around my head, and their whine was unrelenting. I thrived on the swamp noise and drew strength from all of it. I was so glad to be far away from the farm that all the tumult of the swamp was music…the music of freedom from abuse. But this time, my face and hands were not protected by wood ash or Arsène's salve, and I had a hard time of it, swatting and flailing the insects with my free arm, waving them away as best I could. But always, they returned to attack, managing to even get into my ears, despite my thick wet braids.

Flickering lights finally appeared far ahead, a beacon, through the shimmer of raindrops heavily dripping from overhanging branches. I made for the lights, feeling somewhat light-headed from the soaking and the chill, but warmed by the possibility of having found my refuge, praying that this was to be Arsène's cabin, and not some strange outlaw of the swamp. I knew I had to get out of the soaked clothes and into dry ones, or I could come down with fever. By then I was shaking all over, and my lips felt blue.

By the time I reached the bank in front of that light, I could see that it was Arsène's camp, as he passed by a window, his long black hair illuminated by the flickering light of the fireplace. The pirogue ground and bumped up to the bank, and I made the sign of the cross in gratitude for my safe journey. "Thank you, thank you," I said, as the boat jerked to a stop in the black mud of the bank.

Stepping from the boat onto the bank, my boots sank into the mud with a slurping sound, and I tripped, further weighing down my soaked skirts with thick muck. "Hello!" I called, fearful he might shoot into the darkness if he thought I was an intruder.

"Hello!" he responded, and immediately he slid the bolt and opened the front door, stepping out onto the steps, lantern held

high. A black and tan deerhound bolted from the cabin, barking
a chilling warning, until Arsène quieted him with one loud "Gator,
NO!" The hound stopped immediately in his tracks and waited
quietly until Arsène joined him near the bank.

I have often thought back upon that night and all that glow
of the lantern's light meant to me. Its humble swath of light,
warm and yellow, casting away the darkness of the wet night, and
also the darkness of my mind and heart. It lent strength to me
on that night's quest with its promise of comfort and safety. I
can still see that golden light as clearly as it appeared that dismal
night, casting a beam of refuge and promise before me when
my whole life seemed in ruins, and so wretched as to be intoler-
able. That simple act of Arsène's, holding the lantern high, also
marked the end of one long chapter of my life, and the beginning of the new, vastly different life that was before me. But, of
course, that night I had no idea of the dramatic change that was
swiftly coming. I had only a dim awareness of relief, and was
concerned mainly with getting dry and warm by the comfort of
Arsène's fireplace.

"It's Sidonie," I announced.

"Sidonie!" he called in disbelief.

"Yes, it's me. I have trouble." Suddenly I was ashamed of my
story. Now I would have to explain what happened, and it was
all so terrible, I hated to have to tell it. I felt my face go red in
the shadows as I carefully made my way up the bank, dragging my
skirts, even yanking them, as they snagged on roots. Drawing a
deep breath, I stepped onto the rough planks of the porch as he
followed, staring at me in astonishment, trying to fathom what on
earth I could be doing in his camp in the middle of the night. Gator snuffled around me, catching my scent.

"Come in. Come in. I'll get a blanket."

I stepped into his shack, which was little more than a room,
cluttered with hunting and fishing equipment. His fireplace was
half the size of the one at the farm, and there were only two chairs,
a small table in the center of the room, and a cot in the shadows of
the far corner. Various heaps of belongings were stacked on crates
against the rough walls, including a pile of dried pelts, which lay
on a trunk near the door.

"Come here by the fire." He drew a chair closer to the banked fire. Hanging the lantern on a hook, he stumbled in his haste to grab a blanket from the cot. "We have to get you warm. Quickly, get out of those clothes and wrap this around you." He turned away to give me privacy, going to the door and looking out.

I didn't hesitate for a moment to get out of those clammy clothes. Stepping out of my two skirts, I took off my chemise, and wearing only my undergarments, the clothes in a sodden mass at my feet, I wrapped up gratefully in the blanket. Then, huddling by the fire, I chattered and shivered like a shipwrecked sailor.

"You need to drink something that will drive that chill out of you." He crossed to a crate under the window and reached down for an earthenware bottle, then poured some in a cup and brought it to me. "Drink this all down. It's *vin de soco*. It will warm you. My mother makes it."

Muscadine wine is delicious, and within minutes, I was holding out the cup for more. When he brought more to me, his eyes showed how worried he was. "We can't have you getting sick. Why are you here in the middle of a stormy night?" Gazing at me in wonder, he frowned and shook his head.

"A big fight at the house. I had to leave. I just couldn't stay there any longer, and I couldn't think of anywhere else I could go."

"A fight? With who?" He looked puzzled.

"My sister. My cousin." I waved a hand in dismissal. Gator, his dog, came inside then and tilted his head as though he too wanted to hear my story. "I'm too tired to tell you about it. It's enough that I can't go back there…ever again." I felt my face flush with emotion, and surprised myself at the strength of my conviction. "Never!"

"All right. All right." He raised his hands as though to say that was fine. "But you have to let them know somehow that you're safe."

"What do I care about what they think? Let them worry all they want to. I'm sure they're glad I'm gone." Gator, startled by my tone, jerked his head, ears twitching back and forth. "I *know* they're glad I'm gone. Now I'm out of their way!" We waited then for a few minutes before either of us spoke. Arsène stared at me as though wondering what to do. Gator kept watching me to make sure I wasn't going to do something crazy. I sat quietly, breathing hard, and trying to collect myself.

"But, Maurice. He's my friend. He would never forgive me if I didn't let him know you were safe."

"They mustn't ever know where I am. Promise me, Arsène. Otherwise I'm going back out there into the swamp at once!" I gripped his coarse sleeve, pleading with my eyes.

He placed a comforting hand on my own. "No, no. You can't go back out there. You must stay here by the fire and let me help you."

"Do you promise not to tell them where I am?" My voice sounded hysterical.

"But, if Maurice comes out here looking for you, he'll kill me if he finds you here. I know him too well."

"He'll never think I've come all the way out here. Never."

"I hope you're right...or it's my neck." He made a slicing motion with his forefinger across his throat.

"Believe me, Arsène. I wouldn't do anything that would harm you." Throughout this exchange, my blood rose, and because of being so agitated, the shivering stopped. I began to feel calmer as the wine and the fire warmed me. Gradually, I became so relaxed that I felt sleepy, and had to blink to keep my eyes wide open.

Arsène noticed my eyelids growing heavy and smiled. "I told you my mother's wine would warm you. Would you like some beans and biscuits?"

My stomach had been queasy and tight from all the arguing at home, but I realized I had grown hungry from my long wet flight through the swamp, so I nodded drowsily. He lifted a black pot from a corner of the hearth and set it on the fire dogs.

"It's still warm, but I'll make it steaming hot for you. Then you can go to sleep on my cot. I'll sleep over there." He indicated a corner by the door where various crates and piles of pelts were stacked.

"I can sleep in the corner. I don't want to take your bed." I said.

"Oh, no. We can't have that. A young lady needs a proper place to sleep. I'll sleep over in the corner with Gator. We'll be fine." He uncovered a tin plate of biscuits and buttered one for me. "Here. Start on this."

I took a bite of the biscuit, then embarrassed myself by eating it too quickly. He laughed. "Here. Have another one." He buttered another, and handed it to me. Steam rose from the black pot and the smell of sausage and beans was wonderful. I eyed the pot like a hound watches for something to fall from your plate. He ladled out a bowl of it and handed it to me. "Careful you don't burn your mouth."

"Who taught you to cook like this?" I asked after the first mouthful.

"My mother. She's the best cook around."

"Where does she live?"

He gestured with his head. "Tucked away far up the bayou from Alcide Delcambre."

"So why are you here and not with her?"

"Because once I saw this camp, I knew I never wanted to leave."

"And when was that?"

"When I was fifteen, and my father brought me here fishing. It was an abandoned camp, and I felt so much at home that it seemed like it had always been my home. I left my parents after that, and told them I had to live out here on my own. They understood. They said I took after my grandfather. He was a swamper too, him."

"Don't you get lonely out here by yourself?"

"By myself? Do you hear that?" He pointed at the window. "Listen!" A chorus of night birds, frogs, insects, and the howls of a *pichou* echoed in the theatre of the night right outside his camp. "How can you say I'm alone? I have so much company out here."

"Don't you miss people?"

"I see people when I go to town to trade and get supplies. That's enough for me."

I finished the beans and he took the bowl from me. "Do you want more?"

"No, no. That's plenty. I will sleep well now. Thank you so much for taking me in."

He poked the fire with an iron rod. "Who would let you stay out there on such a night?" I yawned, and that made even Gator yawn. "You need to go to sleep now. In the morning I'll make us a big breakfast."

Meekly nodding agreement, I gathered my blanket around me and rose, making my way to the narrow cot and settling myself onto the thin moss-filled mattress. He spread my wet clothes before the fire, arranging the two skirts to dry between the two chairs. There was a carved headboard propped against the cot. In the dim light I could make out wriggling snakes and alligators, a bear and a fox, a hawk and frogs. It was smooth and worn, and I passed my hands over the carvings. "These carvings are beautiful."

He shrugged. "Something to do on those long evenings when I'm not out trapping or fishing." He arranged my boots a few feet from the hearth. "Your boots will be dry tomorrow, and I'll be able to scrape all this mud off for you."

"Thank you," I mumbled, then overcome with fatigue, I turned my face to the wall, snugged the pillow under my head, and barely managing a soft goodnight, I was lulled to sleep almost immediately by the crackling of the dying fire and the rhythmic songs of the swamp.

13

STUNNED

"My dear Athos, you seem to me to look at things on the dark side."
The Three Musketeers - Alexandre Dumas

T he next morning, I awakened to Arsène rekindling the
fire, and opened one eye to see him poking the glowing
red embers and the hot gray ashes with an iron rod. He
then added two split logs to the still smoldering and black charred
wood from the night before as Gator silently watched. Stirring
within my blanket cocoon, I took pleasure in the thin light filtering through the window, casting a pale unworldly hue over the
snug little cabin. It was so small compared to our farmhouse, that
I might have been on a houseboat. Despite the turmoil of the
night before, I felt peaceful in that pearly early morning light.

Silently, I watched Arsène work at the fireplace, noting he was
wearing thick black socks, his worn boots leaning against the far
end of the hearth, one flopped against the other. Looking around
the room to where he'd slept, I could make out a pile of canvas
and *pitre* sacks in a brown heap near the door, and felt a fleeting
pang of guilt for putting him out of his bed. As I yawned and
stretched, Arsène glanced quickly over his shoulder, holding the
poker aloft.

"Good morning. You slept all right?"

"Oh, yes, thank you so much. I slept hard." Huddling in the blanket, I wondered how I was going to step into my clothes that he had folded over a chair.

He smiled shyly, hair falling into his eyes. "Would you like some coffee?" He reached into the fireplace for the pot, fitted with a hand-sewn cotton sack that held the grounds brewing in the steaming water.

"Oh, yes, please." My voice was timid, and I felt self-conscious as I held out a hand for the dark coffee he brought me in a tin cup.

"I have no milk. I'm sorry."

"No matter."

He looked away. "Do you want me to step outside so you can get dressed?"

"Thank you."

First checking the biscuits that were rising nicely by the freshly banked fire, he quickly left the room with Gator trotting close behind. Blinking, I wiped the sleep from my eyes, and gratefully sipping the strong coffee, enjoyed the privacy. Arsène was such a gentleman, quite unlike my rude brother. I said a quick prayer of thanks to the Blessed Mother for his hospitality and my safety and comfort. Then, carefully setting the coffee cup on the floor, I unwound myself from the blanket and scurried to my skirts and chemise, which although still mud splattered and bedraggled, were warm, dry, and inviting.

Once dressed, I rubbed my hands over my face to fully wake up, and sat on the chair waiting for the biscuits to be done, while finishing my coffee. They baked on coals on the flat lid of a black pot. The fireplace hissed and popped as I tried to adjust to my new surroundings, for this was the first night I'd spent away from home my entire life, other than the occasional overnight at the grandparents' as a small child.

Presently Arsène returned, but only after first rapping on the door. Crossing to the fire, he checked the browning biscuits and sausages. "It looks ready," he pronounced. He set about serving breakfast on tin plates, positioning a rough homemade table between two chairs, so we could settle in for our meal. Pouring me fresh coffee, he waited until I took up my fork, and only then did he begin to eat.

When we'd finished, I offered to wash the plates, but he shook his head as he gathered them up and placed them in a pan by the door. "I'll take care of it later."

"In the river?"

"No. I collect water in a cistern." He busied himself straightening up the heap of canvas and sacks he'd slept on, then continued putting the cabin in order as I folded my blanket and tucked it neatly at the foot of the bed.

"Have you thought about letting them know where you are?" he finally asked.

I felt a chill race up my spine. He was going to betray me and tell them where I was. "No, please! They mustn't know where I am!"

"I have to let Maurice know you're safe though."

"*Mais*, no. Then they'll know I'm here with you. You promised!"

He waved a hand in assurance. "Yes, I promised. I did. Don't worry." He seemed surprised at the panic in my voice. There was a pause, the only sound the fire crackling and snapping. One of the back logs rolled forward and sparks flew past the hearth and almost to my skirts. "Careful!" he called.

I jumped back, pulling my skirts around me. Arsène scooped what was left of the biscuits and sausage grease into a pan for Gator and carried it outside. "Are you going to be all right here by yourself?" he asked as he went out the door with Gator trotting behind. He kneeled down with the pan right outside the door as Gator got busy at his food. "Gator and I usually get out in the swamp at dawn. It's better for fishing. This is late for us."

"Take me with you?"

He looked surprised. "If that's what you want. But why? Don't you want to take it easy after being out so late?"

"No. I love fishing. Papa used to take me out with him. He taught me a lot."

"Well, come on with us then."

I hurried to join him outside before he could change his mind. "I'm going to check my cross lines. If you want to help, you can knock worms off the catalpa leaves and put them in this." He handed me a battered pot and a cane pole, then nodded toward the catalpa tree. We often picked worms off catalpa leaves for bait. In the swamp, mostly cypress and tupelo gum trees grow, but Arsène's camp was built on a ridge. Because of this ridge, he had two spreading willows and a catalpa. The willows' graceful, airy branches trailed in the slow current near the pirogue. The catalpa grew near the cypress planks that Arsène had fashioned into a makeshift stand for cleaning fish.

Dutifully, I knocked some fat worms from the tree with the pole, then collected them into the pot. After Gator and I had comfortably settled ourselves into the boat, he shoved the pirogue off the bank, and we drifted along on the water, its surface greenish as it reflected the green canopy of leaves overhead. A light breeze refreshed me, and I was surprised at how little it took for me to feel happy despite all my problems.

The sun filtered through the towering trees, and I contentedly watched the shades of green change with the shifts in light as I breathed the rich scent of this wildly growing and teeming natural greenhouse. As we glided along, Arsène's pole dripping water, I stared at a multitude of egrets, herons, and ducks among the knobby roots and cypress knees. Waterbugs danced as if drunk, and lily pads showed off their creamy yellow blooms spiking strong and erect.

He slowed the boat, sliding alongside a cypress stump. He grabbed a jagged edge of the rim of the wood to stop the boat, then abruptly plunged his right arm deep into the dark hollow up to his shoulder, grunting as he strained to grope beneath the dark water. Watching closely, I fully expected him to come up with a struggling catfish, but he withdrew his arm with a disappointed expression, swinging it to flick off water.

We proceeded toward the first crossline, strung between two young cypress trees. Cypress grows so slowly, and these two, about a hundred years old, were still not two feet in diameter if measured above the swollen base. The *ligne de travers* was strung deep in the water, and he pulled it up like a clothesline, checking the individual lines and hooks dripping and dangling from it. He had caught a blue catfish, a yellow catfish, and one fat water moccasin. Gator was so well trained, he sat serenely in the stern, never once nosing the catch.

My eyes widened as he hauled up the charcoal four-foot snake that had drowned on the line. He cut it loose and tossed it into the boat. "Bait," he muttered as he set about unhooking the catfish and slipping them into his sack. Eyeing the moccasin, I wondered that I'd never been bitten in all the times I'd visited the woods and the banks of the bayou. We had lost one five-year-old boy to snakebite in St. Beatrice the year before, but I had only heard of one other case. Our villagers and neighbors knew how to keep their eyes open in the swamp, and always wore their boots, wary of deadly serpents. Moccasins were so aggressive, a friend of Hippolyte's claimed to have been chased by one all the way to his pirogue, until he managed to hop in and shove off from the river bank.

Maurice and Hippolyte had one drop into their pirogue from an overhanging branch, but Hippolyte said he'd snatched him up by the tail, swung him around his head, and spun him off into the swamp. Knowing Hippolyte, I had no trouble believing this story as I knew he had enough naturally overflowing energy to swing an alligator around in circles by the tail and spin *him* off into the water.

After Arsène had checked some more lines he'd tied to overhanging myrtle bushes, we finally headed back for camp with four catfish and one *gaspergou*. "I'll take some to my mother after I drop you off," he told me as we drew near to the camp. "While I'm gone, why don't you go and start us some dinner with these?" He handed me two of the fish in a sack. "I'm going to leave Gator with you for protection. You won't have anything to worry about with him around." Gator, brown eyes glinting in the light, gazed at me as though to say: *He's right. You have no worries with me around.*

As the pirogue grazed the bank, I jumped out and scrambled up the bank with mud sucking at my boots. Gator sat in the boat until Arsène gestured at him to follow me, and then we both watched as Arsène pulled away with a wave of his hand, insects screaming all around us.

When Gator and I entered the cabin a few minutes later, I breathed deeply of the comforting safe smell of the place as the smell of the smoldering ashes bit at my nose. This new sanctuary meant safety to me, and so glad that I could contribute to my temporary new home, I added a few pieces of wood while I planned how I would cook the fish. After drinking the last of the coffee, still hot, and by then, so strong it would keep me going for hours, I led Gator outside to clean the fish.

Arsène kept a knife tied to the cleaning table by a string. After scraping and gutting the fish, I tossed the multi-colored innards to Gator. He sniffed at them, then turned away as he was so well fed, so I tossed them into the dark, slow moving waters that flowed by the camp. Something large snapped at the purple and yellow innards and made concentric circles as it disappeared beneath the surface, then snapped again at what entrails still floated. I smiled at the completeness of the swamp. It needed nothing and lacked for nothing. And I felt complete within its embrace as well. Grateful and whole and without any desire to leave it. I filled a bucket with swamp water and squatting on the bank, rinsed the filets, then stared out at the shadows playing on the water as flashes of sunlight filtered through the thick canopy of leaves.

A dragonfly skittered over the water and its wings shone with iridescence in the mottled sunlight. I supported my chin with the cup of my hand and continued to stare at the drama of the swamp, wanting nothing more than to be Arsène's friend and somehow continue to stay in this wilderness. This seemed impossible as for me to purposely remove myself from the community and isolate in the great swamp alone as an unmarried woman would have been incomprehensible to the villagers. But at that point, I no longer cared what any of them thought. If I were married and went into the swamp with my husband, that would be acceptable, but after my first experience with love, and the wrenching letdown it had all been, I doubted I would ever be able to venture into that territory again.

Gros Louis had taught me a lot about the swamp when I was younger, and of course now I had the assistance of my new friend, Arsène. And since I no longer cared what any of them thought back home, what could stop me from doing what I most wanted to do? How do we ever know when we are doing the right thing? Sometimes what we believe to be right, doesn't turn out to be right at all, but we can only see that when we look back on it later on. So I'd learned to do what feels right at the time. If it turns out to be the wrong thing later on, then at least I could tell myself that I acted according to what I believed was right at the time.

But sometimes, I'd learned, decisions seem both right and wrong at the same time. Then, owing to this confusion, it is not so easy to make a choice that I won't regret later. And, that particular day, I felt confused as well. Conflicting loyalties thrashed about in my body and mind. I felt drawn in part to the acreage at our farm, the hounds, the garden I'd tilled, seeded, and weeded for as long as I could remember. I even felt a tiny shred of loyalty toward Maurice and Yvonne, but all these feelings paled next to the exhilaration I felt tasting freedom in the mysterious and wonderful swamp in this rough cabin surrounded by barrels, nets and stacks of traps.

After this period of rest by the dark waters, I returned with Gator to the cabin and sliced salt meat, potatoes and onions for the black pot, which I hung on the iron crane over the banked fire. Gator and I sat contentedly by the hearth as I stirred, waiting for Arsène to return before adding the fish.

Gator heard his return before I did and raced excitedly out the door to greet him. When he stomped into the room, I blurted out: "I don't ever want to leave this place. I love it here!"

He laughed. "You can't keep them worried about you forever."

"They can worry all they want. What do I care? They're miserable people so let them be miserable!"

He stared at me for a long moment, then looked away, his face in shadow.

"How long may I stay here at your camp without bothering you?" It was out of my mouth before I knew it. I surprised myself with the question and the way I was pushing him for an answer to a question I knew worried him. Uneasy, he shifted his position from one foot to the other without answering, then walked to the window and looked out.

"Never mind then. I'm sorry I asked." His reaction pained me. "I can tell I'm worrying you by being here. I'll leave." My shoulders slumped in surrender, and my heart felt heavy.

"No, no," he hastened to say without turning from the window. "I enjoy your company very much."

"But it makes you uncomfortable. I know that." I carefully added the fish to the potatoes and onions, gently so the filets

wouldn't break. As the delicious smell rose, Arsène turned from
the window and arranged the table and chairs for our supper. We
didn't speak again until the fish was ready, and then he took over
at the pot and served us. After placing our plates, he poured us
each a cup of wine and we sat to eat.

At one point, he pushed his sleeves to his elbows revealing a
gray string with nine knots tied on it circling his wrist. I recog-
nized it as the work of a *traiteur*. Frequently, they knotted strings to
be worn as part of a treatment. Prayers were given for each knot,
to be repeated for a healing.

"What were you treated for?" I asked.

"Oh, this?" He held up his wrist. "I caught a fever one week in
September. Maman tied it on me."

"Oh, yes. I remember now, you told me your mother treats."

"She's blind. I believe that gives her powers in other areas.
She's *very* good at what she does. The fever lifted by the next day."

"Do you see your mother often? I'd love to meet her. Could
I....some time?"

He looked at me hesitantly. "Maybe one day." Then he quickly
turned his eyes toward his plate.

"You want to say something to me, don't you?"

He started to take a bite of fish, then put his fork down. "Sidonie. You know my position here. You are a young girl. You're
engaged. We have no business being alone together. And here in
my camp."

"Yes, I know. But what can they do? I can't go back there." My
voice cracked in desperation. Gator raised his head at the change
in my tone.

"They at least need to know you're safe."

"And as for Jean Claude..." I rushed on, "he's probably dead.
Do I have to stay alone all my life because I'm promised to someone who isn't even here anymore? And most probably a corpse by
now?"

"Don't say that. It's bad luck. We don't know he's dead."

I pressed my lips together so I wouldn't say anything to further upset him. Then shaking my head, I determined to drop
the subject, and took a bite of dinner. Arsène could do whatever
he wanted. I would not return to that withering, dreadful sister

of mine…or the deceptive Emile. Then, I remembered Solange. "But Solange…" I muttered.

"Who?"

"My mare. I have to get her. I can't trust Maurice to take care of her. They are so angry with me now. Who knows what they'll do next?"

"I can't believe Maurice would let your horse do without. He will take proper care of her, I'm sure."

"You don't know my family. They are hateful! He's probably drunk right now, and doesn't even remember if he fed her or not." I surprised myself at the venom in my voice and the hatred in my heart.

Arsène watched me for a moment, then stood. "I'll be back. I'll think about what to do while I'm gone." He abruptly left with Gator hurrying behind to catch up with him.

It occurred to me to return to the farm by myself to check on Solange. I'd made it through that lightning and thunderstorm by myself. Surely it would be easy for me to return on a quiet, dry night to quietly check on her. Before they even knew it, I could fill her feed bucket and trough and be gone, melting away into the night. Going outside to tell Arsène of my plan, I discovered he and Gator were gone, but the pirogue was still there. Figuring he was doing some chores, I returned to the cabin and lay down for a nap, drifting off immediately, the cicadas and birds lulling me to a deep, refreshing sleep.

When I awakened from my nap, my mouth was dry, and I poured water into a cup from the jug on the table, and sat outside staring out at the water. I daydreamed of days in Papa's boat when we'd lazily fish on the bayou, him telling me stories and teaching me how to fend for myself. His large hands were, as he put it, "My gig. These are my gig." He would hold out his broad hands and laugh from deep in his throat, ending with, "heh, heh, heh." His hands truly were his gig. Many was the time I'd seen Papa catch frogs with his bare hands while Maurice or I held the lantern.

I felt a stab of sorrow as I dreamed about the old days, and my upbringing by this strong, funny man. Papa made everyone laugh, and even my mother, so busy and without much time for playing, would stop everything and laugh uproariously at him, sometimes throwing the apron over her face as she gave into gales of laughter. "Laughter makes you stay well, you," he'd say, and then he'd flash that gap-toothed smile. I knew Papa would be proud of my navigating safely through the swamp to Arsène's camp, and that pleased me.

In the middle of my daydream, Arsène quietly joined me on the porch. "I've decided to take you myself to feed your mare."

"But," I protested, "you have things to do. I don't want to be any more of a bother to you."

"No. I want to do it. Anything I have to do can wait." He hooked thumbs in his belt and looked at the sky, as if to end the discussion.

14

A DEVASTATING SECRET

"I am Vicomte de Bragelonne," said Raoul,
blushing because he was unable to name his father,
as the count had done.
Twenty Years After - Alexandre Dumas

T he shadows were lengthening as Arsène poled our way to the bank by the farm. I helped him drag the pirogue onto the grassy mud, and then, wordlessly, we hastened through the woods, Arsène leading the way. We hurried so as to take care of Solange before dark. Smoke from the fireplace drifting through the woods meant Yvonne was cooking supper.

We slowed at the edge of the woods and walked quietly across the clearing toward the stables. I led the way to the rear door of the stables so we could not be seen from the house. The stables were dim and shadowy at that time of day, and the smell of oats and hay and manure from the neglected stalls bit at my nose.

"I told you he wouldn't take proper care of her," I whispered. Maurice and Theotiste were gone, but there was no sign that any attention had been given to Solange so far that day, and I quickly set about feeding her oats and hay and molasses. Solange nudged me hard, snuffling with her velvet nose, and whinnied a complaint about my absence. "I'm sorry. I'm so sorry, Solange," I said as I nuzzled her. "I'll be back tomorrow. I promise." I felt hot tears well up in my eyes, as one of her ears moved forward to show she was listening. I had never failed to tend to her, and I was angry that Maurice would not take care of her even for just one day. I hated him, despite Sister Claire's telling me to love these people.

Arsène helped me clean the stalls while Solange chomped at her feed, and we tossed manure into the wooden cart outside for the garden. We forked fresh hay in for bedding, and we filled her trough. "Maurice must not be back from last night's hunting or fishing. I can't believe he would neglect a horse for no reason," he said.

She must have seen me carrying a shovel full of manure to the cart, for all of a sudden, just as we were preparing to leave, Yvonne leaned out the kitchen window and called: "Sidonie!" She gasped. There was a pause. "Sidonie! Come here this minute!" she barked, and I could tell by her tone that she felt no remorse for her behavior the night before.

At this point, the hounds scrambled from beneath the house, and yelping and excited, bolted for the stables to greet us. Midnight especially displayed such affection that he almost knocked me over by jumping up and leaning his paws on my shoulders. I fussed with them and patted and hugged them, then returned the shovels to the tack room. With a sinking feeling in my stomach, as though I'd swallowed a stone, I began to slowly walk toward the house, the hounds bouncing around me. Arsène stood attentively near the stables, leaning on a pitchfork and watching as Yvonne stepped out on the porch.

I stopped about twenty feet from the porch, the late afternoon sun weakly warming my skin. Her face was pinched and pale and her forehead furrowed as she squinted at me. She thumped the broom she held onto the floorboards in warning. "Where have you been?" she demanded, biting off each word, almost spitting in anger.

"Away," was all I offered.

"And where did you come from?" She jutted out her chin toward Arsène.

"My camp," he said evenly.

"Where did you go last night? Emile and Maurice and Hippolyte stayed out all night calling for you and wandering soaking wet all through the woods with lanterns. They came back to eat, then went right out again. No sleep for any of them. All because of you, you wicked girl!"

Meeting her withering gaze, I stood straight and tall as a tree. "I came back to look after Solange."

"And I asked where you were last night!"

"She stayed in my camp. She was wet and cold, but she's safe now." Arsène stepped forward and spoke boldly, narrowing his eyes at her as though to warn her she'd gone far enough.

"You stayed the night with *him*?" She jerked her head toward him and thumped her broom again as though it were a weapon.

"Yes. What of it? I couldn't sleep in the boat!"

"You're just a young girl! You do not stay away from home ever! And with a man!" She shook a finger at me, then stepped forward, jaw clenched.

"Is this my home any longer, Yvonne?" I asked, voice dripping malice.

"Not for long if you won't behave as you ought!" Her finger shook with anger.

"I'm coming back for Solange as soon as I can. But I'm never living here again. Of that you may be sure." I turned to go.

"Where do you think you're going? Get in the house this minute!" A shank of hair fell from her cap, and she stepped forward again, her limp so pronounced, she almost stumbled.

"I'm going back to the camp. I can no longer stand being near you and your vicious temper."

"My temper!" she snorted. "My temper! It's not temper. It's more than that. It's rage at such a wicked girl! No respect! No sense of right and wrong. How could you turn on us like this? And leave me, lame as I am!" Two white spots showed at the side of her mouth and nose as her cheeks grew red with emotion.

I drew myself up as proudly as I could and turned around once more. "I no longer have to listen to your ravings, Yvonne. I'm going now."

"Oh, go on then, you ungrateful little wretch! Get out of here!" she sputtered. "Evil child. I wash my hands of you. I have done everything I could."

I resumed my exit back toward Arsène, where he stood watching her, transfixed by her rage.

"And you!" she shrieked, shaking her finger at him. "I'll send Maurice after you, working against us like this, taking her in. I'll bet I know why." Her voice shook.

Arsène raised his voice for the first time. "She could have died out there in the storm last night!"

"Died? Her? Ha! She's a little swamp rat. She's not even one of us." Yvonne suddenly pressed a hand to her mouth and, eyes wide, stood stock still as I whirled to look at her and see what she was carrying on about. Hunching her shoulders, she abruptly turned and limped back into the house.

I stared at Arsène, eyebrows raised in question, as if to say, *What a mad woman!*

But he looked at the ground and wouldn't meet my eyes.

"What?" I asked him, a tingling at the back of my neck. "What is she talking about? Do you know something?"

He turned toward the woods, still avoiding my gaze. "We're losing the light fast. We need to head back."

"What do you care? You go all over the swamp at night." I snatched at his arm. "Arsène. You know something. What is it?" I braced myself in the certainty that something was coming that I didn't want to hear.

"Come on." He took my arm and guided me toward the woods as the hounds followed along, snuffling the ground, seemingly unaware that anything was wrong.

"Stop ignoring me." I halted.

"Please, Sidonie. I'll tell you when we get back to camp. Let's go now."

Shivers chased up and down my spine. I tried to make sense of what she'd said as she began clattering pans in the kitchen. Then, when the yellow glow of a lantern spread through the dark of the kitchen window, I recovered sufficiently to follow him toward the pirogue, hurrying so we could get back to the cabin before I exploded with curiosity as to what all this could possibly mean.

We didn't speak all the way back to the camp. My thoughts raced, going over and over Yvonne's words, but I knew better than to try to get Arsène to talk before he was ready. Whining mosquitoes began their cloud of attack, and I huddled within the protection of my clothes, wishing I'd used his mother's salve before we'd left the camp. An alligator slid into the black water in the gloom as we glided by a high bank that hid his cave. Arsène avoided a moccasin hanging from a dead branch over our heads by silently pushing my head down out of range of the dangling serpent.

As we neared the camp, Gator barked and greeted us, leaping off the porch and racing to the bank. "*Bon soir*, Gator," Arsène laughed. *Nous sommes arrivée!* Impatiently, I tugged and yanked on the pirogue to drag it up onto the bank, as Gator leaped and wagged his tail so hard, it beat at my skirts. He sniffed at my ankles, smelling my hounds, as we all headed for the cabin.

Once inside, Arsène motioned me to sit at the table while he poured us each a drink of *vin de soco.* "Drink this. You're going to need it," he advised, then got busy poking up the fire and adding a few logs. He hadn't looked at me since the incident with Yvonne, but I kept my eyes on him as I waited in the chair, slowly sipping wine.

"It's a long story," he finally said, as the fire came to life and we basked in the warmth of it. Gator settled himself by the hearth, paws crossed, staring at the fire, eyes reflecting the light. Arsène took the other chair and drank some wine as shadows from the hissing flames slid across his dark face. Then he sadly turned his head to gaze directly at me.

"I have always known," he began, clearing his throat.

"Known what?" I felt heat rising in my boots and edged my chair further from the fire. My stomach still felt like I'd swallowed a stone, and I knew I wasn't prepared for what he was trying to say.

"There's so much you don't know." He stared into the fire as though looking for something there that could help him find the right words for whatever was so difficult for him to tell me.

"*What?* Please tell me whatever it is!" The hair raised on the back of my neck, and I was losing any patience I had left.

"All right. My mother," he began again, then paused.

"Yes, your mother..." I tried to help him.

"My mother died. When I was a little boy."

An owl hooted outside, the sound soft and muffled. Gator raised his big head, eyes alert.

"My father married again two years later. Claudine is my step-mother."

"Your stepmother? Yes?"

"I think of her as a mother though. I was so young when my mother died."

"I'm sorry that you lost your mother so young."

"Yes, *merci*." He rubbed his face wearily with his hands. "For as long as I remember, I have called Claudine my mother, but I can't even recall what my real mother looked like. I was only six."

"No wonder you can't remember."

"And Claudine did everything she could to be a mother to me. She never once made me feel I was a *beau-fils*. She raised me very carefully. Even though she is blind, she managed to do everything for me." He paused and took another drink of the wine.

"Blind?"

"Yes. She walked in back of her father when he was chopping wood and got hit on the back of the head when he swung the ax back. She can see only dim shapes. But she makes herself do almost everything she has to do each day. She is the strongest person I know. Not much can stop her once she makes up her mind to do something." He crossed a leg over his knee and leaned forward. "But my stepmother, Claudine..." He twisted his mouth as though to delay what he was going to say.

"Yes?" I wanted to shake the story out of him at this point.

"See...Claudine is your mother too....except she is your *real* mother." These words tumbled out in a rush. He spoke so fast, I almost couldn't make out what he'd said, and even thought for a second or two that I must have misunderstood.

My eyes widened in shock, and I tilted my head. "What? What did you say?"

He spoke slowly this time. "Claudine is your mother too...your real mother."

There was a long silence, broken only by two moths batting themselves at the globe of a lantern hanging near the window.

"But how? Why?" I stammered, as I sat frozen.

"When she was about your age. She was already blind. And she had wandered into the cornfield by her house. And she was..." He bit his lip.

"What? What do you mean?" I felt like the top of my head was going to blow off.

"She was attacked…and…"

"And what?" I almost yelled, barely able to contain myself.

"She was attacked! Thrown down on the ground! Violated!" The words hung in the room between us.

"What do you mean?" I felt hysteria rising all the way up to my throat. "What do you mean?"

"Violated. Violated." He spread his hands out helplessly. "Don't you see?"

"Who? Who did this to her?"

"No one knows to this day." He shook his head and finally looked at me. "My mother, Claudine…our mother, still has no idea who it was. And because she was blind, her parents convinced her to give you up to relatives. They were too old to care for a baby. Claudine depended on them for her care. And they couldn't take care of you too."

I stared at him, mouth open in astonishment. "But you knew this all along? Everyone in the village knew this? And no one ever told me?"

"Not everyone knew. Some did. Most didn't. Family secrets."

"How can you keep something like that secret in such a small village?"

"I never spoke of it to anyone. Maybe a few times with Claudine…sometimes with Maurice. I'd ask him how you were doing always. That's all."

"That carved bird. That was from you then, wasn't it?"

He nodded.

"Then we're related. You and I?"

"Not really. My father married Claudine when he was in his fifties. Claudine was still very young. But you and I aren't related, no."

"Then you are a *beau-frère* to me."

He smiled for the first time since we'd left the farm. "And I've always been glad of it. I liked thinking of you as part of the family…even though you weren't with us…and didn't even know."

We sat in silence as the crickets rasped outside and the fire sizzled and the scream of a wildcat pierced the night. Gator worked his paws rapidly as he dreamed of chasing something. Arsène poured us more wine, and I sipped slowly allowing the story to set-tle in my mind. When I'd gathered my thoughts for a while, I final-ly spoke. "I'm glad to have a brother like you. Even if you aren't a real brother. You're at least the way I thought a brother should be. Maurice has always been cold and disapproving and...he's never stuck up for me...not ever. Not one time. I always thought that a brother should do that...stick up for a person. Defend a person. Like you did today with Yvonne. I should have known from the way he acted that something wasn't right. I should have figured out a long time ago that he wasn't even a blood relation."

"Maurice has always been like that. He stays to himself. Even when he's with Hippolyte, his best friend. He hardly ever has any-thing to say."

"How could he be otherwise around Hippolyte? He never shuts up, him." I laughed. "But how? How did I get to Papa and Maman?"

"Your parents are second cousins to Claudine. On Gros Louis' side. It was arranged for them to take you as soon as you were born. Your mother stayed home out at the farm and didn't go into the village for some months. The villagers just believed she had another baby. Who was going to tell them differently?"

Now that the shock was wearing off, I was beginning to like the story. "Now there's really no reason for me to go back."

He nodded. "You won't have to if you don't want to. You be-long with us now."

"I always did. I just didn't know it. And it doesn't even mat-ter that Maurice and Yvonne are so impossible to live with. It just doesn't matter any more." I sat up straighter, feeling lighter the more I learned. "But you don't even have a suspicion of who my father could be?"

"No. And I've often wondered about it over the years. Maybe it was a drifter. Somebody just passing through and long gone now."

"To think my father, any father, could do something like that." I shook my head. "I'm ashamed for him, and I can't even put a face to him."

"There's nothing you can do about it. Put him out of your mind. Worrying about him won't do you any good. Think about the people who love you instead. Claudine and me."

I nodded. "I will. Thank you for telling me all this...even though it took you almost eighteen years to do it. When can I meet her?"

"Who....Claudine? Why I hadn't thought about it. For now, I'll fix us some supper, and then we'll decide when's the best time. All right?"

As if in answer, Gator growled deep in his throat as he continued on his dream chase.

"How about tomorrow?" I asked, eager to meet her, wondering if I even looked like her. "Or better yet, we could go tonight, couldn't we?"

Arsène laughed. "Not tonight. She goes to bed early, and we haven't even eaten supper yet. Maybe in the morning."

15

NIGHT VISITORS

"My dear fellow," said d'Artagnan to him, "you persist uselessly,
and I protest that the situation is bad..."
Twenty Years After - Alexandre Dumas

After supper, Arsène wanted to go out in his boat, and asked me if I would feel safe alone. "Oh, yes. I feel very comfortable here now," I assured him.

Once he left, I set about tidying up the cabin and trying to absorb the news of my mother. It was too much for me to understand all at once, and I thought maybe after a night's sleep, it would be somewhat easier for me to take in. When I was preparing for bed, I thought I heard a strange noise out on the water and what sounded like low muttering. Then Gator raised such a piercing yowl that even the alligators must have dived for cover.

Cold fear flashed up my spine, and I eyed the shotgun by the door, moving quickly toward it. Gros Louis had made sure I knew how to use a gun at an early age, and that night I grabbed it up and stayed very still, pressing myself beside the door as my heart hammered.

"Sidonie. Are you there? It's me. Open the door." It was Maurice. My heart sank. He had come out to drag me home. My stomach clenched, and I waited, holding my breath. The last thing I wanted to do was to see or talk to him. *Go away! Go away! Go away!* I said to myself over and over.

"Sidonie. I know you're in there. Open the door."

He couldn't know I was in the cabin. I could have gone out in the boat with Arsène for all he knew. Gator kept howling and barking and pawing at the door, and still I waited frozen in place.

And then Emile called. "Please, Sidonie. I know what happened with Yvonne today. Please, my darling. Let me speak with you. I have come all this way to beg you to listen to me." His words drove a sharp pain to my heart. Pressing my lips together, I remained silent, but confused. I had been through too much that day, and hearing Emile's voice was more than I could stand.

"Please let us in. Or just open the door a few inches so I can see you." I heard them slapping at mosquitoes and stomping their boots on the porch. I peered through a sliver of a crack at the door and saw Emile standing just inches away. He looked so pitiful and bedraggled that I softened just enough to call out.

"You must not come any closer," I warned, my voice muffled against the thick boards of the door. "You may not enter. Say what you have to say, then leave."

"Thank you, that's all I ask. Just hear me out. I am telling you the truth, I swear before God." Maurice held a lantern high, and shadows danced around Emile. He spoke toward where he heard my voice, and his mouth was within a foot of my own. I felt the warmth I always felt near him beginning to rise, and it was difficult to keep from flinging open the door and rushing to him.

Maurice stepped away then and leaning against an upright of the porch, turned around to stare out at the night. Always the hunter, he was more interested in the swamp than anything Emile and I had to talk about. I leaned the shotgun back against the wall and tried to calm Gator.

"Sidonie, I must convince you. There is no truth to what Yvonne is saying. I have never had anything to do with her. I swear it on the grave of my daughter. *Le bon Dieu!* What must I say to make you believe me? You must believe me. I love you. I want to marry you. I am dying inside!"

What with Gator carrying on, still clawing at the door, it was so hard for me to think. My mind whirled with confusion. Part of me wanted to let him in to hear what he had to say face to face, but another part kept reminding me of my anger toward him and the humiliation of Yvonne's accusations.

"It would be so much easier if you would let me in so you could see in my eyes that I'm telling you the truth."

"Open the door, Sidonie. He won't touch you," Maurice called.

Touching me was not the problem. My losing all control and beating on his chest with anger was my fear. My other fear was that I'd shame myself and throw myself into his arms, all anger forgotten.

"Listen to your brother, and please open the door. I won't touch you."

At that, I held Gator by the collar and flung open the door. "Brother? My brother? And just who is my brother?" Breathing hard and overcome with emotion, I threw my words at both of them. "Arsène is my brother. Or haven't you heard about the latest ravings from Yvonne?"

Breathing hard, overcome with emotion, I planted my feet wide and held Gator tightly as he growled with menace. "It's all right. Shush, boy."

"Damn!" Maurice clapped a hand to his forehead.

Emile reached out with both arms. "What is this? What are you saying?"

Maurice turned his back on us and stepped off the porch. "I'm going back to the boat. I need a drink."

Emile ignored him. "What has she said now with her evil tongue?"

"Ask Maurice. It seems he's known about it for all these years."

"You tell me. What has she done to you now?"

Suddenly, I felt exhausted with all of it. A wave of tiredness washed over me so that I didn't have the strength to deal with any of it for a moment longer. I pulled Gator back into the room and led him to the hearth. "Come in then. But only for a few minutes...and I'll tell you about it."

He followed me inside, barely glancing around at the primitive room. He stayed well away from me as I sat in a chair keeping a hold on Gator until he settled himself by my side. "It turns out that I'm not who I thought I was. My real mother's name is Claudine. She is Arsène's mother too...stepmother." My voice was weary.

He snapped his head back. "What? But this can't be!"

"Oh, it's true all right. Arsène told me all about it this evening. Right here in this room."

"Arsène told you his mother is *your* mother?"

"No one ever said a word to me in all these years. It was all a big secret. There were reasons…." My voice trailed off. "But, now that Yvonne's hatred of me has boiled over…the truth has come out."

"My poor Sidonie. All that you have been through, and now this." He made a helpless motion with his hands. "Oh, if only you'd let me comfort you and hold you in my arms."

My head hurt. I wanted to cry. I wanted for him to hold me, but instead I took a deep breath and pointed to the door. "It's time for you to leave now. I said only for a few minutes."

He gazed at me with sad eyes. "You've been so hurt. Take it from me…years older than you. Love is not that common. When we find it, we must protect it. Not throw it away. It may never come again…not in a lifetime." He took a step forward, then remembered himself and stepped back.

I closed my eyes, pressing my hands to my temples. "Please, my head hurts. It's been a terrible day."

"You know how in love with you I am," he said softly. "Please believe me. She has lied to you about me. I don't know why."

"She has no reason to lie. Why would she?" I could feel the blood pounding at my temples. "I need to stay out here in the swamp where there's peace for me." My shoulders slumped in weariness.

Neither of us spoke for a few minutes as he stayed in his place, and I held my head despairing of things ever working out. Outside the swamp was alive with the steady scream of insects and loud croaking of frogs. A bull alligator made a loud moaning sound as he blew air out of his nose.

"Very well." He sounded defeated. "Against all my better judgment, I'll leave you alone."

The thought of him leaving pained me, but I kept my eyes down so he couldn't see that in my expression.

"And," he continued, "when I do see you again, I hope you will have decided that between Yvonne and me, I'm the one you should believe."

As he turned and walked toward the door, I glanced up and watched him leave, inwardly cringing as he stepped over the threshold, on his way out of my life again. He closed the door quietly behind him, and my hands began shaking as hot tears trickled down my face. I rested my head on my arms on the table and listened to the swamp sounds, keeping my eyes closed so my headache would go away. The crackling of the fire lulled me, and I finally drifted into sleep until the bull alligator made such a bellowing noise again that I jerked my head up. It sounded like he was right outside the cabin, but I remembered that swamp noises carry for miles, so I laid my head back down and dozed off again.

Arsène returned later with a sack full of frogs. Gator bounded to greet him at the door, and I rubbed my eyes trying to wake up. "How come you're not in bed asleep? It's so late."

"I fell asleep right here." I was just half awake and didn't even tell him about the visitors.

He settled the sack against the wall. "About thirty frogs in there. They'll keep until morning. Then I'll clean them and we'll take them to Claudine. You'd like that?"

"Oh, yes, I'd love that."

"Well then, that's what we'll do," he said. "So you get to bed and I'll put out the lantern, so we can both get a good night's sleep. It's been a long day." Gator nosed and sniffed at the sack of frogs. "Get away from there, you," Arsène ordered. Gator backed away and sat staring at the sack. There was some croaking coming from the frogs and a bit of stirring around. "They'll be quiet as soon as I put out the lantern."

While I spread the blanket for sleep, Arsène spread a thick layer of sacks on the floor for his makeshift bed, and then with a mumbled goodnight, I stretched out under the blanket, falling asleep before he'd even blown out the lantern.

16

CLAUDINE

"It's a manifest happiness which God sends us!"
said Athos, with evident joy.
Twenty Years After - Alexandre Dumas

A silver mist swirled through the swamp, thick as smoke, when we set out the next morning. It was so thick, I wondered how Arsène could even guide the boat through it to Claudine's house. He had left Gator at the camp and set a bucket with lid and a covered pan of the cleaned frogs in the center of the boat. As he poled through the heavy fog, I huddled into my tightly wrapped shawl, chilled and damp from the delicate gray mist.

The fog shrouded sounds so that the swamp remained quiet, and I became lost in the thoughts swirling in my head like the fog itself. *What if Claudine didn't like me? How would she treat me? Would she treat me like a stranger? How could she not have sent for me before this? Did she even want to see me? Would she cut our visit short? Would I cry? Would she?* But the thought that kept repeating in my worried mind was: *Would she like me? Would she want to spend more time with me? Or would she politely tell me to go back to Yvonne and Maurice?*

I tried to stop the endless fearful questions, but that was as useless as calling a hound home when he's busy chasing a rabbit. If anything, my thoughts spun faster and faster the more I tried to calm myself. *My real mother's house! I was coming home in a way I had never even dreamed! What was this going to be like?*

Her property ran along Rat du Bois, a bayou flowing into the
Atchafalaya River. Once he'd turned the pirogue into the bayou,
it wasn't long before he pointed toward the woods to our right.
"Watch over there. We're getting close."

Staying alert, I strained to see through the fog. Within minutes, I could just begin to make out the dark shape of a long house
set back from the water. "I see it! I see it!" I called, so excited that
I rocked the boat. Silently, Arsène worked the pirogue up to the
bank.

Without a word, I got out and helped pull the boat to ground,
as a small black dog raced from the house, barking excitedly, tail
wagging. "Hello, *Minuit!*" Arsène handed me the pan to carry, and
he toted the bucket as he led me toward the house, still without
speaking. The friendly dog escorted us, dancing merrily from one
of us to the other. The sun had begun to burn off the fog, and I
could make out fig, pecan, and persimmon trees on each side of
the cypress house, with a wide porch that stretched all along its
width.

"Claudine will be in the kitchen. She sits there often in the
mornings with her coffee." My stomach clenched as we stepped
up on the porch, and I realized I was holding my breath in anticipation. He called her name at the door. From the back of the
house she answered, "Come in, come in."

As we stepped into the gloom of the front room, cool air touched
my skin, and I could smell a variety of drying herbs. Bunches of
herbs hung upside down from the rafters. In a corner of the room
was a small altar, a low wooden table covered with candles, some
flickering, some guttered out. A pot of earth, a pouch of tobacco,
and a pipe lay beside a carved wooden cross, which I recognized
as Arsène's work.

"Claudine. I brought Sidonie." Arsène took my arm and guided me through the flickering shadows of the front room to the
kitchen beyond, where Claudine sat at a table by the stove.

She leaned forward squinting. "Sidonie," she whispered.

I stopped, frozen in place. Arsène pulled me forward. "Come
on," he encouraged.

She spoke louder, half rising from the chair. "Sidonie!" The
chair tipped and began to rock backward as though it might fall,

but she grabbed it setting it straight. As we came closer to her, I gasped in surprise. I did look like her! Except for the half-closed eyes deeply set in the shadows of her face. She was thin like me, and our hair was worn in the same fashion, a thick black braid.

"Hello," I said shyly as I studied her face, amazed that her features were so like my own. The same nose and a similar mouth and chin. Any questions in the back of my mind that Claudine was not really my mother were now laid to rest.

"I've heard so much about you. Please, come sit here with me." She pulled the chair next to her away from the table. "Arsène, please pour us some coffee. There're some beignets there too. And one pear tart left that you two can split. Will you bring them on a plate?"

"I brought frogs. I'm going to make a supper for us. All right?"

"Of course. Of course. That would be very good," she said without turning her face from me. She reached out a hand once I was seated, and I took it. She squeezed it briefly, then released it. "You've been having some troubles I hear."

"Yes, and Arsène has been helping me get through it all."

"And he always will. He's a very good friend to have on your side. And besides everything else, you still don't know what happened to your fiancé, no?"

"Nothing. No word of him at all."

She remained very still as she peered at me. "I'm so sorry for all you've been through." She leaned closer. "I'm not completely blind. I can make out shapes," she told me. "So please don't mind if I stare at you. I've been wanting to meet you for such a long time."

Arsène brought coffee for me, mixed with hot milk, and set a plate of beignets and the tart in the middle of the table.

"I love the smell of your herbs. It's all through the house," I said.

"Oh, yes. There are always herbs drying in there. I love the smell too. Please," she waved a hand at the beignets. "Help yourself."

I still felt nervous and wasn't hungry, but took a beignet to be polite. However, the aroma of the herbs was calming, and my mother's presence was beginning to calm me also. Her voice was soothing and just by being near her, I began to feel good. Arsène leaned against the stove, drinking coffee. No one spoke for a few minutes. The only sounds were songbirds outside the open back door. Then tears wet Claudine's eyes, overflowing onto her cheeks. She wiped her face impatiently with her sleeve, shaking her head slowly.

"Don't mind me. I'm crying because..." she offered, "because..."

"I told her," Arsène blurted.

"You told her?" she asked, disbelief in her voice. "You really did?" Her face crumbled and her shoulders began to shake, then her lip trembled, and I suddenly knew what to do. I took her in my arms and held her tight.

"Yes, I know now. I finally know the truth," I said, my eyes wet as well.

She pulled away from me. "I knew this day would come. I just never knew when." She smiled. "And it's just as I thought it would be...wonderful." She fidgeted at a gold chain and locket, flicking the locket open with her fingernail. She held it out for me to see. Inside was a tiny curl of hair. "There...you see? I snipped this from your head when you were born...before they took you away from me."

I touched it lightly with the tip of my finger, and then she snapped it shut once more and let it fall back onto her blouse. "I'm so sorry about what happened," I whispered.

"At least I knew you were safe. I always knew that." She patted my hand and pressed her lips together.

"And I'm still safe, but never will I go back to my old house."

"Why?"

"Because I can't stand it there any longer. I want to stay far away from them, out in the swamp with Arsène."

"But you can't stay with him. That won't do at all," she protested.

"Why? I love it there at his camp."

"What's wrong at home?"

"Ever since Gros Louis and Eliate died, I've been unhappy there. And now it's much, much worse."

"Your sister and brother? They're not good to you?"

"Maurice and Yvonne? There is no love lost between us. None at all. No."

"I'm so sorry to hear that." She turned her head toward Arsène. "What do you think about all this, you?"

He paused, crossing his arms. "Whatever Sidonie wants to do is all right with me."

"But she can't stay with you. It just won't do." She took a sip of coffee as though to make time to think. After a pause, she spoke again. "Do they know you're not willing to go back there?"

"I don't know anything about them, or the way they think. My last visit...when Arsène took me to see about my horse...it was terrible there. Yvonne was furious and yelling and carrying on. I just can't stand it any more."

"Do you want to stay here?" She put down her cup with great care.

"Here...with you?" I looked around wildly at Arsène. "Here? With you...my real mother?" Excitement coursed through my body, and such a wonderful rush of joy that I could barely contain it. Half rising in my chair, I looked from one to the other of them. "Oh yes. Yes! I would love that so much." It was more than I ever expected or even hoped for, and worth all the turmoil of the past few days just to hear her say that.

"Good!" She smiled and clapped her hands. "Then it's settled."

"Oh, yes, and I can help you. I know Arsène does. But, I can too. I know how to do so many things. I always did a lot of work at the farm. Yvonne is lame, you know. It's hard for her to get around, so she stays in the house most of the time."

She nodded. "Yes, I know. I have received many reports about you over the years, and I know how capable you are."

"Thank you," I said, embarrassed by the compliment. I wasn't used to hearing such things. "And Arsène tells me you are a *traiteuse*."

"Does that interest you?'

"Yes it does. But I've only received one or two treatments in my whole life."

"I'm so glad you hardly ever needed one."

"What sort of treater are you?"

"I treat for anything. Fever, sprains, heat stroke. Anything at all. I offer prayers, herbs, tonics, salves, amulets." She motioned toward shelves on the wall in back of her lined with various jars, tins, and bottles of all different sizes. "It depends on what's wrong. When you're finished with your coffee, I'll show you around the healing garden."

"I'll start on the stew then," said Arsène.

"Yes, you do that while I show her around. Make us a supper, and we'll all eat together to celebrate Sidonie's first day home… where she has really belonged all along."

She took my hand and we stepped out onto the back porch where still more herbs hung drying. "Bring a basket with us. The pears are ripe and more are dropping every day." I picked a round basket from a nail, as Claudine pinched a leaf from one of the plants spreading against the back steps and handed it to me. "Here. Crush it and chew. It's spearmint."

The back yard was cool in the shade of a multitude of trees. *Minuit* joined us on our excursion, keeping pace beside Claudine as she pointed out the different trees and plants on the property. Along with the *plaquemine* or persimmon, were the magnolia, sassafras, mulberry, fig, pecan, paw-paw, pear, and camphor trees scattered throughout the property. There was also a grand garden with a multitude of thriving plants in a great variety of shades of green. Claudine guided me through each row, lightly touching leaves as we passed and calling out their names as if they were children.

Besides the healing properties of such common vegetables as carrots, pumpkin, and beets, onion, and mustard, there were *fevi*, or okra, citronella, *herbe a chien*, *guimave*, or marshmallow, *patte de chat*, or cat's paw, *baume*, or mint, ginger, horseradish, *tête de cabri*, mauve, boneset, and the spreading *mamou*.

There were pepper plants and, toward the rear of the property, *eronce* or wild blackberry, elderberry, *chardron* or thistle, and plenty of comfrey with plantain growing in its shade. Deeper into the woods beyond, I could see plenty of dewberry and a great tangle of even more blackberry bushes.

"Do you use all of these in your treatments?" I asked as I leaned over and petted *Minuit.*

"*Mais, oui,* and I hunt many more in the woods when Arsène has the time to take me for walks there. I can hunt on my own by touch and by seeing the shapes of the leaves, but it's much easier when he's with me. He knows all the plants very well."

"You must never go alone. Snakes!"

She laughed as we strolled past the lovely plaquemine tree, and she reached for a ripe fruit. "Oh, they wouldn't dare bite me. But, if one did, I'd know what to do about it. Besides, sometimes I need something, and I can't wait for Arsène to go with me."

"I'll go with you. And you can teach me too."

"I can tell you already know your plants, Sidonie. But there're always more things I can teach you."

"I'm sure of it."

"Always remember, if there's a disease, God has provided us with a cure for it."

She swept an arm in a graceful half circle, indicating the woods and the garden. "All we have to do is to open our eyes and be grateful for His gifts."

"I will remember. But how did you learn all this? Who taught you?"

"My parents knew the plants. They grew much of this." She made a sweeping motion with her arm to indicate all the property, including a barn, a smokehouse, a *cabinet,* and some other out-buildings. "They learned a lot from an Indian who used to live a bit further up the bayou. I remember him coming around when I was little. He was very old back then. But he brought us gifts, and told us how to use them. Sometimes he'd hold my hand, and I remember how rough it was." She rubbed her own hand as she spoke. "Sometimes he'd frighten me because he approached the house so quietly - like a shadow. I used to call him Shadow Man, but his real name was Sparrow."

I picked half a dozen mottled brown and gold pears from the ground, leaving a few of them that had worm holes or rotten spots. When we began walking back toward the house I thought to ask, "Why does Arsène wear the string with knots tied in it?"

"He has special prayers to say with each knot."

"So it keeps him safe?"

She nodded, as we approached the back door.

"Would you make me one?"

"Of course. Anything you like."

Later, after we'd eaten the frog stew, rice, and biscuits that Arsène made for us, Claudine fashioned the string for me. I recited the special prayers along with her, and she tied it on my wrist. I felt protection as she did this, but I already felt protected just by the sound of her voice and being in her presence.

Meanwhile Arsène cleaned up the kitchen, and announced that he was leaving us to go back to the camp. "I'll be back in the morning with your boat. I'll pull it behind. Then we can go back to the farm so you can get your belongings. She can bring her little mare here, yes, Claudine?"

"Anything. Anything at all that you want," she said.

"Don't bring Maurice's boat. I'll have to return it to the farm sometime."

"Don't worry, I'll take care of that. You all don't need anything else for now?"

"You go on. We're going to make up her bed in your old room, and we'll be fine," my mother said, and we walked him to the front door, waiting together in the doorway until his boat rounded a curve of the bayou and vanished from view.

17

BOURRIQUE!

D'Artagnan looked by turns at these two women, and could not but confess that nature had committed a mistake in their formation: to the great lady she had given a venal and perfidious soul; and to the waiting-maid, a loving and devoted heart.
The Three Musketeers - Alexandre Dumas

rsène returned next morning before I even had the coffee made. He'd already eaten breakfast, but joined us for a second breakfast of eggs and sausage. There were honey, blackberry jam, and pear preserves to choose from for the leftover biscuits from the evening before.

Claudine's property was on the outskirts of the swamp and closer to St. Beatrice than Arsène's camp, so it was still early morning when we got to the farm. As we quietly approached, Yvonne was tossing a dishpan full of water out the window. Arsène went directly to the stables to tend to Solange, and ignoring Yvonne, I wasted no time scurrying up to the loft to gather my belongings. I couldn't take my trunk or pillow or blanket, although I would have liked to. But I stuffed everything else I owned into a sack and hurried back down the ladder with it slung over my shoulder. During this time, Yvonne kept demanding I tell her what I was doing, where I was going, and on and on. I said absolutely nothing to her, which of course, set her blood to boiling.

By the time I left by the front door, her face was so red, it was verging on purple. She looked so strange, I almost laughed in her face, but I restrained myself and hauling my things, walked fast toward the stables. Arsène had readied Solange for me in the meantime, and was leading her out into the yard. He took the sack from me and explained how best to travel on horseback to Claudine's.

"I'll bring your things with me in the boat," he said. "Let's go now before she has a heart attack. What a *bourrique*! Now I know just how bad it gets around here for you!"

Yvonne was by then stomping onto the porch, swinging the broom like a weapon.

"*Arrête, toi! Arrête, toi!*"

"Hurry! Go! She's going to have a fit…or worse a heart attack the way she's going! I'll meet you at Claudine's. Go!" He held the reins for me, and I raised my skirts, climbed up on Solange, and we took off without a backward glance. We were very far down the road before Yvonne's shouting fully faded into the distance.

* * *

Later that day, when we were all together again at Claudine's, and after Solange was settled in her new stall, we sat down for white beans cooked with deer sausage and onions that Claudine had fixed for us while we were gone. Then we lingered around the table with pralines and coffee before Arsène left once more for his camp.

Claudine went outside to work in her garden, leaving me alone to put away my things. Before doing anything else, I wrapped the precious necklace Emile had given me into the folds of one of my skirts, placing these safely under the thin mattress of my cot. I had not yet had a chance to return it to Emile, but I knew I must do that. I really didn't want to return it because it was the most beautiful thing I ever owned, and it would be hard to give it back. I sighed, knowing my conscience would never allow me to keep it after all that had happened between us.

Later on, when twilight was slowly weaving itself into the fading afternoon light, and when it was becoming what Emile called:

Entre le chien et le loup, I helped Claudine prepare a *gumbo des herbes* using four different freshly picked greens from the garden.

After supper, she asked me to read to her, so I read a few chapters from the beginning of *Twenty Years After* as we sat around the kitchen table before it got so black outside that we decided it was time for bed. *Minuit* was already asleep on his old quilt on the floor of Claudine's bedroom. We'd had a long day, and were both ready for sleep also.

I carried the stub of a candle in with me to my new narrow room, and watched the jumping, nervous shadows cast on the walls by the flickering candle flame for a while as I sat on the edge of the bed pondering all the changes that had come about so quickly in my life. A whippoorwill serenaded me, and my eyelids grew heavier with every repetition of that melodic nightsong.

I felt so safe and peaceful there at my mother's, and knowing that Solange was close by in her new stall where I could care for her, made me feel even more secure. Finally, I blew out the candle and stretched under the blanket already feeling right at home. The night sounds were not nearly as loud at Claudine's there on the edge of the swamp as they were at Arsène's camp in the heart of it, and within minutes, I was sound asleep.

18

A GREAT MISTAKE IS RESOLVED

D'Artagnan uttered a cry of joy.
"Ah," said he, "there is then justice in heaven!"
Twenty Years After - Alexandre Dumas

During the next few idyllic days, Claudine taught me how to make ointments and salves and which herbs to use for certain infusions. We also baked together, making fig and persimmon cakes, and pear pies and tarts. Arsène joined us each day with fresh fish or turtle or game. After dinner at midday, we would sit around the kitchen table drinking coffee and eating pastries or cakes.

Arsène gave me the job of looking after his horse, Rubis and Hercule, Claudine's mule, which suited me perfectly because I was used to taking care of horses and loved taking care of any animals. I took over the care of Beau and Belle, the two hounds as well. Although my mother was able to do almost anything around the place that she needed to, it was difficult for her and very time-consuming. My help meant she had more time to work with her potions and the many preparations she made up for her treatments.

A few times during the first days in my new home, people would come by boat or horseback to seek a treatment. She'd take them inside the front room and talk with them for a while, then say French prayers over them, making the sign of the cross over and over again as she treated them. If further remedies were needed for their ailments, she would go to the kitchen and select powders, potions or salve from her shelves of ingredients while they waited quietly in the front room or out on the porch.

I kept my distance from the visitors, giving them their privacy, but carefully observed them as they came and went. They always seemed happier when they left Claudine's presence with a look of hope on their faces, and they seemed to walk a little easier, no matter how miserable they appeared upon arrival.

One night before bed, we were sitting around the kitchen table by candlelight, and I told her about Emile and Yvonne and how the whole disgraceful business had broken my heart. I didn't much like telling the story because I had been able to push it out of my mind with all the new things going on in my life. "And that's how I came to be in the middle of a rainstorm trying to find Arsène's cabin and hardly able to see, it was coming down so hard."

"We're so lucky you weren't hurt or lost."

"I was never so determined. I'd have found him no matter if I *had* gotten lost."

"I'd like to meet this cousin of yours."

"Meet Emile?" I said, alarmed. "But why, Maman?" It was the first time I'd called her that. The word had come out without warning, and it seemed to hover in the air between us, making her smile.

"Why? Because he's so important to you. Because I want to hear what he has to say about all of this."

"He denies all of it. He says it's all lies."

"And maybe none of her story *is* true," she said.

My eyes opened wide in surprise. "But how can we possibly know that?"

"If he's right in front of me, I can tell if he's speaking the truth."

"Right in front of you? You mean bring him all the way out here?"

"I can send Arsène for him. If you say it's all right, of course," she added quickly. My eyes wandered about the shadowy kitchen as I pondered this, thoughts tumbling around in my head. Sending for Emile gave me even more anxiety than I'd felt while telling her the story. But the frail hope that Maman could get to the truth gave me courage, and I found myself agreeing to her plan.

"If you really want to meet Emile, well, that will be all right with me," I finally said.

She smiled. "It will be much better this way. It's always best to speak about a difficult situation straight out to the person's face. Surprising things happen when people sit together and speak directly from the heart."

"It's not easy though. I mean the thought of him coming out here."

"It will be all right. Mention it in your prayers tonight. Pray that it will work out well for all concerned."

"Thank you, Maman. Any help you give me with this will be so good. It's like a knife in my heart whenever I think about what's happened between us."

"I'll tell Arsène when he comes tomorrow, and then....we'll wait and see what happens next."

* * *

Within two days of her speaking with Arsène about this, a boat scraped the mud of the bayou bank, and as soon as I heard this, my hands began to tremble, my heart began to race, and I felt a lump in my throat. I ran to the front door and looked out into the drifting mist of the early morning, and as I peered into the cool silvery air, there were Emile and Arsène tugging a pirogue onto the slippery muddy long grass.

My first thought was to run back to the barn, but I tried to compose myself by staying very still there by the doorway. Just the sight of Emile made my heart race. He crossed the yard in long strides and ran up the steps of the porch. "Sidonie!" was all he said as he regarded me, his eyes reflecting gray in the morning mist.

"Hello," was all I could manage.

"Your mother wants to see me." He stayed very still. "May I come in?"

"Yes, she's in there." I pointed feebly toward the back of the house.

"Aren't you going to walk inside with me?"

Arsène came up behind him, clapping him on the back. "Go on into the house. Claudine will be glad to see you."

Stepping out of the way, I made room for the men to pass, then followed at a distance, not wanting to be with them in the kitchen, but not willing to miss any of the encounter either. I hung back by the doorway to the kitchen as they drew near to the table where Claudine sat in her usual place. Arsène introduced them.

"*J'ai content a rencontre,*" Claudine said.

Emile briefly bowed. "*Je suis enchantée, Madame.*"

"Please, sit here beside me." She patted the chair next to her. "And thank you for coming all this way."

"Thank you for inviting me. It means so much." He took the chair beside her and settled himself as Arsène brought him a cup of coffee.

She leaned toward him. "My vision is extremely poor," she explained. "Please don't mind the way I look at you. It must seem strange, but I can only make out shapes. I wanted to meet you because Sidonie has told me about you."

"Yes?" There was hope in his voice.

"Lately she has had so much to struggle with. Too many worries for such a young girl."

"Oh, yes. I'm well aware of that."

"And, I wondered if you'd be kind enough to tell me what you make of all her troubles."

He cleared his throat. "Yes. But first and foremost, I would like to congratulate you on the safe return of your daughter."

"Thank you. God has been good to us."

"Most certainly, Madame." He placed the palms of his hands flat on the table. "And I would like you to know, as her real mother, that I love Sidonie and want to marry her."

"Yes? And you are certain of this?"

"As certain as I've ever been of anything." He turned his head toward where I still hovered in the doorway, looked me fully in the eyes, then turned back to Claudine.

"And what about Jean Claude? If he is found?" she wanted to know.

"Forgive me, Madame, but I cannot honor this arrangement. The parents who adopted her are passed on, and they're the ones who made this match. Sidonie had nothing to say about it, and she doesn't love Jean Claude. Hardly knows him really."

Claudine nodded, sitting very still as she contemplated this, while I waited, barely breathing, in the doorway. Finally she spoke. "And, what about Yvonne's accusations?"

"None of that is true, I promise you. Not one word of it. I have never been alone with her, not even for an instant, and have no idea why she would make up such a vicious story. Her motivation for doing this is a mystery I cannot unravel no matter how hard I try."

"Would you mind holding my hand while you say that again?"

Emile gently took her hand in both his large ones as he repeated his words. "And I will swear it on the Bible. None of it is true," he added.

Maman sat quietly, eyelids fluttering as he held her hand, and finally she exhaled a deep breath and squinted toward Arsène. "I believe him," she pronounced.

My heart leaped. "Maman!" was all I could say.

"Yes, Sidonie. I believe him. He has been very wronged for what reasons we don't know...yet. But," she nodded to Emile. "It will all be revealed. Of this, I am certain."

Emile smiled and raised his hands toward the ceiling as he turned toward me. "*Merci a le Bon Dieu. C'est formidable!*"

Arsène clapped a hand on Emile's shoulder. "I told you she knows the truth when she hears it."

Emile's face had changed from somber to joyful. "It's true. It's true. Thank God for that."

Claudine asked him, "Have you eaten?" He shook his head.

"Arsène, please fix something for all of us. Maybe some rolls and coffee. Sausage and eggs. And Sidonie, come and join us."

Emile stood and pulled out a chair for me, lightly touching my hair as I sat down. He pushed my chair in as we all settled ourselves and Arsène began working at the stove.

"Thank you for believing me, Madame. It is such a relief. You have no idea." He took my hand.

"And please call me Claudine."

"Yes, Claudine, thank you. And now that I have your trust, may we marry just as quickly as possible? I can't tell you how happy that would make me."

"Sidonie?" Maman turned toward me. "What do you think? What would you like?"

I began to laugh with pleasure and relief. "I can't keep up with all this. So much has happened so fast. I can't think straight right now."

"It's all right. It's all right. I'm sorry to push you like this. But after what happened, I'm so afraid of losing you again. It's been a wretched nightmare for me," Emile said.

I leaned toward him, reaching out, wanting only to embrace him. "Thank God it's over," he said as he closed the space between us to hold me in his long arms, rocking me to and fro.

I could have stayed there close to him for hours, but aware that we weren't alone, I drew back and straightened up once more. The sausage sizzled and Arsène broke eggs into the skillet. He brought a plate of glazed rolls to us, setting it in the middle of the table. "You can start on these," he said as he gave us each a plate. "The rest will be ready soon."

I was too excited to eat, but took a roll to be polite. "The next full moon. It's three weeks away. That would be a good time," I blurted.

"Emile. Consult the almanac there, and give us that date, please." Maman pointed to a thin white pamphlet dangling from a string hooked to a nail on the wall. Emile took it down and paged through it, looking for the date of the next month's moon.

My excitement was interrupted by a sudden thought of Jean Claude. "But…what of Jean Claude? What if he comes back in the mean time? What then?"

"What of it? Would that change anything between us?"

"No, no. That's not what I meant. But what do we tell him?"

He looked up from the almanac. "We simply tell him we love each other and are going to be married. What else is there to say?"

"I know Jean Claude for years now," Arsène said from where he worked at the stove. "He loves his freedom. He's like Maurice and Hippolyte. They're not cut out for marriage, them. They're out all night almost every night anyway. What would any of them do with a wife at home?"

"You see? Nothing to worry about," said Emile, turning a page of the pamphlet.

"He's obviously not the one for you anyway," said Maman.

Emile broke in. "I found the date. The next full moon is All Souls' Day."

"A blue moon," said Maman.

"Perfect! Because one only finds love like this in a blue moon," said Emile, his face joyful as he showed me the date.

"That's good then," I said, nodding and taking a deep breath as though to finalize the plan.

"No! Don't get married on that day. That's a witch's holiday," Maman warned. "Not on All Souls' Day. How about All Saints' Day?"

I nodded. "All Saints' Day then."

"That's better," Emile agreed.

"And now that we have a wedding date, let's eat!" said Arsène as he brought a platter of sausage and eggs to the table.

* * *

After we'd eaten, Emile asked Maman if he could take me for a walk.

"You may sit with her on the porch. But no further away than that."

"You don't have to worry. We've been alone many times before," I said.

"You wouldn't have been if you'd been living with me," she said gently. "And now you are living with me....for just a little while longer."

"Of course," Emile assured her. "We will follow your wishes exactly." He took my hand and led me from the kitchen back through the front room and to a bench on the front porch. "Now you can tell me everything that has happened since I left for New Orleans." *Minuit* joined us and settled himself beside us, lowering his face between his paws as though he too wanted to hear my story.

Emile put an arm around my shoulders, and I tilted my head back against his arm and told him the whole story. How I'd returned home that day to a fight with Yvonne. How she'd fallen and sprained her ankle; the fire at the convent the next day; Arsène's bringing the corpse out from the swamp; the visit to the constable and Doc's office; my flight into the swamp the day he returned from New Orleans; the subsequent days at Arsène's camp; and how Yvonne carried on when we brought my belongings and Solange to my new home.

"And now that I've finally found my real mother, I'm very happy," I told him. "It won't change my love for Gros Louis and Eliate, who I always believed were my parents, and who loved me. But I love Maman also...and as though I somehow always knew her. It's very strange how at home I feel with her even though we've been separated all those years."

"*Le sang ne trahit pas.*"

"It must be true. Blood doesn't lie."

We sat in silence for a while after I'd finished telling him everything. The songbirds sang sweetly, the crows cawed, and a fish splashed down in the bayou so that a fine spray flew up, glittering with iridescence in the mottled sunlight. He pressed my hand to his lips.

"I'm very glad for you, *chère*, that you found Claudine at long last."

"And after all that, now you're here. It's almost too much for me."

"No, no. You'll see. You'll get used to all the changes. Because they're all wonderful changes."

I leaned my head against his chest, and we remained quietly watching the bayou. All of nature was washed in a golden haze that day, and I wasn't sure if the golden hue was really there, or if I was seeing the bayou through a filter of bliss. A great blue heron stood on one leg in the shadows of a gum tree, waiting for a fish, and the warm south breeze caressed us, murmuring: *All is well. All is well.*

19

CLUES

*"I was suspicious of it, mordioux!" said d'Artagnan,
spending himself in vain efforts,–"I was suspicious of it…"*
Twenty Years After - Alexandre Dumas

T he next day, Emile and Arsène and I decided to travel to the camp where Arsène had found the body. "The camp belonged to an old man who was a friend of mine for many years…Virgil Dupuis," Arsène told us. "He lived out there by himself most of his life. He didn't want or need anything he didn't have handy right out there in the swamp. He was completely happy to be left alone. But I'd visit him anyway. We'd sit out on the porch and talk and drink wine, or we'd go fishing. He lived to be almost a hundred, but you'd never know it to look at him. He looked healthy until the day he died. I'm the one who found him. It looked like he died in his sleep."

As we floated slowly past one of Arsène's favorite catfish holes, we drifted through an overhanging willow branch and the silky strands of a cobweb caught in my hair. Arsène carefully picked out each strand. "I took his body into town so what was left of his family could bury him there. His niece and nephew hadn't seen him for years because he stayed out here all the time."

"Sort of like you? You would never need to go to town if you didn't want to, no?"

"Yes, but I make sure to see Claudine every day…and I go into town for supplies and my friends visit now and then. I used to take supplies to Virgil. Coffee, sugar, things like that. But none of his family ever ventured out there. I think they were afraid to…that is, if they even knew the way."

As we rounded a bend, Virgil Dupuis' camp came into view, the cabin overgrown with vines and other greenery. Even the cistern was covered with vines. A few feet from where the men dragged the pirogue onto the slippery bank, Arsène stopped and pointed at a place on the ground that was a jumble of sodden leaves and twigs. "This is where I found the body of that dead man I brought to town." A ray of light filtering through the trees angled directly at the very spot.

I peered down to examine it. "A lonely place to die," Emile remarked. Silently, we all closely examined the area, looking for anything that might reveal what happened to the man as I recalled the sickening smell of the corpse the day we carried it to Doc's office.

"He must have been careless," Arsène said. "Whoever the man was didn't know the swamp, or how to survive in it. Then too, he might have gotten himself lost."

"Maybe he was hurt and dragged himself to this spot," offered Emile.

"Maybe he got drunk and passed out here. And that's when the alligator tore into him," said Arsène. But as closely as we examined the ground, we found nothing but packed earth, mud, and the mass of sodden leaves and broken twigs.

I poked the tip of my boot at some of the leaves and pondered the possibilities of the mystery man's last night on earth. The whole idea gave me a creepy feeling, and I shuddered at the thought of alligators attacking him.

"Did Leroy Viator come out and search the camp?" Emile asked.

"Yes. The next day. He came to find me at my camp and asked me to show him where I found the body. He spent a few minutes looking around. Poked at the ground around this spot, stirred the leaves and the mud with a stick, then he went over there to the cabin and looked around for a few minutes."

"What did he have to say?"

"Not much. He figures the man had an accident out here, somehow hurt himself and was lying on the ground when an alligator found him."

I winced at the picture in my mind. "A strange business," said Emile, shaking his head. "It doesn't sound like Viator spent much time investigating."

"Maybe ten minutes altogether. Then he wanted to get back. Said he had to go to a funeral that afternoon." Arsène shrugged. "That was it. He dropped me off at my camp, thanked me, and left."

We wandered toward the cabin, and I noted how similar the old cistern was to our own at the farm. The soft weathered gray of the narrow cypress boards contrasted with the vines, thistles and elderberry that grew all around it.

There were a few scattered holes around the campsite. The dirt that had been excavated lay in mounds at the edges, heaps softened and blurred by the recent rains.

"Somebody's been digging," Emile said.

"What would they be digging for out here?" I wondered. We approached one of the holes and peered down into it. There were a few inches of black water at the bottom, but no indication as to why the hole had been dug.

"It's like an unused grave," said Arsène.

"Let's go into the cabin," I said, pulling Emile by the hand. We creaked over the warped boards of the porch, where there were two old straight back chairs and a crude cypress bench.

"Watch that board!" warned Emile, as we carefully stepped over a buckling board that had pulled loose of its nails.

"I need to come out here and do some work around this place," said Arsène. "If for no other reason than in memory of my old friend, Virgil. He loved this place so much, his spirit is probably still here watching over it."

"I'll come out and help you. I'd like that," said Emile.

"I'll help too," I offered. "It's so peaceful out here." Arsène stomped the wayward board with his foot, driving it back into place. "It wouldn't take too long to get this place back in shape. It's been here a long time, and it'll stay here a long time with a little help from us."

"We could come out here and spend some time fishing if you'd like," Emile said looking at me. "Does that idea appeal to you?"

"I'd love it. And we could cook the fish out here and have a home away from home."

As we crossed the sloping porch, I scanned the weathered uprights, noting one especially that had many cuts and slashes on it. "What did you find?" asked Emile, as I bent to study the marks.

"These slashes look like the marks on our porch where Maurice and Hippolyte throw their knives. When they sit around drinking and talking, they like to practice throwing knives."

He leaned over to study them. "Knife throwing, eh? Could be."

"Do they come out here?" I asked Arsène.

"Those two go all over the swamp. Almost every night they're out here," he said as he crossed to the door of the cabin. "I can tell you one thing. Hippolyte is good at it, him."

"Good at what?" I asked, straightening.

"Knife throwing. I saw him throw once at a moccasin. Pinned him to a tree."

"He showed off at a card game. He threw at a spider on the wall. Perfect shot. So maybe those two know something about the dead man that they're not saying."

"Those marks could be months old. That doesn't prove anything," said Arsène, stepping across the threshold.

"We better ask them about it," I said.

"It wouldn't do any good. They wouldn't let on if they did know anything. Those two are secretive. I've played cards with them enough to know them very well," Emile said as we followed Arsène into the cabin.

"Whoever that man was," Arsène said. "He found this cabin, probably got drunk and was sitting out here at night like a *couillon*...perfect alligator bait."

"Maybe," I said. "But I think he was killed by a human alligator," I muttered.

"Come on," Arsène said. "Let's look around at everything in here. Maybe we'll find something that will help us figure out what happened."

Our eyes had to adjust to the gloom of the cabin. Cypress smells fresh, so even though the cabin was abandoned, the air was clean inside. The room had scant furniture from the old man's years there. A cot, a table, and one chair were visible in the shadows. Pegs on the walls held an assortment of shapeless clothes, and a few shelves held dented pots, jars, and two tin plates.

Crossing to the clothes hanging limply from the pegs, I idly felt in the pockets finding only lint and loose shreds of tobacco. Feeling in the shirt pocket on the next peg, I found a key. "Look!" I turned triumphantly to my companions. "A key."

"Good. That's something Viator missed," said Emile, nosing around the room.

"I would like to know whose it is," I said, and slipped it into a pocket of my skirt.

If the constable didn't care enough to check out everything, at least we would. Kneeling by the cot, I peered into the cool shadows there, seeing little besides gloom and cobwebs. A spider high up on a leg of the cot was busy wrapping an insect with a delicate strand of web. Something small was lying on the floor at the base of the metal leg. It was covered with grime, and I swooped it up and rose with it clenched in my hand.

"I found something else," I announced, and crossed to a window to see it better in the light. "It's a tooth!" The tooth, tobacco-stained, had been broken off. Its edges were jagged and sharp. "It's a broken half of a tooth."

"Maybe it was Virgil's," said Arsène, who was inspecting everything on the shelves.

"Maybe. Or maybe it came from the dead man's mouth," said Emile, who was peering underneath the table.

I slipped it into the pocket along with the key. "I'll keep it safe until we know more." The spiders had been busy weaving webs in all the corners of the walls and ceiling. Hundreds of webs, some new, some old and dusty, shrouded the walls and windows. Only dim light filtered through the thick veils of cobweb at each of the two windows. I stared through the gauzy window, musing over the mystery of what could have happened. Within moments, another possible solution to the mystery came to me. I kept these thoughts to myself for fear Emile and Arsène would laugh at my ideas. As my imagination took over, I saw the unknown man struggling with someone, which turned into a fierce fistfight, and a punch to his jaw. I saw him spit out the tooth as he continued to defend himself against the other man.

As my imagination spun out this story, Emile called, "Sidonie, let's go! I think we've seen everything there is to see in here for now. Your mother is probably wondering what's taking us so long. She's probably got dinner waiting."

He interrupted my reverie, and I turned blinking from the window as I emerged from my daydream and followed them outside. We watched our steps, mindful of the deep holes someone had dug, as we returned to the pirogue for the trip back.

I remained silent all the way to Maman's, as I pondered what may have happened to the mystery man at the camp before he was so horribly attacked and chewed and torn apart. Emile and Arsène seemed to sense my mood, and neither of them interrupted my thoughts as Arsène navigated us along the waterways. It is such a gift to be with friends who don't interrupt you when you're trying to work out a problem in your mind. The swamp is never quiet and there was the usual background of shrill screaming insects, a concert from hundreds of songbirds, and the high-pitched cry of hawks that continually circled above in their never-ending hunt for prey. However, throughout the trip home I was able to work out some possibilities and was most anxious to ask Maman what she thought of the ideas forming in my mind.

When we arrived, Emile and I quickly jumped out to help Arsène pull the pirogue up onto the bank, which had dried and was no longer slick and slippery. I stepped up onto one of the old cypress boards that Arsène had placed there for footing, and then Emile and I, holding hands, slowly walked to the house. *Minuit* ran from around the porch greeting us with loud yips and yaps, then leaped around us with joy. I picked him up, hugging him, and carried him with us to the house.

"I'll go back to my place," he said, kissing my forehead. "I'll leave you alone with your mother now."

"When will I see you?" I asked quickly, hating to see him go.

"When I've given you more time with your mother. Don't worry. I have plenty of chores at the house to occupy me. I'll be back soon though. Of that you can be sure."

"Soon?" I said wistfully, laying my head on his chest, feeling his warmth. Soon seemed too far away, and despite the happiness of being with my mother at last, I didn't like the prospect of separating from him. Not after all we'd just been through. Arsène had gone inside to say good bye to Maman, and then the two of them pushed the boat back off the bank and took off down the bayou as I waved them goodbye with *Minuit* still in my arms.

Once inside, I joined Claudine at the kitchen table and over coffee described our visit to the camp, *Minuit* curled by our feet. "I'm sure Arsène told you about the mutilated body he found out there."

"Oh, yes. I heard all about that."

"Well, we examined everything carefully, looking for any indication of what could have happened to him."

"Yes? And you found something?"

"Oh, yes. For one thing, there were holes dug all around the camp with piles of dirt left heaped beside them. Somebody was definitely looking for something."

"How deep?"

"Very deep. Up to my waist probably."

Maman pursed her lips thoughtfully, tilting her head back as she watched me.

"And we found other things that were strange. I could see marks on the porch that looked like the kind of marks Maurice and Hippolyte make when they sit around practicing knife throwing. It was like they'd been throwing at one of the uprights. There were many gashes in the wood."

"I can picture that in my mind," she said, nodding. "I know what you mean."

"And then inside the cabin, there was something under the bed. It was a tooth."

I pulled it from my pocket and held it out to her on the flat of my palm.

She frowned and took it in her hand, bringing it close to her face, peering at it with half-lidded eyes.

"Then I began to get ideas of what may have happened there."

"What ideas?" She gave the tooth back to me.

"Arsène says Hippolyte and Maurice went out to the camp often. What if they used it as a kind of base when they were out in the swamp? What if one night they went out there and someone else was in the camp? Someone they didn't know. And then maybe this stranger did something they didn't like."

"Such as?"

"I don't know. Maybe he took something that belonged to them. Or maybe they just got in an argument about something. Maybe they didn't want anyone else using that camp. Who knows?" I was getting carried away with the story, and the more I spun my fanciful tale, the more likely it seemed it could have happened that way. "And maybe they were drinking too much. They often do that. And neither one of them is a stranger to fighting." I got up to pour coffee for us, and listened for Maman's reaction to what I'd said.

"Yes, I suppose all that is possible. But what of the holes?"

"Maybe they were searching for something of theirs. Something that was missing from the cabin that they'd left out there. Maybe they thought the man hid it whatever it was," I said as I served her coffee. I served myself and joined her at the table again. "I don't know. I just keep getting these ideas about it. The whole thing bothers me. The dead man. He being a stranger. And if you'd seen how horrible he looked...I can't begin to tell you how awful he looked. What was left of him that is." I shuddered as I took a sip of the strong black coffee.

"But what could be so important that they'd go to all that trouble? Digging deep holes is hard work."

"There's only one thing I know of that would be worth all that effort."

"And what is that?"

"Emile had some gold coins stolen almost a month ago. He brought them here from France. They were hidden in the lining of his trunk."

"Oh really!" She raised her eyebrows.

"Four thousand francs!"

"Four thousand francs! *Mais non!* But, why would anyone hide the coins in the camp? Why not at home? Buried in the yard, or... under a loose board? The camp is so far away."

"I don't know. I'm just guessing."

"Let's say this is what happened though. Let's say it's just as you guessed. What then? You can't prove it. Those two would never admit it."

"I know that. I don't know what to do next."

She paused, idly tracing a finger around the rim of her cup. She looked up suddenly. "I'll ask Arsène to bring them to me. I'll talk to them. I can tell more if they're right in front of me. I can tell if they're lying."

"Do you think they'll come all the way out here?"

"Sure they will if Arsène asks them to. Why wouldn't they?" She patted my hand. "Try to put it out of your mind for now. We'll have our supper, then I'll light some candles and say some prayers. Prayers that will help the truth to come out. It's important to let the spirits know that we're searching for answers to this puzzle."

"And it *is* a puzzle."

"I'm glad you listened for inner wisdom today. That's how you came up with these ideas. That quiet voice inside us will always give us guidance...if we will just listen for it."

"I don't know. Maybe none of it's true."

"We'll see soon enough. Of that I feel sure."

20

AN INSPIRING DREAM

"You do not guess?" said d'Artagnan,
whose eyes brightened up with intelligence.
Twenty Years After - Alexandre Dumas

B
y twilight of the following day, word had been relayed to
Hippolyte and Maurice, and they arrived at Maman's, calling from the boat.

"Go out and ask them to come inside, please, Sidonie." Maman was putting dried leaves into jars and bottles to store them
until needed. She worked on top of a cabinet stationed beneath
her shelves of remedies and potions.

As I stepped outside, Hippolyte greeted me warmly from where
he stood in a wide stance, arms crossed, halfway up the dirt path
from the bayou bank. His favorite hat with the alligator tooth
band was tilted low over his brow, casting his face into shadow.
"Good evening, Sidonie. *Comment ça va?* I haven't seen you for a
while."

"I'm doing fine. And you?" I held the door open, gesturing
toward the front room. "Claudine would like for you to come inside."

"Do you know what she wants with us?" he asked, starting up
the path and beckoning to Maurice to follow. I shook my head.

He lowered his voice as he approached the porch. "You like
living out here in the swamp, you?" he asked cheerfully, a wide

smile lighting up his face as he pushed back the brim of his hat with a thumb. Maurice, frowning, dutifully followed him, lagging behind and making it clear he didn't want to be there. Hippolyte reached the steps, then leaped up onto the porch, skipping the two steps altogether, and landed with a great thump of his heavy black boots.

"I love living out here. I wish I'd moved out here years ago."

"I love the swamp too. No place I'd rather be." He stopped three feet from me, his expression serious. "I should do what Arsène does. Just pick up and land right in the middle of it. Build me a little shack like his...and only come out of there when I have to go to town for supplies. Now that's living!" He smiled again and lightly touched my shoulder, lowering his voice. "I'm glad for you."

"Thank you. I'm glad too."

Maurice, keeping silent, followed along as we passed into the house. We didn't greet one another. I couldn't even begin to acknowledge him with a nod because he kept his gaze averted under the rolled-down brim of his hat. His mouth was twisted into a sneer as he crossed the threshold, and I wondered why he had even bothered to answer Maman's summons if he was so reluctant to do so. I silently thanked God that he was not my brother after all.

Hippolyte ducked as the hanging dried herbs brushed his head when we filed through the shadowy front room. "This place spooks me. I don't want to stay long," he whispered over his shoulder to Maurice.

"Go on in and sit at the table," I said as I motioned them toward the kitchen. Maman had finished working with the herbs and was sitting at the table, looking serene.

"I'm glad to see you both. Come in and join me, please," she said, beckoning them over to the table. I didn't know why she had a cypress branch lying on the table in front of her and a small cotton sack in her hand. I thought maybe it had something to do with the herbs she'd been working with at the cabinet.

Hippolyte took one of the chairs, scraping it back and then settling himself, positioning his hat on his knee. He pulled out a chair for Maurice who was hanging back by the doorway. "Come on, brother. Sit down."

Maurice finally sat down heavily, then leaned the chair back so it rested on two legs, as was his custom. His jaw worked as he sat, silently watching Claudine and rocking the chair to and fro. "What can we do for you, Miss Claudine?" Hippolyte asked.

"Why nothing, really. I just wanted to ask you a few questions if you don't mind."

"Sure. Ask away." He clapped a hand on his hat to keep it from slipping off his bony knee.

"I was wondering if either of you knew Mr. Virgil Dupuis?"

"Why sure we did. Everybody around here knew him, didn't they?"

"Well then, you and Maurice are familiar with his abandoned camp?"

"Yes." Hippolyte blinked in surprise at the question as he lifted his hat from his knee and twirled it with both hands. Maurice, remaining silent, shifted his gaze from Claudine to Hippolyte, then back again to Claudine.

"Do you know of anyone who still goes out there and uses the old camp then?" She spoke in a chatty way as though they were talking about the weather.

"Why do you want to know all this, Miss Claudine? You want us to take you out there so you can visit it?" Hippolyte asked, jiggling his foot and continuing to twirl the hat. Hippolyte always finds a way to somehow stay in motion.

"Oh, no, no, no. That's all right." She laughed and picked up the cypress branch and swished it back and forth a bit, as though she were chasing away flies.

"What then?" asked Maurice, speaking for the first time, his voice impatient.

"Just wondering, that's all." Maman, still preoccupied with the cypress branch, kept swishing it slowly back and forth. After a moment of silence, while Maurice and Hippolyte exchanged questioning looks, she spoke again. "I'm sorry. Would either one of you like a cup of coffee?"

"Oh, no thank you. We've got to be going soon," Hippolyte said. "Is there anything else before we go?"

"Yes. I wondered if you two ever go out there...to the abandoned camp?"

Hippolyte sniffed, stole a quick glance at Maurice, then spoke hurriedly. "Once in a while we might stop off there. You know, if we're tired and need a rest while we're out fishing or hunting; we might just sit around out there for an hour or two...every once in a while."

He started to rise and brought his hat halfway to his head, pausing midway as Claudine leaned forward and asked, "When is the last time you were out there then?" She was no longer smiling and swishing the cypress branch, but very still and peering at him intently.

Hippolyte frowned, then straightened, hastily placing the hat on his head. "Why, I don't even remember. When's the last time?" He looked over at Maurice. "You remember?"

Maurice ran a tongue over his upper teeth, then shook his head. "I can't remember either. It's been a while." He abruptly brought the chair back down onto four legs once more, then rose and turned toward the doorway where I stood.

"You sure you don't want us to take you out there, Miss Claudine?" Hippolyte asked again as he looked after Maurice.

"Oh, no, that's all right. Just curious is all. Glad you both were able to come by, and I thank you for it."

"Anytime. Just ask. We had to come out near here today to check our trot lines anyhow." He clapped a hand on Maurice's shoulder. "Maybe we should go on over to the old camp and check it out. What do you say?"

I moved aside as Maurice passed through the doorway into the front room without answering. Since he was always *contraire*, I wasn't surprised that he didn't even have the courtesy to say goodbye to Maman. Hippolyte, however, touched two fingers to the brim of his hat before following him out. "Goodbye, then." He nodded at each of us in turn. "Let us know if we can do anything for you. Whatever you need. Nice to see both of you."

Their heavy boots made a loud noise as they trudged through the front room, followed by the sound of the front door closing. I sat at the table with Maman, waiting patiently for her reaction to the visit. She rocked to and fro, holding the branch to her chest. "What do you think, Sidonie? You heard them too."

"I don't know. Hippolyte was his usual self. Jumpy. Restless. Maurice was his usual self…contrary…rude."

"Were they telling the truth?"

"I don't know."

"What does your inner voice say?" I had no opinion, so I shook my head.

"How does your stomach feel then?"

I thought a minute before deciding how I felt inside. "Tight. Uncomfortable." I shifted in the chair, impatient as to what *she* thought. I looked at her questioningly.

"If something isn't right, you're going to be able to tell because you're going to feel it. Headache. Stiff neck. Stomach upset. See what I mean? Learn to notice these things."

I thought about this for a bit. "Then judging by the way I feel, I think they were lying."

"Could be," she nodded in agreement. "I think they were."

My eyes opened wide as a thought came to me. "What if they know where Emile's gold coins are?"

She laid the cypress branch on the table and tilted her head back as she watched me. "It's possible."

I felt excitement stirring within. "What if the reason Hippolyte's uncle spent so little time inspecting the camp is because he already suspects they had something to do with the dead man, and he doesn't want Hippolyte to get into trouble?"

"Could be. But none of that can be proved…even if it's true."

"Maybe the truth will never come out. Maybe it will remain just another mystery swallowed up by the swamp," I said.

"Something may turn up. Those two seemed nervous about something. But who knows what? They're certainly not going to tell us."

"They sure left in a hurry."

"Yes, they did," she laughed. "A big hurry." She closed her eyes again, a sign that she was retreating into her own thoughts. I left her at the table, took an apron off a hook on the wall, tied it on, and got busy at the stove while continuing to wonder about our visitors.

It wasn't too long before Arsène called to us from outside. He entered moments later, fresh fishy smells from the swamp wafting from his clothes. "Did they come out to see you yet?"

"They just left. Maybe ten minutes ago," Maman said.

"Did you find out what you wanted to know?"

"Don't know yet. Go ahead and tell him what happened, Sidonie. I'm going outside to get some fresh air." She stood. "I've been in the house long enough. I need to stretch my legs."

After I briefly told him about the visit, he called to her as she stepped out of the back door. "Now you've made those two nervous. They might do something."

"They won't hurt us," Maman said. over her shoulder.

"They're headed back for the camp though. I could go spy on them. See what they do."

"No. They might see you," she said sharply.

"They won't see me. I can be a shadow if I want to be."

"Then take me along," I insisted.

"No! Don't take Sidonie out there," Maman said from the back porch.

"I'm not afraid of those two," I protested.

"Let Arsène go by himself if he wants to."

"Please take me. This whole thing was my idea."

"That's true. This was her idea. And nothing will happen to her if I'm along. I can guarantee that." My new brother taking up for me was a pleasant change after years of living with Maurice who had always done quite the opposite.

"Anyhow, Maman. I had a dream last night about all this."

"Tell us." She stepped back onto the threshold of the back door.

"I was flying over the old camp, and I looked down at it from a distance. I had to keep moving my arms as if they were wings, so I could stay in the air."

"Like a bird?"

"Like a bird. And I could see every detail of the camp as I hovered there. And…"

"And what?" asked Arsène, giving me his full attention.

"I think I know where the coins are!" I blurted out, surprising even myself as I remembered a fragment of the dream that I had forgotten. This portion of the dream came suddenly back to me like a wisp of memory from out of nowhere. Untying my apron,

I turned away from the stove. "Please," I begged him. "Take me there now!" I appealed to Maman with my eyes as well.

"All right, go then," she said. "Go. But keep her safe!" She wagged a finger at Arsène.

"Always," he assured her. "Let's go then!"

21

TREASURE

"Has your grace any suspicion as to who has committed the theft? Perhaps the person has still got them."
The Three Musketeers - Alexandre Dumas

Once we'd come close to the old camp, Arsène navigated us into a cut-off protected by a sheltering stand of trees that lay near the farthest edge of the high ground where the cabin was built. He secured the boat and with his finger to his lips, we crept among roots and vines twisted beneath an overhang of graceful willow branches. By peering through the foliage, we had a semi-obstructed view of the campsite.

Hippolyte and Maurice's voices carried to us before they came into view from around the front porch of the rough cabin. "I just can't figure why that woman kept asking so many questions," Hippolyte said.

"Who knows? Maybe she works spells with all those dried plants hanging from the ceiling. She's probably a witch," Maurice answered, his voice muffled, as they stepped up onto the porch and passed on into the cabin.

The air was dense with the drone of insects and the shrill scream of a hawk.

"We'll just have to wait here until they decide to leave," whispered Arsène. "Are you comfortable enough? It could be a while."

"I'm all right." We were awkwardly hunkered down, and I adjusted myself to a better position by sitting on a fallen log, abundantly covered with springy dark green ferns. Mosquitoes whined annoyingly near my ears, and I was glad we'd smeared Maman's smelly salve on our face and hands. A perfect spider web, sparkling with dew, stretched between two branches two feet from my head. While we quietly waited, I watched the spider busy at work, wrapping a fly in a cocoon to save for a later meal.

It felt like half an hour had passed, and I was stiff all over from sitting still in one spot so long, before the two of them clumped back out onto the porch. "There's nothing here," Maurice said. "Let's go."

"Yeah, I'm ready," agreed Hippolyte. They sauntered off the porch, swatting and cursing at mosquitoes, and made their way back to the boat where it lay angled and secured on the sloping grassy bank.

I adjusted my position again as we waited for them to be out of sight. Cramped and itchy, I was delighted when they were gone and we could get up and moving again. "Let's go look around over there," said Arsène, as he got to his feet and stretched his arms.

Mindful of the spider web so that my hair didn't get caught in it, I hastily scrambled to my feet, brushing my hands over my skirts to get rid of tiny twigs and leaves that clung to the material. Arsène led the way through the foliage and across the clearing and past the spot where he had found the mutilated body. We threaded our way around the deep holes scattered over the property. At one point, I took his arm. "Come on over here." I led him, not toward the cabin where he was headed, but toward the weathered gray cypress cistern.

"What are you doing?" he asked when I stopped beside it.

"Lift me up. I want to see inside there."

"It's just an old cistern. No different than all the rest of them. Who knows how long that water's been sitting in there? It's probably got scum on it."

"Lift me up," I insisted.

He did as I asked and hefted me by the waist so I could grab the top of the rough planks where they were bound by a metal rim. I stretched my head and shoulders so I could look down inside to the dark water. Peering into the gloom of the enclosure, I thought I could see what I was looking for.

"Get up here with me somehow," I urged, a thrill running up my spine.

"How can I? I'm holding you up."

"I can hold on to the rim. You have to get up here." I worked my arms over the metal rim, making myself as secure as I could. Arsène ran for a chair from the porch and carried it back to the base of the cistern, where he set it down firmly to stand on.

"Now what?" he asked as he held on by my side and looked down into the dim interior.

"Don't you see? Look there!"

"I see about a hundred gallons of rainwater."

"The bottom. Look to the bottom!"

"What is that?"

"I think it's a sack of Emile's stolen gold coins." My arms were getting tired, and I was having trouble holding on. "I've got to get down now," I said, "before I fall off."

"Wait! Hang on. I'll get you down." He let go of the rim and held onto my waist. "I'm going to bring you to where I can lower you down." He maneuvered me so he could safely lower me to the ground, and then he jumped off the chair.

"What makes you think that shadowy lump down there is a sack of coins?"

"That was my dream! I just know that's what it is. You have to believe me."

"But the only way I can find out is if I get down inside there and see." He looked doubtful as he considered the problem.

"I can do it myself! It's my dream, I tell you!"

"No, no. Claudine would kill me if she knew I let you do something like that. I'll do it. If you're sure that's what it is?" He looked at me expectantly.

"I'm certain of it."

"All right then. I'll get down in there and get wet if you're so sure. But if I don't find gold coins, I'm not paying attention to any more of your dreams."

"But you won't have any dry clothes to change into."

"That's all right. I can use some of those old clothes hanging in the cabin. My own clothes will dry soon enough."

"Maybe we should just come back later."

"And leave what might be a sack of Emile's gold coins?"

"Why not? If someone was out here looking for them, it doesn't seem like they found them. And besides, if those are Emile's coins, then we might as well give him the pleasure of finding them."

He hesitated. "Well, all right then. It would be better that way. We'll bring him out here. Claudine will want me to bring you back before it starts getting dark anyway." He returned the chair to the porch, and we headed back for the hidden inlet and the boat.

"That was some dream you had," he said as I got into the boat and he pushed us off.

"The spirits are always looking after us," I smiled at him. "Haven't you been listening to Maman?"

* * *

An old man with skin the color of the bayou was just leaving Maman's as we returned in late afternoon, shadows lengthening around us.

"Hello, Chester," said Arsène. "How are you tonight?"

"Better, thanks to your mother," said the white-haired man.

"Claudine can fix anything, can't she?"

"Oh, yes she can. Everybody's been knowing that." He held out a hand wrapped in a cocoon of leaves neatly bound with string. "Burns. She took out all the hurt with that sticky mess of salve she makes up."

"How'd you burn yourself?"

"Spilled some hot grease from the cook pot. Trying to work too fast. That's what happens when you hurry. You make trouble for yourself. But, look, I better be getting back. It gets dark fast this time of year."

"Goodnight, Chester. Be careful. Take care," Arsène cautioned as he led me into the house. I looked over my shoulder at the old man disappearing into the shadowy woods.

"Who was that?" I asked as we stepped across the threshold into the front room.

"Chester? He lives a few miles down the bayou in the woods. They had to let him go from the plantation down in St. Martinville. They couldn't afford to keep him and the others on after the war. He makes do out here by himself."

"Maman!" I called. "They're there!"

We found her in the kitchen with *Minuit,* where she was sorting through and arranging her shelf of ointments, potions and salves. The delicious smell of beef stew rose from the stove which made *Minuit's* nose twitch.

"What's there? What do you mean?"

"Emile's missing gold coins! I'm sure of it! They're lying in a sack at the bottom of the cistern over at the Dupuis camp."

She turned from her work. "That's wonderful! You found a way to get them out?"

"No. We decided it was getting dark and you'd be worried… and besides, it would be better to let Emile have the pleasure of retrieving his treasure himself. Don't you agree?"

She worked a glass stopper into one of the jars. "Yes, probably so. But you couldn't actually see the coins? Just a sack at the bottom of the cistern?"

"But I know that's where the coins are!" I tapped a fist over my heart. "I feel it strongly in here, Maman."

"Good! Then that's all I need to know." She wiped her hands on her apron. "Now let's have supper. I made a delicious *etouffée.* and we can celebrate your good work with a glass of strawberry wine!"

22

ACCUSATION

"And if he does not act right, I will smash him,"
said Porthos; "that's all."
Twenty Years After - Alexandre Dumas

The next morning, as we were enjoying a leisurely breakfast, Emile called out to us as he arrived on Argent, my heart heart immediately began to beat faster as I pushed back my chair and ran out to the front porch to greet him.

"Emile!" I shouted, bursting with excitement and jumping up and down with delight. "We have news for you! You won't believe it! Come inside quickly!"

The morning air, still misty and enveloping him in a golden haze, made him look like an unfamiliar figure in a dream as he tied Argent to the hitching post. "What is it, *chère?* Tell me!" He strode toward the porch, still surrounded by that strange early light, scarf knotted around his throat, face shining. Laughing, he ran up the steps and swung me around with great exuberance.

"The coins! We found your coins! They're safe…wet, but safe."

His face changed altogether as he reacted to my words. "What? You say the coins are safe?" His jaw dropped in disbelief, and his eyes opened wide.

"Yes! Yes! Your coins are safe in the bottom of that old cistern at the abandoned camp! I saw them in a dream, and when we went out there to see, it was just like in the dream."

"But...this is incredible! A dream? You dreamed where the coins were hidden?" He looked more and more stunned as the news sunk in.

"We need to go out there this morning and show you. Can we go there now?"

"By all means. Let's go!" He whirled me around, then released me.

Arsène stepped out of the house onto the porch. "It's all true. She's found them for you. We better get going before someone else figures out where they are."

"Let me go tell Maman, and I'll meet you at the boat," I said, hurrying toward the door.

* * *

When we drew near to the Dupuis camp, Arsène nosed the pirogue in among the weeds and twisted roots of the bank, and we all helped pull it onto higher ground. Holding Emile's hand, I led him toward the bulky cistern, close to the back corner of the cabin. Arsène brought a chair from the porch and positioned it in the high grass around the base of the cistern, motioning for Emile to stand on it.

Wasting no time, Emile climbed onto the chair that rocked as its legs dug into the ground, then he stretched his arms up so he could rest his elbows on the rim in order to look over. After a moment, he laughed with glee. "I see what you're talking about. It could be! It could really be my sack of coins!" He pulled his body up so his torso was halfway over the rim, then rested a hip on the edge, preparing to drop into the water. "Hidden away right here in the middle of a Louisiana swamp!"

"But your shoes!" I called from below.

"Who cares?" and with that, he splashed into the water so that a spray flew up over the metal-bound rim. Stepping up onto the chair as Arsène held it steady, I stretched and pulled myself up in order to look over. Emile was collecting the sack from the bottom, his long legs scissoring back and forth as he stuffed it into his shirt. Then, twisting himself around to kick to the surface, he burst forth from the water with a great whooshing noise, splashing another spray of water and making me flinch.

Laughing with delight, he grabbed the metal rim and flicked his drenched hair out of his eyes. "You've done it, *chère!* You've really done it!" He hauled himself up and over the top as I leaped off the chair into the high grass in order to give him room to descend. But, it turned out he didn't need the chair for he dropped down from the top of the cistern onto solid ground once more. Pulling the sack from his dripping shirt, he held it aloft triumphantly, and swung it into the air.

Arsène clapped him on the back. "Congratulations! We thought you'd enjoy retrieving them for yourself."

"And you were so right!" He opened the drawstring of the sack and looked inside. "It looks like they're all there. I'll count them later. Meantime I need to dry off. Let's go so the sun can dry me off on the trip back."

"And you can get some hot coffee back at Maman's," I added.

"And some *vin de soco* to warm your blood," said Arsène.

"And to celebrate," said Emile, smiling at both of us. "Thank you, *mes amis.* Thank you so very much."

All the way back to Maman's we talked excitedly about the mystery of who could have hidden the coins there. Emile's drenched shoes were drying on the flat bottom of the pirogue on his side of the boat, the wet suede sack drying between his bare feet. "I'm so happy that you found them...I almost don't even care who stole them...or how they got there."

Arsène, standing behind us, poled the boat, let it drift, then poled the boat again. "But we need to know who the thief is, or it could happen again," he warned.

"Yes, it's true. But I forgive whoever did it. My life has not been blameless. People do wrong things. We all get tempted from time to time. Now that I have them back, I'll hide them where the devil himself could never find them."

"I have never been tempted to steal," I said.

"Well, consider yourself fortunate then." He touched my hair affectionately, then wound a strand of it around his long fingers.

"Whoever did this might take something from someone else," I said. "We need to find out who it is."

"It will all come out. One way or the other," Emile assured me as he closed his eyes, basking in the warmth of the sun, his clothes slowly drying. A brilliant silver fish splashed down, making concentric circles that spread out over the surface of the water, and I watched the shimmering sapphire green dragonflies darting through the air as my thoughts aimlessly spun out more possible answers to the mystery.

By the time we reached Maman's, I had formulated an idea that would possibly explain all of the missing pieces of the mysterious puzzle. But I didn't want to speak of any of it, except with Maman, and for the same reasons as before. I felt shy about putting forth my thoughts because I had not yet learned to have confidence in my ideas.

As we entered the front door, I looked up at Emile. "As soon as we've had some hot coffee and shown Maman your coins, will you please take me to see Maurice?"

"Maurice? But why?"

"Because I need to speak with him. I just might have figured out what happened. Close to it anyway."

"Take you to Maurice?" asked Arsène as we passed through the shadowy front room.

"Yes, please, Arsène. You've trusted me so far."

"And that was most definitely a success," Emile said, as he dramatically tossed the clinking sack of coins onto the kitchen table. Maman sat there in her customary chair, folding dried leaves into paper packets.

"I hear the coins!" she laughed as she slid her work aside.

"Your darling daughter was right. And there they are!" he said, slipping his arm around my shoulders proudly.

Maman picked up the sack, felt its weight, then dropped it back onto the table again. "I'm so glad for you, Emile."

"And now she wants us to take her to see Maurice. Would that be all right?"

"Maurice? Why, Sidonie?"

"I'll tell you in a minute, Maman, when we're alone. First, let me pour us some coffee. Emile got soaking wet, and he needs to go back out into the sun to finish drying off."

Once I served them, the two men obligingly took their coffee outside, leaving us alone. I told Maman what I thought I had figured out on the way home from the camp. She nodded when I finished. "Do as you think best. You've been right so far. I'm not going to interfere with your plans. And those two will be with you, so I'm not worried about your meeting with Maurice."

"Thank you, Maman. We'll go, take care of this business, and come directly back here to tell you what happened."

"Go then. I had the strong conviction this morning that all of this would be working itself out very soon."

Kissing her on the forehead, I left her side to join the men at the pirogue, feeling grateful that she had such faith in me. I wasn't accustomed to having my ideas so well received, and it felt wonderful to be so trusted. I wasn't used to anyone paying the slightest attention to anything I said since Gros Louis and Maman Eliate died. It felt so good, I was sure it gave a glow to my face.

"Let's go!" I said to the men as I settled myself into the boat. "The sooner we get there, the sooner we can put an end to all this."

A little more than an hour later back in St. Beatrice Parish, we three were making our way through the woods that bordered the farm where I grew up. Smelling the familiar wood smoke, and the rich rotting leaves of the forest floor as we picked our way around the thick undergrowth, I felt a twinge of sadness that my youth was gone, that youth of the forest, the mushroom gathering, the long silent vigils surrounded by my precious woods and owls and songbirds. From now on, I suddenly realized, those quiet private times in the forest would be those of a married woman, not a lonely young girl.

A screech owl, disturbed from his daytime rest by our passage, made a soft fluttering sound, and my heart grew heavy. Life would be so different in the near future just a few weeks away. I looked back upon the young girl's loneliness of the past and, almost as if I could see her there among a patch of new snowy white mushrooms, I missed her.

But then, I glanced up at Emile ahead, watching for snakes and leading me through the fallen leaves, and I took his hand, grateful for our new life. I was able to shed the old, casting it off like the fallen feathers of the mourning doves and blue jays that I had so often gathered over the years.

As we approached the stable, I heard Maurice stirring around in his makeshift sleeping quarters in the tack room. "Maurice," I called out, knowing he could hear me through the cracks between the rough exterior planks of the stables. Chickens clucked, and I heard their wings whirring as they ran about in the yard. A goose charged us from one of the water troughs, honking with such energy that I needn't have called out to Maurice. He would have known we were coming by the geese setting off the alarm.

Then the hounds, awakening from their naps beneath the house, clambered out, furiously wagging their tails as they bounded to greet us. All of this clamor, yet still no response from Maurice, but that was typical. Soon he would emerge from his shadowy home in back of the stables.

The front door to the house slammed, and Yvonne stomped out onto the porch calling, "What is it?"

Maurice finally showed himself, slowly walking down the center aisle of the stables, moving toward the sunlight, but remaining half in shadow, so that it was difficult to make out his expression. "Maurice," I said. "Please come out with us. I want to talk to you."

"What do you want with him?" scolded Yvonne from the porch. "Go on back to the swamp and leave us alone."

Ignoring her, I kept my gaze on Maurice's face, still half in shadow. "I think I know what became of that dead man Arsène hauled out of the swamp," I began. He remained silent in the shadows, finally stepping into the open entrance to the stables. He blinked in the strong light, adjusted the black eye patch, then pulled the brim of his hat down to shade his eye.

"I think he was staying out there while he did his scouting for that logging company that reported him missing. I think he found something out there that you and Hippolyte had hidden somewhere in that old cabin of Mr. Dupuis." Maurice shifted his weight from one foot to the other, but otherwise remained very still as he regarded me with an insolent expression, his upper lip curling.

"I think you and Hippolyte went out there, not knowing he was there, and discovered he'd found the gold you had hidden. And you got in a fight over the gold coins because he wouldn't tell you where he hid them. Or even admit to it."

Maurice stepped forward, slowly scratching his jaw. "*What* are you talking about?" He looked puzzled. "What gold coins?"

"The gold coins you and Hippolyte took from Emile's trunk."

"Took what? Are you calling me a thief?" He lowered his head and stepped forward again. He reminded me of a bull who chased after me in a pasture when I was twelve. Emile moved closer to me, and I felt Arsène tensing as he carefully watched Maurice.

I continued, undaunted. "Somehow this man died in the fight. Probably because one of you pulled a knife. And you got scared and left him there, thinking whoever found him would believe he'd had some sort of accident." Pausing in my story, I took a deep breath. My heart was pounding from the effort of standing up to Maurice.

He glowered at me, head still lowered, staring up from under that dark brow. "Now you're calling me a murderer? And Hippolyte too? Me, your own brother?"

"You're not my brother," I reminded him, and it felt so good to say it aloud to him.

"And then, you two went back out there again and dug all those holes searching for the gold coins. But you had no luck. Then, Claudine sent for you both, and you got scared all over again. So you returned to the camp yesterday to take one more look around. Am I right so far?"

Holding my head high, I stood as tall as I could and waited, my strong words surprising even me. He stepped completely out of the shadows then, and a light breeze through the passageway blew the smell of old straw and damp and manure from the stables. "No. That's not right! Everything you just said is wrong," he said in a loud voice. He adjusted his stance so he was standing with legs spread and arms crossed, solid and unmoving once more.

"What have I said that is wrong?"

"All of it! This is the first time I've heard anything about any missing gold coins. And I never met this logging scout Leroy Viator was asking about, and neither has Hippolyte. If he had, he'd of told me. And I never saw the dead man until Arsène brought him out of the swamp that day."

"So you say," I answered which made him twist his mouth even more. "The coins, by the way, were lying at the bottom of the cistern the whole time," I added, watching him carefully for the slightest twitch or change of expression.

His face remained still as a stone. "How can you believe that I'm a thief and a murderer? You've lived with me for almost eighteen years!"

"Because it all fits. And I found a tooth that was knocked out, probably in the fight over the stolen coins."

"Hell, Sidonie. You're dead wrong. And I don't know what I ever did to you that you'd turn against me like this." His face grew red with anger. "All I ever did for you was to provide food for the table. Ever since Papa died. Who hunted and fished and trapped for you? Who kept this place together…kept it from falling apart?" He jabbed a thick thumb against his chest. "Me! That's who. Now all of a sudden you make me out to be a murderer? And that's not bad enough, I'm a thief besides. I steal from my friends now?"

"And all those years you're talking about that I lived with you, you hated me all the while! Don't even try to deny it!" I felt my face grow hot.

Emile tugged urgently at my arm. "Sidonie. Calm. Be calm."

I pulled my arm away. "No! I'm sick of him and his meanness and his bad temper!"

"Go on then. But when you find out the truth, you'll come back around here asking me to forgive you for accusing me." He turned abruptly and retreated into the shadows of the stable once more.

"What truth?" I yelled, running after him.

He laughed an ugly laugh, turning his head briefly to look at me. His one good eye glittered in the darkness so that he appeared demonic. "If you'd think for once, instead of wandering around in the swamp making up crazy stories, you'd figure out the whole mess for yourself."

"How? What do you mean? Talk to me, Maurice! You never talk to me!" I came up behind him and snatched at his arm, but he wrenched it free, looking so dark and angry I thought he was going to slap me.

Emile and Arsène ran forward. "Hey, calm down!" Emile shouted. "Both of you!"

Maurice was so angry, he turned fully around, clenching his hands into fists that he held stiffly at his sides as though trying to restrain himself from striking me. "Talk to you? Now it's a sin that I don't talk? How can I talk when Yvonne never shuts up? What do you want me to say? I already told you…I didn't steal Emile's gold. Hippolyte didn't steal his gold. And neither one of us murdered that idiot Yankee! Isn't that enough for you? Now leave me alone and take your friends with you back out to the swamp! I've heard enough!"

"What did you mean *if I knew the truth?* What are you hiding?" I grabbed him again to prevent him from stalking off back to his room. He tore his sleeve wrenching his arm free once more.

"Quit grabbing my arm. Who do you think you are?"

"What are you hiding?" Boldly, I pushed my face closer to his, so close I could smell the straw stuck to his shirt, and the alcohol from whatever he'd drunk the night before.

His jaw worked, and he flicked his gaze for a moment toward Emile and Arsène, then back to me. "I can't tell you more than that," he said firmly, then turned and continued down the walkway toward the rear of the stables. Theotiste whinnied softly as he passed, seeking attention, but Maurice ignored him. Staring after him, confused as to what he meant, I tried to make sense of his words, then turned toward Emile and Arsène with a questioning look, as if they'd have an answer for me. Emile motioned for me to leave to go back to the boat, so I joined them and we started back for the bayou.

"Damn you, Sidonie! You're always causing trouble!" Yvonne shouted from the porch.

"Come on!" Emile took my arm. "Let's get out of here!"

"Go on back to the swamp! And don't you ever come back! You hear me?"

"*Bourrique! Putain!*" Emile muttered as we ignored her, walking fast to the boat, the dogs escorting and prancing around us.

"What do you think he was talking about? I asked both of them when we arrived at the boat. "Can either of you figure it out?"

"I don't know what to think," Emile said as Arsène shoved the pirogue off the grassy bank.

"Let's take the tooth and key to the constable now. Maybe something will occur to one of us on the way," I said, patting the hounds goodbye as we prepared to shove off.

I kissed them each on the top of the head, tears welling up, for they clearly had no idea why I was deserting them. Then getting into the boat with a heavy heart, I watched them as they wagged their tails and danced in circles. "I love you!" I called to them, wiping my eyes. I wished I could take them with me back to Maman's, but they also belonged to Maurice and Yvonne, and I knew I could not take them from the farm.

"Goodbye, goodbye! I love you!" I called as Arsène poled the pirogue toward the center of the bayou. Emile took my hand and kissed it as we glided down the slow moving bayou toward the village, Arsène poling silently at the stern, the sun sparkling on the coffee colored water. My thoughts drifted back to the cryptic words Maurice had spoken.

"If I knew the truth. What is the truth?" I murmured.

"Forget those people. They upset you every time you see them. And if you never want to go back there, we never will."

We glided in silence the rest of the way to the village, as I basked in the dappled sunlight filtering through the trees and felt the warmth of Emile's love. The loud cicadas' drone from both sides of the bayou rose and fell in a soothing rhythm, and I gained assurance from the greenish hues of the trees' reflections on the bayou. I sensed that the answer was close, and realized the truth could not be rushed, but would slowly be revealed. I felt that certainty as we approached the village, and this, along with the sights and sounds of the bayou all around us comforted me.

"The truth will come out," I said to Emile.

"I'm sure of it," he agreed.

The air was clear in the village, less humid and with no haze, so that the crops in the fields and the wildflowers we passed were vivid and bright. As we neared the constable's house, he was working in the garden. When Arsène called to him, he straightened and, leaning on his hoe, mopped at his face while he waited for us to come up from the bayou bank.

As we approached, he seemed wary of us, as though he preferred we had not come. "What brings you into town today?" he asked without the usual polite greetings people exchanged. I walked right up to him in answer, holding out the tooth and key on my open palm.

"What's this?" He raised an eyebrow, and took the tooth first between thick callused thumb and forefinger, holding it close to his eyes.

"I found these in the old camp where Arsène discovered the body."

"Well, well. A tooth and a key. Hmm." He slipped the tooth into his shirt pocket and next took up the key, holding it even closer to his face as he turned it back and forth inspecting it. Finally, he looked at each of us in turn and flashed a quick and impatient smile.

"Thank you for bringing these by. Whose tooth? Whose key? We may never know. A strange business all around, don't you think?"

He paused and scratched his head. "Did you hear that dead Yankee's brother came down here to find out what happened to him? He was convinced enough it was his missing brother going by some moles and old pox scars on his chest. Said his name was Roderick Gilbert. Buried the body himself." Leroy waved a hand in the direction of the village cemetery on the bayou. "He was a nasty piece of work. He kept boldly insisting his brother must have been murdered by someone around here, and he eyed me like I was covering it up. I told him nobody around here even knew his brother. I told him his brother got himself lost out there in the swamp where he didn't know how to take care of himself, and he got himself killed in the thick of it. I told him he'd have been better off if he'd minded his business and stayed at home up yonder in the north where he knew his way around, and where he belonged."

He shook his head, slipping the key into the same pocket with the tooth. "These Yankees," he continued. "They need to stay up there and see to their own business, instead of always trying to mind ours for us. We've had enough death and disaster from the whole lying mess of them up there, and if I never see another Yankee for the rest of my life, I'll be glad of it."

He waved a hand in disgust toward the north and all that lay there. "They love to come down here like we're children, and they know everything, and they're going to tell us how to run things. To hell with all of them! Excuse me, Sidonie, but they're a vicious lot, every stinking one of them." He spat to the side in anger. "They've burned us out, stolen everything they could find, and killed enough of us. You'd think they'd be satisfied by now. The devil take all of them!"

Arsène nodded his head vigorously. "Yes, the devil take all of them!" I made the sign of the cross with two fingers, because it made me nervous to hear any talk about the devil.

"So the dead man's brother is gone now?" asked Emile.

"He's gone. I ran him off. I told him if somebody is fool enough to come down here and wander around in the swamp which he doesn't know the first thing about, why, to my mind, he got what was coming to him, and if he gives me the fishy eye one more time, I'll slap his worthless self in jail. Course then I'd have to feed him besides look at him every day." Leroy stared evenly at Emile, his face flushed with anger as he mopped at it again with the handkerchief. "Like I said, the devil take the whole worthless lot of them to burn in hell!"

Again, I made the sign of the cross with my fingers. "And," he added, "as far as this tooth and key..." He patted his pocket, "Why, I'm not going to lose any sleep over it. Are you?" He ran a tongue over his teeth and surveyed the sky. "Sun's on the move. Got to get back to my weeding."

"Come on, Sidonie. We've got to get moving too. It'll be dark before long," said Emile taking my hand.

Arsène had already begun heading toward the boat. Leroy nodded to me. "Anything else on your mind today? No sign of Jean Claude anywhere?"

"No, nothing," I answered as Emile and I started to catch up with Arsène.

"Well thank you for coming by. Keep safe, you hear?" He bent to his work among the rows of dark green cabbages once more.

"Now that you've done your duty, do you feel better?" asked Emile as he squeezed my hand.

"Yes, I do. It's clear the Constable doesn't much care what happened to that man anyway, and those possible clues don't matter much to him. He'll probably throw them away as soon as we're gone."

He leaned over, mid-stride and kissed my forehead. "And maybe you can put it all to rest now and we can concentrate on our wedding."

I smiled in anticipation of that day.

"And I've been thinking…" He paused to pick a violet and gently tucked it into my hair. "I decided to organize a work party of my card-playing friends, and anyone else who cares to join us….in order to help your friends, the nuns, to rebuild their chapel."

"Oh, Emile!" I stopped in my tracks.

"Yes, now that I have the coins back, thanks to you, I can afford to pay for the cypress they're going to need. I can buy it all from Alcee Boudreau's sawmill."

Arsène turned to see what was taking us so long. "Come on. Hurry up! It's getting late."

I clapped my hands in delight. "That's so wonderful. The nuns will pray for you and your friends every day for the rest of your lives for helping them like that. Sister Claire and all the rest of them will be thrilled."

"It will be in memory of my lovely Catherine and our precious daughter, Amelie. May they rest in peace. And maybe it will in some small way make up for many past sins." He passed a hand over his eyes. "I can only hope."

A mockingbird sang from a tree branch above us. "We, both of us, have everything we need, *n'est ce pas?* And it's good to be generous with our good fortune."

The mockingbird flew in front of us as though showing us the way, then soared to an oak tree next to the pirogue and commenced singing once more.

"I believe our friends will all join in and help the nuns," said Arsène.

"I'm sure of it. I'll bring it up tomorrow night at the card game. We're meeting at Leon Hebert's this time. I'll draw up a sketch of the chapel as I remember it. It was quite small. It won't take us long to rebuild it."

"We could have the walls up and the roof on in three or four days if it doesn't rain," Arsène said as he started to shove the pirogue free of the bank.

"That sounds about right," Emile nodded. "I agree. And more people will come out to help us, once the word gets out."

The mockingbird serenaded us again, this time imitating a different bird call, as we settled into the boat and Arsène poled us once more to the center of the bayou.

23

CHESTER FETCHES US

"Why, my dear fellow," said Porthos, "you are like the raven; you always croak of some ill. Who can encounter us on this dark night, when one sees scarcely twenty yards before us?" Twenty Years After - Alexandre Dumas

Later that evening, when Arsène, Maman and I had all finished our supper and were sitting around the table having coffee, there came a knock on the front door.

"I'll see to it," said Arsène, pushing back his chair.

"Must be trouble at this hour. My people usually come to see me in the daytime," said Maman.

Moments later, Arsène returned, leading Chester into the kitchen. The old man snatched his hat from his balding head, and grasping the brim tightly to his chest, he nodded at each of us in turn. "Sorry to bother you so late," he said.

"Chester needs help, Claudine," Arsène said.

Chester stepped forward, still clutching his hat. "There's a man…" he began.

"Yes?" Maman encouraged.

"There's a sick man at my place. He fell down at my front door. I tried, but I can't do for him. He's too sick now." Chester revolved his hat round and round, blinking often, and shifting his weight from one foot to the other and back again.

"Who is he? What's wrong with him?" she asked.

"I don't know who he is. His jaw's broke. He can't eat. He's too weak to get up. Just lies there."

"Is he fevered?"

"His head's so hot, it'll burn your hand." Chester took a deep breath and appeared to be less nervous as he stopped twirling the hat and regarded Maman steadily.

"We'll have to go to your place then. Sidonie, come help me gather my things."

We gathered a bottle of brandy, cottonade, spirit of balm, nettles and sage, vinegar, and some of Maman's famous salve for pain, which she spooned into a tin. We packed these in the leather medicine pouch that always hung from a peg in the kitchen.

"Do you have a cookstove?" she asked Chester.

"I have an outside campfire."

"Do you have a big pot?"

"Yes, Miss. I have a big pot of water always sitting on the coals."

"Good then. That's what we need. We're ready to go back with you. Lead the way." Arsène picked up the lantern from the kitchen table, and we all filed out through the front room.

"We'll take Rubis and Solange, but we'll have to shut *Minuit* in the house, or he'll follow us into the woods." Arsène took over the directions, quickly closing the back door before *Minuit* could follow. "You take Maman with you, Sidonie. Chester, you ride with me."

At the stables, we all mounted according to his plan, and with Arsène and Chester in the lead, our procession headed toward the woods at the edge of the property. Chester's job was to hold the lantern aloft and the light cast such eerie, wavering shadows as we rode along through the woods, my imagination conjured up all sorts of strange creatures hiding behind bushes and underneath sheltering branches. Creepers and vines hanging from trees caught at our face and more than once, Arsène had to hack a thorny vine from our path. Coyotes yipped from a far distance and their cries echoed in the darkness, making my imagination run away with me even more.

Presently, the smell of Chester's campfire was the signal that we'd almost arrived, and we were at last able to make out the outlines of his tiny shack, nestled in a small clearing of the forest.

Dismounting, Arsène and Chester came over to help Maman and me, and Chester tied the horses to a gum tree at the edge of the clearing. We hurried inside the narrow shack, the doorway so low we had to duck our heads.

A lone candle flickered on a tree stump that had been left inside the dwelling to serve as a low table. Next to the stump was a pallet on the floor, and lying on it was a still figure, covered by a worn quilt, with a moss-filled *sac de pitre* for a pillow.

We drew near the bed, and in the dim light of the candle, saw that the man was lying head turned to the wall, dark hair tousled and wet from the fever. Arsène wasted no time kneeling beside the pallet. He gently touched the shoulder of the sleeping man. "Can you hear me? We've come to help you."

The man moaned and turned his head, blinking in the candlelight as he tried to wet his parched, cracked lips. "Jean Claude!" I cried out, kneeling beside Arsène, and reaching out my hand to touch his arm. He could only mumble as his jaw was so swollen. The bruise from it darkened half his face. His breathing was labored and sounded like something was rattling in his throat.

"All right then. Let me pass. Let me get closer," said Maman, instantly all business. She waited until we backed off to give her room, and then she pressed forward with her leather medicine pouch. "Chester," she directed. "Go bring me that pot of hot water from the campfire, please." She began spreading out her curatives on the stump.

Carefully feeling his forehead, she murmured to him in words we couldn't hear. In the flickering light of the lone candle and lantern, we could see her assess the damage to his jaw, and press, with the most delicate touch, her special salve to the area. "Sidonie," she said without turning from him. "Put that root in the hot water when Chester brings it, and soak those strips of cotton in the water and wring them out for me."

I managed to do as she asked, although the hot water hurt my hands, while she continued to work at his side, pressing the hot cloths gently to his face, and murmuring her prayers softly while we waited behind her for any further instructions. This treatment went on for almost an hour, during which time I repeatedly soaked the cloths and wrung them out. Three or four times she was able to get some drops of a red potion between those cracked lips, so sore it hurt me to look at his mouth.

Finally, she backed away from the pallet, still hunkered down, and surveyed her patient silently as we all observed his breathing. It had slowly grown slower and steadier as she worked on him. "There," she whispered. "That's a little better. We need to get him to sleep for now. But we'll have to bring him back to the house in the morning. Arsène, be thinking how we can safely transport him back to the house. I'll leave that up to you."

"I'll bring him back with me on Rubis."

"Very well," Maman rocked on her haunches and rubbed the small of her back. "I'm very stiff from staying so long in this cramped position. Help me up so I can stretch and spell me for a while, Arsène. I need you to get this down him somehow."

She slowly stood as Arsène took her arm, and bending over the items she'd spread out on the stump, she selected a vial of her elixir. "I'm going to mix this with the brandy, and I want you to give it to him in little sips. Then follow with this." She picked up a jar of broth. "Just get it down him. Very slowly or he'll choke or vomit."

Chester brought Maman and me each a three legged stool, so crudely made that rough bark still covered the wood. "I'm going back out to heat up more water," he said as he picked up the black pot. "Then I'll make you all some sassafras tea."

"Thank you, Chester. That's just what we need right about now," Maman said.

"Sidonie, say the healing prayers with me," she directed, as she folded her hands and settled herself on the stool, watching Arsène as he worked at bedside trying not to spill the elixir.

We softly recited all the French healing prayers she'd taught me so far, and as we slowly spoke the words in the flickering light, I began to rock back and forth, feeling a great sense of gratitude that we'd finally found Jean Claude, and he was still alive.

Arsène, sitting on the edge of the pallet, leaned over Jean and guided small portions of liquid past those swollen lips. His patience and easy manner with the sick man was heartening to see. Jean's eyelids opened enough that we could see how glassy his eyes were, and then he'd shut his eyes again as though too weary to make even that slight effort.

"Is he going to be all right? Will he live?" I whispered to Maman when we'd finished one cycle of prayers.

"I think so," she whispered back. "We'll know for sure if he
makes it through the night."

"So we're staying awake all through the night?"

"Oh, most definitely." She smiled at me. "Don't worry, I'll keep
you awake."

Chester brought us each a cup of red sassafras tea, and we accepted gratefully, the tea so hot that the steam bathed our faces.
Hunched over and cradling the tin cup, I watched Arsène work
with Jean Claude as the raucous night cries and screams from the
forest surrounding the clearing increased with each late hour.

With every sip he was able to get past those chapped lips, I
gained hope that Jean Claude would live. When Maman finished
her tea, she set the empty tin cup on the floor and said, "We'll
start the cycle again now, Sidonie." She handed me a length of
string. "Begin tying a knot in this, one for each prayer. Then tie it
on his wrist when we've finished."

We began the new cycle of healing prayers, and Chester went
outside and then returned a few minutes later with a wooden
crate which he upended and sat on beside us, so we all four could
wait and watch in order to keep vigil beside Jean Claude's pallet
throughout the long night.

24

AN OMEN

He was oppressed and afflicted,
yet he did not open his mouth;…
Isaiah 53:7 KJV

Each time I dozed, Maman true to her word, awakened me with a gentle nudge as we kept our vigil by Jean Claude's bedside. In the cool glow of morning, stiff, chilled and damp, I blinked myself alert, rubbing my arms and face to wake up.

Chester prepared chicory coffee for us at the campfire, and we all drank it gratefully. His brew was dark and strong and helped revive us after the long night. Jean Claude stirred and appeared to be gaining some strength. In the thin light of morning, the bruises on his face were angry red and purple, and the swelling of the left side of his face was grotesque.

"You're doing better," Maman told him. "We're going to take you to my house so we can continue to look after you." She tenderly felt inside his dry lips for damage. "Oh," she said. "You've broken off a tooth." Jean Claude winced, letting out a weak cry of pain as she probed the side of his mouth.

"All right then. I'll leave it alone. But, that's part of the swelling and the infection you're suffering from. You've got to drink more of this. No matter that it's bitter. You've got to get it down."

She presented him with another cup of her special tonic, and this time he was able to raise his head and drink without needing as much help. He made a grunting noise from deep in his throat with distaste after each swallow that he was able to get down.

"I know it tastes terrible, but it will help you so much." She filled the tin cup again. "In a few minutes, I want you to take some more. Let what you got down so far settle first." She set the cup down on the tree stump and said, "Sidonie, please ask Chester to bring another pot of boiling water. We'll apply more compresses to that jaw before we leave for the trip home."

"Maman. The missing tooth!" I whispered.

A shake of her head warned me not to talk about it right then. We'd save it for later when Jean Claude was out of danger. That really woke me up, even though I was still badly in need of sleep. If the tooth I'd found in the cabin was Jean Claude's….that opened up a whole new set of possibilities. I hurried outside to relay her message to Chester and found him squatting by the campfire, minding a batch of biscuits all formed together in a black iron skillet. Arsène was seeing to the horses where he'd tied them by trees the night before, and cinching Rubis' saddle back on him.

"Maman needs more boiling water, please, Chester."

"Oh, I figured that. Got some right here almost ready for her. Got some breakfast cooking for you all too." He smiled at me, holding up a wooden spoon. "Thank the good Lord for your mother. She's fixing that man right up, isn't she? I didn't think he was going to make it." He poked at the fire with a stick.

"Thank you for saving Jean Claude, Chester."

"I didn't save him. God and Miss Claudine saved him. He was on his way out."

"Yes, but if it wasn't for you taking him in and seeing to him and then going to get her, he'd be dead and gone by now."

"Maybe so, but it's Miss Claudine knows what to do when people are in trouble. She's got the gift." He picked up the pot of boiling water by the handle and stood. "God Almighty puts people in your path to help even if you stay all the way out here in the woods by yourself. It's the truth." He blinked and waved steam from his face with a free, callused hand. "Come on. Let's take this inside to Miss Claudine so she can make that man well again."

After Maman had prepared the infusion with more pieces of brown shriveled root from the medicine bag, she wrung the cloths out, gently treating the swelling with more hot compresses. As I watched her work, I thought about what this new bit of information meant to the whole mystery of the dead man. If it was Jean Claude's tooth I'd found, maybe he'd fought with the Yankee scout, and the man had landed a punch to his jaw that had broken the bone, broken the tooth, and led to the infection that had almost killed him.

By the time Chester brought us each a steaming biscuit, Maman had finished working with the hot compresses, and was putting her assorted medicines and packets away. Jean watched us eat and tenderly touched his swollen cheek.

"Don't be touching that!" cautioned Maman. "Leave it be. You're on the mend now. Let's not spoil things."

"Do you think you're up to riding with me on Rubis if I hold you in front of me on the saddle?" asked Arsène who had come in from outside. Jean signaled with his hand that he could.

"All right then. We're going to take you back to Claudine's. She can care for you better at home."

"Chester. Thank you so much for helping Jean Claude," said Maman, "We'll take him away now and see that he's well taken care of. Thanks to you he's going to live." She picked up her medicine bag and walked toward the door with Chester, then spoke softly, her head leaning toward his ear. "But if you hadn't helped him, he probably wouldn't have made it through the night. That infection could have gone to his brain and killed him just like that." She snapped her fingers. "So God will bless you for saving his life."

"That's good to hear because I need somebody to bless me," said Chester. "You sure about that, Miss Claudine?"

"Oh, yes, I'm as sure about that as I am about anything," she said smiling at him. "And next time you need anything, don't hesitate to come ask us for any help we can give."

The men crossed to the pallet to lift Jean outside, and Maman and I went outside to the horses. I led Rubis over to the door to Chester's shack, and the men brought him out and then Arsène mounted so he could help to haul him up safely in front of him on the saddle, while Chester and I raised him high enough so Arsène could get a grip under his arms. Jean Claude groaned, his head lolling, as Arsène got him finally situated.

The sun had begun to burn off the early morning spirals of mist that drifted from the woods over the clearing. A bold ray of golden light angled through the pines, and I took that to be a good omen for Jean Claude's recovery as I crossed over toward Maman and Solange. Chester was already hurrying over there to help her mount. "Wait up, Miss Claudine, I'm going to help you with that," he called as he trotted toward her.

In just a few minutes, our procession was in order, and Arsène took the lead so we could begin the trip back home. "God bless!" Chester called as we waved goodbye to him. "Be careful!" He kept watching as we made our way through the woods. But then after a while, when turning my head to see if he was still watching after us, the trees had swallowed him up.

25

MAURICE

"We have not yet reached our destination,"
said d'Artagnan.
"Beware of encounters!"
Twenty Years After - Alexandre Dumas

O nce he was situated in the bed we arranged for him in the front room at Maman's, and after hours of careful attention, Jean Claude's condition steadily improved, his color began to return, and it was clear that he was on the mend. We all took turns spooning beef broth mixed with healing herbs and watery gruel into his slightly open mouth whenever he was awake. In between, we'd let him sleep, taking care to keep him warmly covered with quilts. *Minuit* trotted along after Claudine as she came and went from room to room, until he finally decided his job was to guard Jean Claude, and so he curled up beside his bed.

One of us would stay alert at bedside when he was sleeping, while the others would doze during those times trying to make up for the long night's vigil at Chester's camp. Arsène was so used to staying up all night that he didn't need much sleep and was soon out hunting fresh meat, Gator at his side, so he could feed us at suppertime. We heard the shotgun blast six times far back in the woods, and within an hour, he returned, emerging from the trees with six squirrels tucked into his belt, their bodies and long tails hanging down below his waist. He immediately set about cleaning them at the edge of the bayou, which was a job that I was used to doing back at the farm when Maurice brought small game home. I offered to help him, but he told me to stay with Maman and Jean Claude in the house and he'd take care of it.

Presently, the delicious smell of browning meat, onions and peppers wafting into the front room awakened Jean Claude. He stirred himself beneath the quilts and tried to sit up. This was such an encouraging sign that Maman and I propped him up against the wall with every pillow in the house. He couldn't make himself understood, his attempts to say a few words were hopeless, but the swelling had slightly gone down which told us he was winning the battle against the infection. We continued applying hot compresses from time to time at intervals and Maman kept his spirits up by softly talking to him.

"You're doing so well. After we help you have some supper, I'm going to give you another sedative, and you'll be able to sleep through the night. By the time you wake up tomorrow, you're going to feel much better."

My job was to take out the small bones, cut and mash the meat in brown gravy so we could feed him such that he wouldn't choke. He was able to make appreciative moans throughout, and before long, the bowl was empty. "Now, you see?" said Maman, smiling. "You've had a nice supper, and you'll sleep safely while your body mends. We'll all be here nearby, so you have nothing to worry about."

He took her hand and made a feeble attempt to smile out of the left side of his mouth. Then she gave him the sedative, and we removed all the pillows but one so he could stretch out flat once more for the night. Maman said a French prayer with all of us assembled, and we watched until his eyes closed and his deep slow breathing told us he was sound asleep.

Arsène made himself a bed on the floor in the front room with quilts, and Maman and I went to our rooms, grateful to be in our own beds at last. I don't remember ever falling asleep so fast. The last thing I remember was curling up and pulling the quilt snugly to my chin, while a whippoorwill, a frequent visitor, serenaded me from the swamp maple outside the window of my room.

The morning proved Maman right, for when we came out from our rooms, Jean was already sitting up again, and Arsène had served him coffee with scalded milk in a tin cup which Jean was able to hold for himself with both hands.

"Now that's a wonderful sight to see," Maman told him. "You're doing so well. We're going to get you up and about before you know it." He tried to answer her, but his words were still muffled, and we couldn't understand him.

"I'm going to make a place for him out on the porch this morning, so he can breathe some fresh air, and have a view of sunlight and the bayou," said Arsène. He set about fixing a comfortable spot for him outside, and we helped him walk Jean Claude to a chair with pillows near the front door so he could see something besides four walls and a ceiling full of hanging herbs. We put his feet up on a crate, and before long, he was giving us a crooked, feeble smile out of the side of his mouth.

We all went about our chores then, making breakfast, feeding and watering the animals, cleaning the stables, setting the house in order, and starting the noon dinner. Someone was always checking on Jean Claude, and now that he could hold his own, we kept bringing him hot drinks of broth, coffee, or herb teas.

By late morning, when the chicken *fricassée* was simmering, and the chores were almost finished, we had a surprise in the form of an unlikely visitor. Arsène was outside with Gator when he alerted us that we had company. Maman and I came out onto the porch to see Maurice securing his pirogue on the bank in front of the house.

He strode up the path to the porch without the courtesy of greeting any of us. His head was lowered, his one eye glaring at each of us in turn as though we were enemies. We all moved closer to Jean Claude in a protective way. *Minuit* growled deep in his throat and stepped forward toward the first step of the porch.

"The word got out that they found you, you sorry mess," he said to Jean Claude. "And look at you, a wreck, and with women standing around to protect you. What a baby!" He shook his head in disgust, stopping short at the steps. "You look like you died and came back to life. You're going to wish you *had* died when I get done with you!"

Arsène hurried up the steps and stretched out an arm, hand held up to stop him from going any further. "He's hurt bad! Leave him alone!" he warned in a tone I'd never heard him use. *Minuit* stood beside him, also ready to defend, still warning Maurice with a low growl.

"He's going to be hurt a lot worse if I don't take him back to the farm. I only just heard what's been going on." Maurice planted a boot solidly on the second step, leaning forward on one knee, still frowning fiercely at Jean Claude, and pushing his hat back from his forehead.

"And what is really going on?" asked Maman.

"It's a family matter," said Maurice, not taking his menacing eye off Jean Claude.

Jean Claude closed his eyes as though to shut out the world.

"A family matter?" asked Maman. "A family matter," she repeated softly. "And would that have anything to do with Yvonne?" she gently asked Jean Claude.

Jean Claude opened his eyes, and the bruising around his eye and swollen cheek turned darker purple as he met her gaze for a moment. He slowly nodded in answer, and kept staring at her as though she could provide an answer to his unfortunate situation.

"You mean, you…" I pointed to him in amazement, finger waggling. "You mean, all this time, it was you…you and Yvonne?" I began laughing from deep within, at first trying to stifle it by pressing my lips together, and looking away. But this didn't work, and the laughter erupted from my throat despite my best efforts so that I shook all over as I gave in to it.

"Sidonie!" Maurice yelled at me. "Quit your laughing! Nothing about this is funny!"

Clapping my hands over my mouth, I tried again to stop, but my body wouldn't stop shaking as I released all the tension of the past week with this unending and embarrassing laughter. I squeezed my eyes shut, so I couldn't see anyone's reaction to this hilarity, but one part of me didn't care how foolish I might look, or what anyone thought, as I gave in to this release.

As I began to recover somewhat from the helpless laughter, I actually heard a click in my head as all the pieces of the mystery fell into place. "Oh, no," I said, eyes opening wide.

"What the hell is wrong with you?" asked Maurice.

"I see it all now. I know what happened. It's clear as the day."
I raised my hands, shaking my head in wonder that I hadn't seen
it before.

"What? What are you going on about?" asked Maurice, his
tone as usual, unpleasant and impatient.

"Jean," I turned to him, hating to cause him more pain in his
condition, but unable to stop myself. "You," I said as gently as I
could, "wanted so badly to escape from Yvonne and fatherhood...
that you were even desperate enough to steal the gold coins from
Emile to make your escape somewhere far from here....maybe
New Orleans or Natchez...I don't know where you planned to go."

Jean Claude winced and closed his eyes tightly again to shut
all of this out, but I pressed on despite his discomfort. "You took
the gold out to the Dupuis camp...and hid it there until you were
ready to leave...then, I don't know how, maybe you were out trapping or fishing in the swamp, and when you went by the camp,
that Yankee scout was there. Here's a stranger using the camp...
and your gold was gone from wherever you hid it. You got in a
fight with him about it when you found him in the cabin. He must
have hit you so hard, he broke your jaw, and your tooth broke off
from the blow. And the fight must have been a fierce one, because
the two of you fought your way outside...and finally you were able
to knock him out is what I guess. And you left him there on the
ground unconscious...and set about searching for the gold coins.
You even dug holes around the campsite in desperation, but came
up with nothing. And maybe it got dark, and you were worn out,
so you fell asleep, and maybe when you woke up in such pain from
your injuries, you found him dead out there, all torn up in that
horrible way...and you got scared and left the camp before anyone
could accuse you of murdering him." I paused as Jean Claude
tilted his head back, eyes still closed, hands tightly clenched in his
lap. Then suddenly, he opened his eyes and tried to speak, making garbled sounds, but just as quickly, he closed his eyes again as
though to make all of this go away.

"And then," I went on, "you tried to stay alive out there in the
swamp any way you could, but you kept hurting worse and worse,
and feeling weaker and weaker as infection set in, and somehow
you made it to Chester's camp before passing out at his door." I

leaned toward him. "I'm trying to piece it all together best I can, but am I close to the truth?" I asked.

He waited a moment as all of us watched his reaction, then he opened his eyes, winced, and closed them again. "Well! Answer her!" barked Maurice. "Is there anything to this crazy story?" We all waited while Jean sat silently, still with eyes closed, breathing fast, a few fingers twitching. "Answer her, or God help me, I'll bust you up where you sit! And none of you will stop me!" Maurice shouted. I ran forward and grabbed up *Minuit* for fear he'd attack Maurice and Maurice would kick him.

Arsène drew himself up to full height and held both arms out like a gate in front of Maurice. "Take it easy! He's all banged up, and you're not going to make it any worse! You can't kick a man when he's down."

Finally Jean opened his eyes, looked at me with pain and shame clearly visible on his face, and nodded once. "You sorry son of a bitch," Maurice said, shaking his head. "All my life I've known you, and I never would have believed this of you."

Knowing Maurice, I was afraid he'd shove Arsène aside to get to Jean Claude. I interrupted quickly. "You'll be glad to know the coins have been found. We found them in the cistern by the cabin. He must have dropped them in there when he heard you approaching the camp. Or maybe he was planning to make that abandoned camp his base while he was scouting the swamp, and he planned to stay there for a while."

"See there! And you couldn't wait to accuse me and Hippolyte. I told you you'd be apologizing one day," said Maurice from his spot on the lower steps.

Looking him directly in the eye, I said, "And I *am* sorry for accusing you...and Hippolyte. I was dead wrong." I turned back to Jean Claude. "And don't worry about going to jail for any of it. Emile will never put you there. He's so glad to get the coins back, I don't think he'll be interested in seeking out punishment. And as far as the dead man, the constable has closed the case. He decided it was an accident days ago, and the man didn't know how to protect himself in the swamp. You didn't set out to kill him, did you?"

Jean shook his head, and for the first time since we'd met up with him, he was able to croak, "*No!*"

Maurice tore the hat off his head and swatted it against his knee. "Well, damn. I can't believe!" He looked up as two fox squirrels chattered and chased each other on a branch by the side of the porch. "Now, that's some wild story to get my head around." He sniffed and ran an arm across his nose, then shook his head.

Arsène and Maman were silent as they thought about these events, then Maurice resumed his menacing tone. "If that all happened out there, it still doesn't change what happened at my house. And I don't give a damn about anything but taking Jean Claude back to Yvonne...where he's going to have to take care of her and that baby she's going to have. Your little escape plan didn't work out, son, and you're going to make it right, or you'll be the one lying on the ground deep in the swamp in the middle of the night. Bait for whatever's hungry and roaming or crawling around out there."

Jean Claude, face flushed, was still breathing rapidly, his distress obvious to anyone looking at him. "I'm against moving him today," said Maman. "I don't care what he's done. He needs to rest. He's got a dangerous infection."

"Well, he's going today. Like it or not. If I don't take him back there to the farm, he'll sneak off again just like he did before." He pointed a finger at Jean. "I would never have thought for a minute that you'd do what you did. All this time we were out searching for you hoping you weren't dead somewhere from a hunting accident. Then we hear you've been found and Yvonne finally owns up to the whole shameful mess. You're going back with me, and you're going to marry her, you. She's not going to be a humiliated unwed mother."

"Jean Claude, I don't think moving you is a wise idea just now," said Maman. "Do you want to go back with him? It's up to you. We'll keep you here if you want to stay."

"We'll keep you safe if that's what you want," said Arsène. "Until you get stronger."

Jean Claude, with a resigned expression on his bruised and swollen face, made a motion with his hand toward the boat. "I'll go," he managed to mumble. He tried to rise, and Arsène hurried over to help him. Maurice came up the steps to grasp his other arm. They maneuvered him to his feet and Jean, though limp and wobbly, seemed somehow energized by all the emotion of the confrontation.

"I'm going to give you some salve and some herbs that I want Yvonne to keep giving him," said Maman, as she went into the house to gather an assortment of supplies.

"Jean Claude," I said as he was gaining his balance. "Don't feel badly on my account. It's going to be all right. Things changed between Emile and I since you've been missing. We're going to be married soon. And you are welcome to bring Yvonne to the wedding."

"You and Emile! Great God Almighty! I can't keep up with all that's going on around here," Maurice complained, slapping the hat back on his head.

Maman came back out of the house with a cloth tied around the medicines and handed them to Maurice. "Tell Yvonne to make this tea up and keep giving it to him. And keep this salve on his swollen cheek. And also hot compresses. For at least two more days. You will see to it?"

Maurice nodded grudgingly and stuffed the package into a pocket of his vest.

Jean was able to get out two words to Maman and me, sounding like his mouth was stuffed with cotton: "*Merci, angelles.*" He gave me another of those crooked sideways smiles, and began to make his way slowly with his escort toward the steps.

When they were halfway to the pirogue, we heard Maurice speak in an easier tone to Jean Claude, "It's not going to be all as bad as you think. At least Yvonne is a really good cook...*beau-frère!*"

26

THE WORK PARTY

"But," said Parry. "I have no tools."
Twenty Years After - Alexandre Dumas

Despite all the excitement of finding Jean Claude at last and his successful path to recovery, Emile managed in the next few days to accomplish his goal of organizing friends to rebuild the chapel for the convent. It proved not difficult to persuade Leon Hebert, Maurice, Hippolyte, Alcee Boudreaux, Gerard, and even Leroy Viator, to help rebuild the chapel. And there was more good news that Emile reported to us one sunny afternoon at Maman's. The word was out in the community, and there would be even more men, outside of their regular card-playing group, who were planning to join in the work.

"I want to be there too," said Maman. "I want to meet the sister who burned it. I can help her with her illness."

"Brigitte."

"Yes. I want to give her a treatment....if she'll allow it."

"If anyone can help her, Maman, it's you," I assured her.

"I can bring both of you out there tomorrow then," promised Arsène, who was cleaning his rifle on the back porch.

I was busy outside also cleaning the globes of lanterns. Emile kissed my hand even though it was streaked with soot. "I'll meet up with all of you tomorrow then, at the convent."

As always, I felt a stab of loss watching him go, and Arsène laughed as he watched me forlornly looking after Emile. "I'm glad I never met anyone that stole my heart. It looks painful. I don't need that, me."

"Just wait," Maman said from the kitchen doorway. "Your time will come, and then we'll see you suddenly spending more time in town than you ever thought possible."

"No, no, Claudine," he shook his head. "That can never be."

"We'll see."

There was still an early morning mist the next day when Arsène picked us up, that cast a silver glow over the surrounding woods. We loaded the four loaves of pecan bread and a *gateau de figue* we baked for the occasion. "I'm sure the nuns are preparing plenty of food for everyone, but we wanted to contribute some sweets for the big dinner at noon," Maman told Arsène.

"Those men will eat all of it. There will be nothing left at the end of the day," Arsène assured her as he shoved us off the bank.

"It's not often I get to take Claudine out," he said while taking up the pole. "This is even more of an occasion than rebuilding the chapel." We passed turtles sunning on logs, and a great heron took flight before us, his wingspan so grand, he appeared to be escorting us to our destination.

As we passed by the old farm, I felt a pang of regret, revisiting my youth there and missing my beloved hounds, picturing them sleeping lazily on and under the porch. I wondered how Jean Claude was adjusting to his new arrangements, and if Yvonne was learning to sweeten her disposition now that she was beginning a whole new family life. I imagined she was enjoying the fact that he was injured and somewhat of a prisoner there so she could be in charge of him, rather than the other way around. Time would tell if he could manage to live with her overbearing manner; or if he would pick up and disappear again into the night.

When Arsène had glided us further down Bayou Perdu, he slowed the boat and poled us over to the bank, to a spot as close as he could get to the convent by water. Once Maman's feet were safely planted on the bank, I took her hand and guided her along through the vines and low hanging branches, keeping an eye out for roots and snakes and any other pitfalls that might harm her.

"How much further do we have to go?" she asked, wiping her face with the shawl she wore loosely tied around neck and shoulders.

"Only a little ways more," Arsène encouraged. "We're almost there."

By the time we arrived on the road that ran along the front grounds of the convent, Maman was smiling. "This is wonderful," she said. "I need to get out more often. I stay home because it's easier, but the change feels so good."

We walked quickly down the rutted road, hearing hammering and men calling to one another before we even rounded the bend where the convent came into view. "They're already at work. I'll go on ahead and join them. You two take your time," Arsène said.

As he hurried on ahead, I watched him catch up to the workers and shook my head at all the changes in our lives since I'd first traveled to Arsène's camp in the swamp. Since that lightning filled, drenched night, the two of us, both Jean Claude and myself, had new homes and new families, and Emile, within a matter of days, was about to have a new family as well. If I had been told just a short time ago all this would take place, I would never have believed it to be possible. It was like a dream, except that this time it wasn't a dream. I swung Maman's hand. "So much has changed, and in such a short time. It's almost too much to be believed."

She nodded. "It was time for it. I could tell change was coming. All the signs pointed that way. I just didn't know how it would happen."

"What signs?"

"Oh, if you get used to reading the signs, you can tell...by little things that happen all around you. The world is always talking to us. It just takes a while to understand the message."

"I don't understand."

"Notice everything around you. All the time. It's all speaking to you. Keep your eyes open every minute of the day. If you learn to read the signs...and you will... you will know what I mean."

"But, like what?"

"Hmm, well, it's like..." she began, then paused and took a deep breath. "...say a feather flutters into your hand or a butterfly lands on your shoulder, or mushrooms grow in a certain unusual pattern. It's so hard to explain." She took another breath. "Let's say a spider is on you…that's a sign of money coming your way…but seeing a spider first thing in the morning, now that's bad luck. *Araignèe le matin, chagrin.* Or maybe you hear a certain bird call, or something whispered on the wind."

"But how do you know what these things tell you?"

"You reach out with your deepest self, and…" she searched for the right word, "You *mingle* with it. That's the only way I can explain what I mean…and by mingling with it, and waiting, you begin to know what the world is telling you."

I shook my head. "I don't know if I'll ever be able to do that. It sounds too mysterious."

"But that's just it! It's not mysterious at all…once you learn how to recognize the signs. Just wait, you'll see one day." She squeezed my hand. "You're just starting out. Give it time."

"Time! Everything takes so much time! Look how long it took for us to find each other."

"Don't worry about time. There is no time as we know it. It's all God's time. And when you learn, really learn patience, you'll find that it doesn't matter if something takes years, or just hours. It's all the same."

"Maman!" I was confused by this talk we'd had. Signs all around us? The world speaking to us? Time has no meaning? I was having enough trouble trying to get used to all the changes that had happened so quickly in our lives, and now she was telling me this? It was all too much for me. And yet I didn't doubt her words. I knew in my heart that what she taught me was true, because I had so much faith in her.

"You have the *way*. You just don't know it yet." She squeezed my hand. "But as for now we must get to work helping the others." We had reached the convent by then. The workers, including Arsène and Emile, carried planks from a wagon loaded with cypress toward the site of the new chapel. Some of the others were already erecting part of the frame and even starting on the rafters.

"Do you see Brigitte?" Maman asked.

"I'll take you to her right now." We stepped up our pace and crossed the grass toward the walkway that led to the garden where

Sister Claire was standing with a basket filled with greens, watching the men at work.

"Sister Claire." I waved.

"Sidonie!" She turned, beaming. "Isn't this just the most beautiful sight to see? All these wonderful helpers. And isn't our Lord so very pleased today to see all their good works?" She set her basket on the grass and came toward us. "And you've brought a friend?"

"Yes, Sister Claire. This is Claudine Dugas. My real mother." I felt a rush of happiness as Claire took Maman's hands and clasped them together in her own.

"Your real mother?" she asked.

"It's a long story. I'll tell you all about it one day." I handed her the baked goods for her basket. "These are for you. Maman and I were up baking well before dawn."

"Thank you so much." Claire kneeled and carefully placed the wrapped breads and cake into her basket.

"I've heard so much about you from Sidonie," Maman said. "She's been with me for the last week. Thank you for befriending her and helping her. It's meant so much to her."

"Oh, yes, of course. She is a charming, good person. And she is always welcome here. And so are you, Miss Claudine."

"Thank you. That is good to know because I've really enjoyed the trip over here today. I'm so used to staying home because of my blindness. I see you, but you're a dark shape, and I can't really tell what you look like."

"I'm very plain, round, and white-haired," laughed Claire.

"Don't listen to her, Maman. She has a beautiful smile and blue eyes that always crinkle when she laughs."

"I'm sure of it. I can tell a lot about a person from their voice," Maman said. "I'm sure you all are very busy, but do you think it would be all right if I met with Sister Brigitte some time today?"

"Why certainly. She's in the cookhouse right now helping to prepare the midday dinner for the workers."

"She's back to her old self?" I asked.

"Yes, she most certainly is. We've calmed her down. These fits she has pass in time."

"I've brought some herbs with me. I believe they will help."

"A lot of people come to see Maman for treatments," I explained.

Claire picked up her basket. "Oh, I see. Well, then, come along with me, and we'll go find her." She turned toward the cookhouse, and I took Maman's hand as we followed along.

The air inside the cookhouse was hot from the great wood burning stove and four of the nuns chopped and mixed ingredients at a long worktable. Steam billowed around two sisters who stirred great pots with long wooden spoons. Maman wiped her face again with the edge of her shawl, and Claire seeing how warm she was, went to fetch drinks for us.

"Sit there," she said, bringing us cups of tea and motioning to chairs set against a whitewashed wall. "I'll bring Brigitte over to you in just a minute."

We sat and sipped the tea gratefully as Claire crossed to the worktable and whispered to Brigitte who was rolling dough out on a floured portion of the table. Brigitte looked over at us, clapped the flour from her hands, and the two of them moved toward where we were sitting. "This is Sister Brigitte." Claire began the introductions. "And this is Sidonie's mother, Miss Claudine."

"I'm happy to meet you," Brigitte said.

"*Et moi aussi,*" Maman said. "I've brought you some special herbs for tea that I thought you might try."

"That's very kind of you. Thank you. It's good of you to think of me."

Claire brushed a spot of flour from Brigitte's face, as Maman reached into her pocket and drew out some folded paper packets, pressing them into Brigitte's hands. "If you simmer a few tablespoons of these herbs in a quart of water for about a half hour, then strain it for tea, and drink it throughout the day, you will feel well and stay well. If you don't like the taste, you might add some honey." Maman smiled at her and folded her hands in her lap.

Brigitte sniffed the packet. "They smell good. What are they?" she asked in a timid voice.

"It's a blend from my garden of healing herbs. It's my special mixture and if you like the effects, let Sidonie know, so she can bring you more."

"Thank you." Brigitte slipped the packet into a pocket.

"And now, may I hold your hand for a minute or two?" Maman held out her hand and Brigitte, nodding, slowly reached out to her. Maman stood as she held her hand, and her lips moved as she said the French healing prayers. Claire and I watched as the cooks continued to chop and stir, and the hammering outside continued at a steady pace.

It felt good to see Brigitte's expression change during this treatment. At first she looked slightly confused, but gradually her face smoothed out, the lines of her forehead disappeared, her breathing slowed, and her eyes closed. When Maman finished, she released her hand and smiled. "There! Thank you for trusting me."

Brigitte started to thank her in return. Maman shook her finger. "No, no. Don't thank a treater. Healing comes from God."

"Well," Brigitte said with a quick look at Claire. "If I can't thank you, then I must get back to help the others."

Claire nodded to her and Brigitte returned to her work. "You came a long way today," Claire said to us. "And I hope you will be able to stay and eat with us at noon. I think you'll enjoy yourself if you do."

"Thank you, I'm sure of it," said Maman.

"Come. Let's get out of this hot kitchen and see how the men are doing," said Claire as she took our empty cups. As she led us from the cookhouse, the delicious smells from the stove followed us out the door into the cool morning air.

"What did you think?" I asked Maman softly as we followed along.

"I think Brigitte is going to do very well."

"Look!" called Claire, pointing toward the work site. The frame for the chapel was half in place and Hippolyte was high up riding the rafters, one leg slung over and swinging, the other just hanging, as he hammered furiously, whistling all the while.

"Watch it!" yelled Maurice, who was looking up at him from the ground, shielding his eyes with one hand. "You're going too fast."

"I always go too fast, brother. That's the way I am. You know that," Hippolyte laughed, immediately resuming his whistling.

Alcee swung up on the wagon. "I'm heading back to the mill for more lumber," he called to anyone within range.

"At the rate they're going, they'll be finished before we know it," said Claire. "Who would have thought they could work so fast. It's remarkable! I think I'd better go help with the cooking. Maybe you'd like to sit there in the shade near the roses. Their perfume is heavenly today."

As we made Maman comfortable on a bench in the shade by the garden, three men of the Latiolais family arrived on horseback. Emile greeted them with a welcoming wave. "We're glad to see you," he called.

Hippolyte, still aloft in the rafters, waved his hammer. "Halloo!" he cried.

"Quit waving that hammer over my head!" complained Maurice. "Or I'll come up there and knock you out!"

"Don't scare me! I scare easy!" mocked Hippolyte, but he did stop swinging the hammer.

Presently Doc arrived in a horse-drawn wagon, his silver hair shining like a halo in the bright sunshine. "I brought my special tonic for any man who gets too worn out to work." He waved a corked bottle of spirits.

"Isn't this wonderful? So many neighbors offering their time and labor for us," said Claire beaming.

"I'd like to help too," I offered.

"Good. Then come along with me," said Claire. We left Maman by the flowers and followed the brick walk toward the cookhouse. Once inside, the heat pressed upon us once more, and she put me to work chopping onions in a spot near Brigitte at the worktable, while Claire went to relieve someone at the cookstove.

Toward noon, Claire asked the men to set up planks on sawhorses, so we could begin bringing out the food. I went outside with her, and by this time two of the Boudreaus had joined the work party, along with Pierre Arcenaux and Jean Delcambre. The progress on the new structure had already come so far along, it took my breath away.

Looking around for Emile, I found him on his knees, hammering the foundation for the floor. Just the sight of him, intent and so hard at work, his tanned skin glistening, shirt wet against his skin, touched my heart. All of them working so hard to help the convent touched me. I felt a tear come to my eye that so many would be so willing to give up their time to do so much for the sisters.

Claire and I helped two men place the sawhorses where she wanted them. We straightened the planks and wiped them down, making ready for the tablecloths we would be placing over the long makeshift tables. "There. That's going to be fine the way it is," Claire said. "I'll go tell the others we have it ready for them out here."

By the time the nuns had carried all the bowls and pots of steaming food to the tables, the rich smells of the stews, gumbos, and *grillades* carried on a light breeze to the men. They threw down their tools, mopped their faces with handkerchiefs, and hurried to the pump to splash water over their faces, hair and necks, laughing and sputtering as they refreshed themselves and got ready to eat.

Claire quieted everyone with a call for prayer, and as everyone respectfully bowed their heads, she thanked our Lord and Savior for bringing us all together in the blessed work of rebuilding the chapel. "...and thank you, blessed Lord, for our friends and neighbors who have given of their time to work so hard for us here today. May we remember all our blessings as we continue with this beautiful day. Amen."

There were echoes throughout the assembled people of her *amen*, and a moment's polite pause after the blessing. Claire stood smiling at the head of one of the tables, stirring a gumbo, and quietly directing two of the sisters where to place a heap of long freshly baked French loaves.

As the workers filed in line to fill their plates, Emile found me and took my hand. "I'm so glad you're here with Miss Claudine to see all this," he said softly near my ear. "It's a great day! And it's even better because you're here to see it."

"You know I want to be with you as often as I can."

"Very soon we'll always be together. I can promise you that."

We laughed then as Hippolyte cut in front of Maurice in the line. Maurice started to say something harsh about it, but as Claire passed close by, he thought better of it, and settled for simply scowling at Hippolyte.

"I wonder how Jean Claude is getting along," I asked Emile, as we watched the line move quickly along from our position toward the end.

"Maurice says he's still weak, but better because Yvonne is presenting him with food all day long."

"She's going to make him better fast, now that she's got him all to herself."

Emile smiled. "She has him where she wants him now."

"But what if he rebels and runs away again?" Hippolyte and Maurice wandered off to sit on the grass over by the pump, and in a few minutes Leon Hebert joined them. The line moved forward faster as most of the men had filled their plates and were sitting on the grass, eating quickly and with great appetite.

"She can't nail the doors and windows shut," he shrugged as he guided me forward. "Still maybe this time he'll stay. Now that he must be so grateful to be alive...and out of jail besides."

There was such a variety of food that we couldn't possibly fit all the choices on one plate. I tried not to take too much so Emile wouldn't think I was greedy...but I was very hungry by then. Using some restraint, I spooned brown gravy over rice, and chose some *moque choux*, field peas, *etouffée*, and glazed rolls and prepared two plates for Maman and me. We carried the dinners over to where she sat on the bench.

"I'm going to ask Arsène if he'll take you both back home after this," Emile said as we squeezed onto the bench next to her.

"Oh, I'm fine," she protested.

"I know, but it's been a long day for you. You're not used to being so far from home," he said gently.

"Yes, that's true, and it *is* a long trip back," she agreed.

When we finished our dinner, Emile left us to find Arsène, and I picked up our plates and helped by going around collecting and stacking more empty plates to carry back to the cookhouse to be washed. On my way I paused by Claire. "Emile thinks Arsène should take Maman and me home now. He thinks she's had a long day already, and it takes a long time to get back to her house."

"That's a sensible idea. I hate to see you go, but I'm so glad you could both be with us today."

"We enjoyed every minute of it."

"And your mother's kindness has already changed things. Brigitte looks calmer and happier than I've seen her in a while." Claire placed a small bowl on top of my stack of plates. "Here's another for you."

Hurrying back from the cookhouse, I found Maman and Arsène by the tables. Arsène had his arm around her, and they were talking as they began to walk toward the road.

"Come on, Sidonie. We're headed back," he called.

"Wait! I want to say goodbye to Emile. I'll catch up!" I ran to where Emile had begun working again. "We're heading back, so I'm going to say goodbye for now."

He took my face in both hands and kissed my cheeks, which made my skin glow and feel hot. I touched my fingers lightly to my face. "Are you wiping my kiss away?" he laughed.

"No. I'm making sure it stays there."

He gazed at me solemnly still holding my face in his hands. "I'm grateful for this project, you know." He indicated the chapel with a gesture. "Because it keeps my mind off you during this interminable wait until our wedding."

I pressed my hands against his for a moment to let him know I felt the same way, then took my leave, hurrying to catch up with Maman and Arsène. As we glided along toward home that day, I kept thinking of Emile, daydreaming about our new life together. As we passed the various creatures of the swamp, and regal herons standing like statues all around us, I also mused as to what these signs might mean according to Maman's way of belief.

"Mingle with it," she said earlier that day, and that's what I tried to do from time to time during that trip in order to better understand her meaning, but my thoughts kept returning to Emile. I was filled with him, and the memory of his touch and his kiss caused my skin to tingle. I sighed with pleasure at the memory.

"Tired?" asked Maman, who looked tired herself. She wasn't sitting up quite as straight as she normally did, and her shoulders slumped just a little.

"No, Maman. I'm all right." The truth was, I felt far from tired because of all the excitement of the day.

"Then it must be something else I'm sensing. Are your thoughts faraway on Emile? Am I guessing right?"

"Yes, Maman. My thoughts are faraway on Emile. But they're also here with you and Arsène. And I am watching for signs all around us as we pass by."

She smiled. "That's what I like to hear. Keep your eyes open and watch for me as well. And as for Emile, you'll be with him soon enough. But this beautiful day gliding along the water as we are now will never come our way again."

27

A WEDDING GIFT

"Do you see?" interrupted d'Artagnan.
Twenty Years After - Alexandre Dumas

Many a time in the nights following, I would awaken with wonder about our upcoming wedding day. Those restless nights when moonlight lay across my bed were more tolerable as moonlight soothes my spirits and my soul. But, with or without moonlight, time seemed to pass so slowly that I had to keep reminding myself that I needed to learn to have patience as Maman tried to teach me. But I still didn't know how to *learn* or to *have* patience.

And then one day, to my great surprise, Maurice and Hippolyte appeared at Maman's, and I heard them call out while I was collecting herbs and vegetables in the garden. When I rounded the house with my basket, they were wandering up the well-worn path to the house. It was Hippolyte, as usual, who spoke first as they approached. Maurice was hanging back in his typical manner, eye patch askew.

"I brought you something," he said. Puzzled, I must have frowned, for he said, "Don't worry. It's a present...for your wedding day." He smiled fully at me, and the sun glinted on his strong even teeth. He held out a package, and he looked so eager for me to take it, that I hurried forward to oblige him.

"A present? What is it?"

"Open it, and you'll see." He watched expectantly as I took it from him.

"For me? Really?"

"Go on. Open it. It won't bite," he laughed.

The stiff brown paper crinkled as I carefully unwrapped the gift, and as I slowly uncovered the blue silk that lay neatly folded within, I gasped, then touched its softness lightly with my forefinger, fearing I'd mark its delicate pale color. "It's silk!" I exclaimed, somewhat in awe. I'd never owned anything of silk in my life. Home woven fabric was all we had ever worn in my family.

He drew himself up even straighter and craned his neck to glance at Maurice, who was slowly chewing on a stalk of sweet grass. "Of course it's beautiful," he blinked slowly. "You think I'm going to give you some ugly old rag for a wedding present?" Stuttering something, I touched the material lightly again.

"You deserve it," he said in the gentlest tone I'd ever heard him use. "I brought it back from New Orleans the last time Maurice and I went down there to trade hides and pelts. I thought I was bringing it back to give my mother for Christmas, but it turns out I was bringing it back for you." He blushed and gave me a crooked smile.

"Thank you so much! It will make a beautiful wedding dress."

"You're welcome!" He jerked his head toward Maurice. "We like Emile, don't we, *frère?*"

Maurice muttered something, which might have been a yes. I looked from one to the other, still marveling at the fine gift. "Would you like to come in and have coffee with Maman and me?"

"No, we have traps to check this morning. Thanks anyway." He waved in farewell and bolted away from me, and Maurice lost no time in shoving the pirogue off the bank. I held the fine silk to my chest, as a pleasant serenity washed over me. All things were settling down once more after the upheavals of the past weeks. And soon it would be another full moon...and my wedding day.

I watched them until they were out of sight down the bayou, then hurried to the house to show Maman the surprise gift. She was busy at the cabinet mashing dried herbs into grease for a salve as I laid the silk, still in its wrapping, on the kitchen table. "The strangest thing happened, Maman."

"What was that?" she asked turning her head.

"Hippolyte and Maurice were just here. Hippolyte brought this to me as a wedding gift. Feel how soft it is!"

She came over and touched a finger to the silk. "And why is it so strange that he would bring you a wedding gift?"

"He's always been friendly, but this is so unexpected from a rough swamp rat like him. And after all I accused them of...stealing the coins and maybe even killing that logging scout."

"Obviously he forgives you for that."

"Maybe because he's so glad it all worked out in the end."

"It certainly has seemed to, hasn't it?"

I felt the peace of mind that comes with problems being sorted out. And as we sat together that day at the table, I began to design the wedding dress in my mind.

* * *

That night I had a strange dream. Lying in bed as the haze of dawn crept through the window, wisps of the dream floated in my mind while I lay half awake, trying to remember all of it. I was able to recall the sound of hard, loud knocking on the door of the dream house, which was a cypress cabin on an unnamed and unfamiliar bayou. The knocking was insistent, and I tried to open the door, but couldn't, despite tugging and yanking on the iron latch.

"Who's there?" I kept calling, while struggling in great frustration.

"It's me, your father," came the deep, rumbling voice on the other side of the thick cypress door.

"Who are you?" I called frantically as I continued to tug uselessly at the latch.

"Open the door, and you'll see," the voice insisted.

Then I recalled another part of the dream. Gros Louis stared at me from behind a fence at the edge of the woods back on the farm where I grew up. He didn't speak, just stared at me, and his dark brown eyes looked so sad, that I felt terrible in the dream as though I'd hurt him somehow.

I felt a stab of pain in my heart. What if Gros Louis in heaven, who had always tried so hard to raise me well with Maman at his side, was hurt that I was so concerned with my real father's identity? What if he and Maman were hurt that I had found my real mother, and had so quickly grown so close to her?

Then I remembered the rest of the dream. As he stayed beyond my reach on the other side of the fence at the edge of the shadowy woods I called out, "Oh, Papa. You were always my father. You loved me much more than my real father, or he would have shown himself to me by now. Please, don't be hurt. I love you so much, Papa, and you will always be my father. This is only curiosity. I want to know. It's a puzzle that's all. If I ever find out who he is, he'll never have the love I have for you, dearest Papa."

He never did speak in the dream, but he did vanish then from the woods. And somehow, I sensed that he'd been satisfied with my words. As I lay there in the warm bed, the cool moist air of morning drifted in the window, and I smelled the coffee and beignets that Maman was making for us. I felt happy and content. I had Maman and Arsène...and Emile. And soon, most likely, I would have my own babies to love and nurture and teach. Just as Gros Louis and Eliate had loved and taught me.

If I never found out who my father was, I now had the blessing of knowing my real mother. Knowing her had explained so much about my own ways because in so many of those ways I was like her. It explained, for instance, why I had always been more religious than other members of the family back at the farm. It explained too, my closeness to Sister Claire and the rest of the nuns at the convent, and a lifetime of saying prayers so often during the day and night. None of these traits were shared by the rest of the family.

My intense love of the outdoors, the birds and animals, and all the rest of nature was another quality that I inherited from my real mother, and I was so glad of it. "Good morning, Maman," I greeted her happily as I entered the kitchen. "The coffee and beignets smell wonderful, and I can't wait for breakfast!"

"You won't have long to wait, *chère*," she said from the stove. "It's almost ready now."

28

ALL SAINTS' DAY

"You set my mind at rest, d'Artagnan."
Twenty Years After - Alexandre Dumas

A few days before All Saints' Day, Maman arranged for us to travel to the little cemetery set in a clearing further back into the woods, where her parents and grandparents were buried. "We have to weed and clean the graves and place flowers." Most everybody we knew did this in the days before All Saints', whether their family gravesites were on their property or in the village cemetery.

We cut roses which I carried in a jar of water as Arsène and Gator and *Minuit* escorted us to the tiny family cemetery through the sweet gum, hackberry, pine, swamp maple, and scrub oaks to a regal stand of old and graceful live oaks. The branches were shrouded with gray moss, and the oaks formed an almost perfect semi-circle surrounding the graves, which was why that special spot had been selected so many years before.

I had a peculiar feeling as I approached my real grandparents' and great grandparents' graves for the first time. It seemed strange, unlike when I visited my other family graves. I felt no pull toward speaking to them as I did to the others, nor did I feel they somehow heard me or watched over me, as I believed the others did. I suppose it may have been because I felt anger toward them for discouraging Maman from keeping me. I had not known the

depth of my anger toward them until I stood over their graves, gazing at the flat mossy stones.

Maman, always sensitive to the slightest detail, detected my
mood. "You must forgive them, *chère*. They did the best they could
by me. They did not have the strength to look after you as well. If
you don't have it in your heart to forgive them on this occasion,
I'll bring you back again next year, and maybe you will have found
a way to forgive by then."

"Maybe, Maman. But for now, I'm full of resentment."

"It will pass, I believe. As for now, let's see about weeding
around their graves."

She pointed out two gravestones, black with age. "You don't
need to feel badly towards your great grandparents. They had
passed on before you were born, and had nothing to do with the
decision to give you up."

Arsène kneeled and began to pull weeds, so I crouched beside another patch of high grass, runners, and weeds and began to
work. Maman sank slowly to the ground, making herself comfortable in a spot where she could work and began to hum a tune.

"What is that pretty tune?" I asked.

"Just a little nonsense song my mother used to sing around the
house. It just came back to me while I was sitting here."

"Maybe that's a sign she's watching over you right now," I said.

"*Mais, oui, chère,*" and she resumed the tune once more.

When we'd pulled out all vegetation a few feet away from the
four graves, we stood and clapped the dust and dirt from our
hands. "That's good. Now we can brush the stones clean," Maman
directed. She pulled a stiff brush from her skirts, and Arsène took
it from her and dutifully began scrubbing the stones.

"When he's done with that, we'll leave a rose on each grave,
and we can go home knowing we've done a good job today."

"Excuse me please for asking, Maman. But don't you feel some
anger too?"

She sighed. "I did. For a long time. But I've learned that anger poisons heart and mind. It harms us. So I had to release it."

"How did you do that?"

29

A SECRET REVEALED

"Go then, Monsieur," said the queen, dismissing Athos with a sign,
"You have got what you wished to obtain,
and we know all we want to know."
Twenty Years After - Alexandre Dumas

The morning of our wedding was chilly, but the sun continued to gain strength so the thin light began to warm the
cool air. I had only an old brown handknit shawl to wear
over my beautiful blue silk wedding dress. I hoped the morning
would continue getting warmer, so I could take it off as it spoiled
the effect of the delicate dress and, of course, my precious sapphire necklace.

There was so much excitement in our house about the upcoming wedding that the blood hummed in my veins, and I felt a fluttering sensation moving all through my body and mind. I could
scarcely think, I was so excited, and the smallest task seemed difficult to perform.

Maman brushed my hair for a long while until it shined, and
she tied it with a silk bow using a scrap of the leftover material. I
had no appetite for breakfast, but she made me chew a biscuit with
fig preserves anyway. "You must eat to settle yourself. You don't
want to feel shaky on your wedding day," she warned.

We had traveled early that morning to Emile's where the wedding was to be held. He and Arsène had set up long plank tables

the day before for the great assortment of bowls and heaping platters of food to be served later in the day. Maman and I had cooked for two days and more food would arrive with the guests. The delicious smell of roasted meat and baked goods filled the house.

Friends from the village began arriving mid-morning by boat, horseback and wagon. All of Emile's cardplaying friends arrived with their families, except for Jean Claude and Yvonne. Hippolyte and Maurice arrived on horseback, accompanying Hippolyte's parents and sister who arrived in a wagon, closely followed by Leroy Viator and his wife in theirs.

The drinking began even before the wedding on the way to Emile's house. By the time most of the guests had arrived, Hippolyte and Maurice were so bright-eyed, I knew they had been at it all morning. When Emile saw me in the blue wedding dress shimmering in the sunlight, he rolled his eyes heavenward. "You are even more beautiful than I ever imagined." His expression was so loving, and the tan leather vest he wore looked so soft, I wanted only to fall into his arms and hold him close. But I was snatched away by friends who led me off to get ready for the ceremony, just as I was leaning forward to go to him.

When a priest came around our village sometime toward the end of the following year, we'd say our vows before him, but in the meantime, it was up to Leroy Viator to marry us. By mid morning, the sun was brighter and I left the shawl behind as I stepped out of the house, with Maman beside me, in the beautiful silk dress. Arsène escorted me to where Emile waited with Leroy, and the people pressed around to see and hear. By the time Leroy pronounced us man and wife with all the people watching solemnly, Emile gently kissed me, and this brought pleased murmurs and even cheers from the assembled friends.

Then we jumped the broomstick and as everyone clapped and laughed, they began singing old songs about married life that had no titles, but were known by their first lines only, such as: *La fleur de la jeunesse* and *Je me suis marie. Je me suis marie* made Emile and everybody else laugh and point at him as it is about a hen-pecked husband.

The musicians were gathered together to the side of the yard, in front of the garden. Bertrand, one of the village fiddle players was there, and Doc Seifert with his accordion, and a cousin of Bertrand's with the triangle. Leon Hebert joined them with a pair of clacking spoons to help keep rhythm. They started with a waltz and the dancing immediately began.

It is the custom for an Acadian bride to dance with every man at the wedding no matter how young or old or infirm. And we did that. I enjoyed all the dances, but longed to be with Emile and caught his eye as often as I could while the men waltzed me around the great circle of grass.

When it came Hippolyte's turn, he hung back by the porch with Maurice, then relented and came forward to dance with me. By then I could see he was very drunk. He reeked of liquor, and my eyes widened as he haltingly took me in his arms. He slurred his words, and his eyes were half closed, so much so, I wondered if he'd be able to finish the dance, but he stumbled his way through it.

"Do you like my wedding dress?" I asked him, trying to act as if nothing was amiss.

"It's beautiful." He managed a lopsided smile as the song mercifully came to a close. "Thank you," he said as the music wound down. He placed his hands carefully on my shoulders and blinked at me, eyes bleary. "Be happy. If he doesn't treat you right, let me know right away."

I tilted my head in surprise. "Emile? Don't worry. I know he'll be very good to me always."

He looked troubled. "I mean it, Sidonie. Just let me know and I'll take care of it."

"How could you possibly be worried about Emile?"

"Never mind!" he said abruptly, instantly releasing my shoulders. He turned to go, and I was glad of it because the air was smelling sweeter already. The aromas of all the rich food we would be eating shortly wafted from the house.

"Hippolyte," I called, so that he turned around. "What's wrong? What's troubling you?"

"Nothing's wrong," he said, then loped back toward Maurice who was leaning against a post of the back porch watching us.

And then I took a step back as if I'd been slapped. It all became clear in an instant. The gift of the silk. The concern about my being treated right. It was Hippolyte all the time. He was the one. I ran after him and grabbed his arms, forcibly turning him around so I could look him in the eyes.

"It's you, isn't it?"

"Me what?" He blinked in confusion.

"You're my real father!" And I knew it with every part of me at last, and it didn't matter whether he admitted it or denied it. I knew it was the truth. We stared at one another, my hands still grasping his arms. He bit his bottom lip, a stunned look in his eyes.

Anyone watching us must have wondered at the peculiar way we looked at one another, both of us motionless, as everyone near-by danced rapidly in a two-step. Everyone that is, except for Maurice who leaned against a post at the porch, quietly observing.

As the music changed to a slow ballad, Hippolyte looked down for a moment. When he brought his gaze up, his eyes were watering, and I didn't know if it was from all he'd had to drink or sadness or both. He brought his attention back to my eyes, seeming to have made a decision. "I was only fifteen, Sidonie. Can you please forgive me?" He let out a groan and tears spilled over onto his cheeks. He wiped them away impatiently with his sleeve and this motion reddened the rims of his eyes, so that he looked even more forlorn.

"I'm so sorry. It all hurts so deep...right here." He jabbed his heart two times with his fist. "I was crazy. Drinking corn liquor in the field that day. The sun burning down on me." He shook his head, squeezing his eyes shut as though to bury the memory.

"After I sobered up, I couldn't tell anybody. I was too scared to go to jail." He clapped a hand to his forehead, looking away. "But I hurt inside all the time for what I did...and I think Uncle Leroy always suspected me...but he never came right out and said anything. Just acted differently around me from then on." He gulped and pressed his lips together as though he'd said enough, and began to turn away, shoulders slumped.

"Hippolyte!" I said sharply. "Don't ever turn away from me... not ever again!"

"I can't stand what I've done." He choked on the words.

"Look at me!" I insisted.

He did as I ordered, and I grabbed his arms. It was some-what of a shock to look at him now that everything had changed between us, because I realized for the first time that there was a similarity in the shape of our eyes and cheekbones. I wanted to say something else, maybe even harsh, but different words welled up from within me, and instead I found myself saying, "I forgive you."

He nodded, wiping his eyes again, this time using both hands. The music grew louder so I leaned closer to speak to him. "But why did you never tell me? I wouldn't have hated you for it. At least not for long. You know me too well for that."

"I wanted to. Many times. But I couldn't bring myself to do it. I was afraid you'd never speak to me again. That you'd hate me and look down on me. And I couldn't blame you for that."

"Never speak to you? And you really believed things between us would stay bad after that? After all these years that we've known each other?"

He nodded and grimaced. "But I was always there. At your house. Every day. Always had to make sure you were doing all right." His face was smudged with the tears and the flying dust the dancers were kicking up.

"Is that why you stayed such constant friends with Maurice all these years?"

"We've always been friends. Since we were little boys."

"Does he know?"

"I think so. It's possible. But we never talked about it." He shook his head a few times.

"You've put Claudine... Maman, through hell."

"I know," he groaned again, face flushing.

"Someday you'll have to speak to her."

"I know. I'm not ready yet."

"One day. Let me know. I'll go with you if you like."

I was accidentally knocked into him then by a passing couple as the music shifted to another song, and I took the opportunity to hug him. He looked so forlorn and so desolate, I couldn't help myself.

"Thank you for not hating me, Sidonie. I'm so sorry for what I did. But I'm glad you're here. If I hadn't been so bad, you wouldn't be."

"And for now, everybody's safe." I leaned back to look into his eyes once more. "And I really do forgive you. But Gros Louis will always be my father in my heart."

He nodded sadly. "I know. I have no right to that."

"Go on over there with Maurice. I'm going to dance with my husband now." I smiled at him. "It will all work out in time."

He looked mournful as he started over to join Maurice at the porch, and I looked around for Emile. Still feeling the impact of what had just occurred, I felt the need to find him quickly and lean on him for strength. Feeling almost dizzy from this revelation, I wanted nothing more than to be with him. He stood by the musicians, hand over his eyes to shield the sun as he searched the dancing crowd for me. I raised my arm. "Emile!" I called, but my words were drowned out by the music as I pushed through the fast moving dancers. He saw me and hurried forward, a broad smile on his face and arms outstretched. "This is my happiest day," I called to him as he reached me and threw his arms around me, whirling me into the dancers. I was truly home at last.

Made in the USA
Lexington, KY
21 March 2014